CODAGENESIS

CODAGENESIS

Wayne Campbell

SACRAMENTO, CALIFORNIA

To request written permissions for authorized reproductions, contact the author at authorwaynecampbell@gmail.com.
Visit www.wayne-campbell.com for more.

ISBN: 9798373558839

Cover photo by Engin Akyurt
Cover design by Wayne L. Campbell using Gimp 2.10.32 and Canva

For Aaron

PROLOGUE

Bend, Oregon
April 3, 2080

A sea of faces, reddened from fear and anger, crowded the glass panes of the Bend City Hall doors. The frames bent and creaked as the mob pressed against them. A crack here, a spiderweb there appeared as the crushing weight of Bend's citizens became too much for the doors to bear.

Anxious and under-armed police officers and city security guards formed ranks in the lobby; when the crowd inevitably pushed through they knew they would be overwhelmed in seconds. Two million inhabitants feared for their safety as the virus sped through the city. Many in the mob showed signs of infection.

A few of the officers and guards peeled away from their positions and ran off. Those who remained cast looks about their comrades. One police officer stepped forward and took a few paces before turning around to face the cadre. Wordlessly, he unpinned his badge and held it up. He turned to face the citizens pushing and pounding on the glass. Arm still raised, he opened his hand, letting the badge fall to the floor. He turned back to his comrades and saluted. After dropping the salute, he strode through them and walked out of the lobby, peeling his uniform shirt off as he went.

The remaining officers and guards followed suit. Soon, the crowd was only addressing an empty lobby, a floor littered with polyester the only witness to their pleas.

Mayor Gerry Karch was on the phone in his office calling every number he could find for Ziggurat Consolidated. Every line had been disconnected. He ripped off his tie, feeling as though he were dangling from the gallows at its tightness. Sweat and grit poured onto his starched collar. He slammed down the receiver.

Breathing heavily, Karch moved to the window. The crowd swarmed like angry ants below. His eyes rested on the snow-covered Cascade Mountains, which glistened white under the bright Central Oregon sun. Every day before, he had enjoyed seeing their majesty from his office; that day, he wished he were anywhere but his office.

"What are we going to do?"

"Sir, we should get going." Robert Parrell, Karch's Chief of Staff, stood calmly on the other side of the room. Karch turned from the window and gathered his jacket from the coat rack.

"How did it come to this, Robert?" The two men exited the office and entered the elevator across the hallway. "We did everything Ziggurat asked, and still we've been shut out."

"We're one small city compared to the rest of the world, sir." Parrell mashed the button marked **ROOF**. "Clearly we didn't meet the criteria for Ziggurat's relief protocol."

"Those sonsabitches have installations here, why couldn't they spare room for some of our people?"

"It could be that they're already overcrowded, sir. And they may not have had enough supplies for their own, let alone the rest of the city."

Parrell's calmness and reason was maddening, but it was also the reason Karch had hired him. Karch's temper and tendency for gaffes had nearly cost him re-election two years prior. A *ping* signaled the arrival of the elevator. Static erupted from Parrell's radio as they stepped in.

"Dunleavy here...broke...glass...inside..."

Parrell switched off the radio. Though the transmission was staticky, it was clear that the head of security across the street was reporting that the mob had breached the doors and were now flooding the building. It would be a matter of minutes before the masses made their way upward to the offices of the mayor and his staff. Karch was thankful he had the foresight to evacuate the building hours ago at the first signs of unrest. Parrell and Karch remained behind to attempt last-ditch efforts for contact with Ziggurat.

The elevator glided slowly upward as the two rode in silence. It halted at the roof and rotor wash whistled through the door as it opened. Parrell and Karch hustled toward the waiting helicopter. Karch cried out and crumpled in front of Parrell. Parrell rushed to Karch's supine body on the helipad and knelt beside him. Karch clutched his chest as blood poured out profusely under his hand. Parrell removed Karch's hand from the wound, which made a wet sucking noise. Swearing under his breath, Parrell jammed his hands on top of the wound and pressed.

"Ah, Jesus!" Blood streamed from the wound and from Karch's mouth.

"Hang in there, Gerry!" Parrell looked around frantically for the shooter. They were so high that there was only one other building from which the shot could have come. Parrell's eyes sought the rooftop of the Wells Fargo Tower on Wall Street. Squinting, he thought he could see the hint of a silhouette resting on the parapet.

Parrell felt a hard *thud* in his chest; at the same time, a sharp pain cut through his torso. He tried to stand but staggered and fell on his back, blood flowering on his crisply pressed shirt. A tight, clean hole in his shirt, just a hair to the left of his tie, indicated where the shooter's bullet had entered. Karch lay motionless at his side. Parrell's vision tunneled before the world went dark. The helicopter pilot, knowing he could do nothing, hit the throttle and flew off into the deep blue high desert sky.

Within just a few minutes, the mob reached the roof access and spilled out onto the helipad. Their momentum slowed as they found their leader and his right-hand man sprawled out on the concrete. Jagged circles of pooling blood surrounded the bodies, staining the crisply painted **H** on the helipad. Several of them let out wails of anguish before hurling themselves over the edge of the roof.

The world as they knew it had ended.

Thirty-three miles southeast of City Hall, Grayson Brooks paced the corridors of a bunker underneath Pine Mountain. He had been assigned to the facility just three months before, not long after Ziggurat Consolidated announced that the stolen virus had been released into the general population on New Year's Day; a Monday, of all days. He had whipped the security team at the facility into shape quickly to keep the scientists and civilian workers both calm and productive.

Ziggurat's offer of employment had come at the right time. A mine had shredded his right leg while his rifle squad was on a recon mission in North Korea and had caused irreparable damage.

Grayson spent six months in physical therapy at the Navy hospital in Busan, but he was left with a permanent minor limp that no amount of rehab could fix. After returning stateside, the Marine Corps—in its infinite wisdom—had decided that he was a liability as a sergeant in the field due to his injuries and tried to relegate him to riding a desk with a promotion to lieutenant. He was having none of it and opted for a medical discharge.

Grayson had been approached by a Ziggurat recruiter after a physical therapy session one morning at the VA clinic in Bend. The pay and benefits seemed too good to be true, but some checking around with old military buddies that had similar jobs proved that Ziggurat's offer was legitimate. After the hell of dealing with TRICARE and attempting to set regular appointments at the VA clinic, he jumped at the opportunity. Shortly after that, he found himself in the Ziggurat bunker located under an old observatory east of Bend.

Ziggurat had assigned him some of their doctors to attend to his leg as part of his benefits package. Miraculously, Grayson's leg no longer bothered him. Whatever the Ziggurat doctors had done to fix his injury had worked. He was grateful to have been relieved of the pain and stiffness of his maimed leg. The only part that bothered Grayson was that he couldn't remember some of his time at the bunker, having been sedated for the first three weeks as the doctors worked their magic.

In the distance, Grayson heard commotion in one of the labs. He rushed to the end of the corridor and slid to a stop as Keona Sage, his former second-in-command, burst through a door backwards, pumping rounds into the lab from the pistol in his right hand. Grayson drew his own pistol.

"Drop it, Keona!"

Keona spun and leveled his pistol's muzzle at Grayson. Both men stood their ground, staring each other down, each daring the other to move. Keona spun and sprinted up the corridor, reloading and holstering his pistol as he ran. Grayson grimaced and took off after him. His legs churned below him in a comforting rhythm. He hadn't felt that in some time. He was gaining on Keona. Four steps behind. Two steps behind.

Grayson grabbed a fistful of shirt but was caught off guard as Keona dropped and twisted in a way he hadn't expected, sending Grayson flopping to the floor and his head bouncing off the tile. His ears rang and his vision blurred for a moment.

"Stay down," Keona growled as he jumped up. Keona continued his sprint down the corridor and out the bunker doors. Grayson stood carefully and dusted himself off, reeling slightly from the hit his head had taken. Two of his guards came around the corner and placed their hands on his arms.

"What's going on?"

"You've been ordered to report to the meeting room."

Grayson let himself be led into the meeting room, a plainly-decorated area that looked much like any small-town city council meeting room. He noted, with some alarm, that there were two Ziggurat Consolidated judges sitting at the daïs at the front of the room.

"Grayson Brooks, you have been charged with dereliction of duty." The judge who spoke had a humorless face. Thinning white hair capped a tall forehead, rheumy eyes, and a mouth which seemed pulled downward at the corners by heavy weights. "There will be no room for such cowardice in the coming new world."

"What? What are you talking about?"

"This evening, approximately five minutes ago, you drew your weapon on a dangerous escaped patient and refused to either capture or kill him."

"Patient?"

"Yes, one…" The judge adjusted his glasses and read from a document in front of him. "One Keona Sage. A patient within the psyops program."

"Was he a willing participant?"

"Not that I am obligated to answer, but as it appears you two were friends as well as co-workers, no. He was removed from your program due to his…gifts."

Grayson wriggled against his captors, whose grip felt suddenly looser. Fear etched their faces, if momentarily, as they adjusted their grips to again hold Grayson fast.

"So you kidnapped him?" Grayson's face was reddening.

"No. We simply, ah, transferred him from one program to another." The judge smiled, a smile without humor. "Now, Mr. Brooks, back to the matter at hand, do you have a reasonable explanation as to why you did not kill or capture Mr. Sage?

"I told him to put the weapon down and engaged in a foot chase. He threw me to the ground and my head hit the concrete, which dazed me. I couldn't physically continue my pursuit."

"Be that as it may, you still did not fire upon the patient nor successfully capture him." Grayson began speaking, but the judge held up a hand to signal silence. "Therefore, it is the ruling of this court that you be sentenced immediately to fifty-five years in stasis, at which time you will be eligible for parole."

"By what authority are you entitled to this action?!" Grayson demanded, the language he chose surprising him.

"By the authority of Ziggurat Consolidated's Memorandum of Understanding with the Executive Branch of the United States of America, to wit, the internal handling of discipline. Ziggurat is responsible for some of the most secret projects and holdings of the United States government, and, as such, must treat matters of malfeasance such as this with the utmost care, speed, and firmness."

A pod rose from the center of the room and opened. It looked like it would barely contain Grayson. The guards, for whom he had been commander just minutes ago, stripped him down to his underwear and tried heaving him into the pod. They were stronger than they looked, but Grayson grabbed the sides of the pod and held fast. The metal around the door began bending under his fingers. For a split second, Grayson watched the divots become near-perfect forms of his grip.

"BAILIFF!" The judge stood and barked the word, his fear clearly evident on his face. Grayson roared as he felt a pinprick in the meat of his shoulder. He looked down and saw a syringe dart sticking up from his arm. The bailiff's pneumatic weapon was steady on Grayson. Grayson threw one guard off and was about to charge the bailiff when two more darts hit him in quick succession. Grayson suddenly grew weak.

The guards regained control of him and heaved him into the pod.

"This is ridiculous! I was doing my duty! You have no right…"

"We have *every* right, Mr. Brooks, as stipulated on page 27 of the employment contract you signed, in which you agreed to these terms."

Grayson suddenly regretted not having read the fine print. He was strapped down to the backboard and the glass door was sealed. Just as quickly as the sedative in the darts had begun to work, he was becoming clear-headed again. He struggled against the restraints, which were already beginning to fail. The judge slammed a hand onto the desk, panic beginning to take over the once-calm eyes and face. A long syringe darted from the pod wall to insert itself in his upper arm. His heart rate slowed, and he was suddenly very, very tired. As his head dropped forward against the forehead strap, Grayson saw stars floating before his eyes.

Look at the stars, look how they shine for you... Grayson's drifting consciousness called up a song from the turn of the millennium.

Darkness fell. He was spared the discomfort of the varied tubes and wires being thrust into his body meant to keep him alive in stasis. The guards slammed the door shut and locked it; luckily, the damage from Grayson's hands didn't impede the door, the door lock, or the door seal.

They wheeled the pod to the closest cell in the bunker's jail. The guards quickly connected the power and data supply cables that rose through the concrete and bolted the pod to the floor.

Not long after, another pod was brought in and stood up next to Grayson, this one containing Keona. Ziggurat had made it nearly impossible for a psyops patient to escape their facilities, and anyone who tried was not punished lightly.

The guards turned off the lights in the cell and locked the door behind them. The computers in the cell worked silently, compiling vital signs, pumping fluids, and controlling the stasis environment.

The cell was silent but for the nearly imperceptible sound of the computers' power supply fans. The silence would persist for some time.

LAZARUS MEN

ONE

His head throbbed. He opened his eyes, but he saw only darkness. He blinked. Blinked again. Same. *Have I gone blind?* But no; in the distance he could see two faint pinpoints of green light, one of which was blinking steadily. His night vision was coming around. He steadied his breathing and waited. There—the outlines of the room were forming. He reached out a hand. *Thump.* Hard and cold.

"Pod," Keona said thickly. He smacked his tongue a few times. So dry. He pushed on the glass in front of him, but the pod's door didn't move. He pushed again with the same result. Keona closed his eyes, focused, and breathed. He put his hand lightly on the glass and began pushing outward. The glass cracked. Spiderwebbed. Exploded outward in a hail of shards.

Keona opened his eyes again, pulled off the mask covering his nose and mouth, and exited the pod. His arm tugged him back, and he realized the nutrient tubes were still attached. Keona pulled them out and tugged off the waste collection device that circled his midsection. The only sound was that of computer power supply fans and the crunch of broken glass underfoot. In the darkness there was now one green and one red dot of light. He turned and saw his old friend still in stasis.

"Sorry, Grayson. No time for grudges on exit."

Keona exited the cell and began searching the locker room next door. The bunker smelled musty, as though he were in a hot attic, though the air was pleasantly cool. He found a full guard uniform in a locker along with a backpack and a pistol. *Shirt and pants are a little loose, but they'll do.* The boots were nearly a perfect fit, but he filled out the wiggle room with an extra pair of socks. Keona stuffed the pistol into the lower right cargo pocket on his shirt. In the backpack were several full spare magazines for the pistol and two boxes of ammunition.

After searching the rest of the lockers, his pack was loaded with first aid supplies, several pairs of wool socks, an empty canteen, an emergency blanket, and a rain suit. He had seen some pre-packaged food bars in a breakroom, but they had been covered in thick layers of dust. Keona began to wonder just how long he had been in the pod.

Keona returned to the cell and stopped at the workstation next to the pods. Keona tapped his finger on the monitor to wake it up;

the resulting blinding light gave him an immediate headache and he quickly turned down the brightness as low as it would go. A lockscreen greeted him with the date in the lower right corner.

23:18
Monday, June 12, 2484

Four hundred and four years. *Well, that's just great.*

The lockscreen asked for a password. Keona tapped in the first thing that came to mind: **ABCD1234**. Voilá, he was in. Lazy guards.

A few taps told him that the power on his pod had failed, which ceased the oxygen supply and spurred Keona's brain to begin waking up. Grayson's vital readouts were strong but his pod showed near full power. The best Keona could figure was that a relay or bridge between the batteries attached to his pod had failed somehow. The air exchangers must have been on a separate system; by the smell of the bunker, no fresh air had circulated inside for at least a week.

Keona powered off the monitor. He stood in the dark, allowing his night vision to come back and for his mind to adjust to being on a virtually alien planet. As the gray shapes of the computers and pods began filtering into view again, he left the cell through a set of double doors. As he walked, he held his hand behind him. The footprints in the dust vanished as quickly as his boots left the floor, the dust settling back in on itself.

Keona easily opened the door leading into the entrance corridor thanks to the fail safe. The door was meant solely to keep the outside air out and the inside air in. He closed it behind him, mindful that Grayson may someday need to leave. There was no way for Keona to know who—or what—what could breach the exterior door after he left. At the end of the entrance corridor, he pushed against the exterior door. As expected, it would not budge. He checked the card reader, just in case, but it had been powered off and would be of no use; the door's fail secure had engaged.

Keona sighed and moved in front of the door. Arm extended, he thought of the door open. At first, nothing happened. Keona concentrated; a deep groan reverberated through the door. A squeal perforated the groan moments before the door hissed open. The smell of petrichor and pine filled the entrance corridor.

Keona drew the pistol from the cargo pocket on the shirt and held it before him. He exited the bunker cautiously, uncertain of what he would find beyond the door. Keona stepped out into the moonlit evening.

"Unbelievable."

The last time he had seen the outside of the bunker, only a few scraggly Ponderosa and Lodgepole pines stood among the juniper and sagebrush that graced the top of Pine Mountain. Now he craned his neck to find the tops of a crowded stand of Ponderosa pines, about eighty feet up. They looked inky black against the moonlit sky, of which barely a slice could be seen. The night hummed with crickets and other nocturnal creatures calling to each other.

Keona turned back to the entrance of the bunker and thought of the door closed; it squealed back into place. The night sounds immediately around him stopped as the creatures were startled. He inspected the door and hinges, satisfied with the patina of rust hiding his exit. The door hinges looked like they were on their last legs, which would be good news for Grayson when—if—he woke up.

Keona took a few tentative steps away from the bunker mouth, his eyes scanning the area for any potential threats. The air was crisp and clean, no foul odors hiding on the breeze. The creatures were again stirring, welcoming him into their world. What little light penetrated the Ponderosa canopy allowed him to weave through the trees in the direction of Bend, which suddenly seemed very far away.

TWO

Splip.

Splip.

Splip.

Moisture from the dense fog fell from the giant Ponderosas' pine needles and splattered in slow rhythm on the duff below. The air was cool, just shy of cold, and the sun couldn't penetrate to the forest floor. No breeze swayed the limbs of the trees and the fog simply hung where it was. The stillness was a comfort. The absence of sound and movement was the absence of enemies.

Juniper Scanlon surveyed the outer ruins of the bunker before her. There was evidence that the tree roots had cracked and buckled the concrete apron, though it remained intact. It looked like it was a self-healing concrete, which had grown around the roots and filled in the cracks, giving the concrete a strange, bumpy surface. Beige pine needles littered the entranceway and the surrounding structure of the bunker mouth. The door was intact and looked as though once upon a time it had a nice, polished sheen, judging by the hints of silver that peeked from the orange rust covering the face. She shuddered. The last time she had seen a door like that was from the inside as she threw it open and ran into the darkness. Bitter memories flooded her thoughts for a few moments before she shook them away. This was not that time, nor the same bunker.

Juniper looked over the hinges and saw that rust had nearly devoured them. She went back to the truck and returned to the door with a winch hook. She attached the hook to the bottom hinge, activated the winch, and watched with satisfaction as the hinge shrieked and popped free. Juniper did the same with the top hinge, and the door fell with a loud *clang*.

"Keep it down, willya?" Ben Cooley, her foraging partner, was still trying to sleep off the previous night's drinking binge. He sat up and rubbed his temples as he rolled out of the cargo bed of the large, creaking monstrosity they drove, an old personnel transport designed and built many years before they were born.

"Maybe you should lay off the shine for just one night. Whaddaya think?"

"One night. Some night."

Juniper picked up her short rifle and a flashlight from the truck bed and stalked away into the bunker. Thin shafts of weak light strayed into the entrance of the bunker. She shook the flashlight, flicked it on, and swept the beam left to right. The bunker looked desolate. Water stood on the floors and dribbled down the walls; the forebay to the bunker had clearly begun failing and might only stand a few more years.

Juniper slowed her pace as she reached the interior door, beyond which was the first junction. She hesitated, unsure of the direction she should go once she passed through. The last bunker she had been in was constructed in roughly the same configuration, so Juniper opened the door and went right. She continued sweeping the corridor with her light, noting the several doors lining the corridor. At the end was a double door.

Juniper reached out with her left hand and steadied her rifle barrel on her left arm as she pulled at the door. A little movement. She tugged again, and the door gave a little more. Frustrated, she yanked as hard as she dared, and the door flew open. She quickly scanned the room with her light, though it was clear no one was going to be in the room. Juniper lowered the rifle as she stepped inside and lit a magnesium flare to illuminate the room.

A man's semi-masked face appeared in front of her.

She screamed and fell backward. Her backside hit the concrete as she swept the rifle barrel upward and fired two rounds in fast succession. Her rounds bounced off the man and she let off the trigger, fearful she might be struck by one of her own bullets. As

Juniper regained her composure, she realized that the man was contained in some sort of enclosure. His eyes were closed, and he looked as though he was in a deep sleep. The mask he wore covered only his nose and mouth. Juniper got up and moved closer, rubbing her backside as she walked. She looked over the pod. There were no visible wires feeding energy to it. She turned to the whirring bank of electronics; one green light was on next to a series of markings. Juniper noted that the same markings were etched on a sticker near the pod's glass door.

G. BROOKS 20800403

A red light appeared next to another series of markings heavily obscured by dust.

Light bounced off the walls as Ben came in the door, quickly sweeping every nook with his own rifle.

"You all right? I heard you fire."

"Yeah, yeah, I'm fine," Juniper said. "This guy just surprised me, that's all." She pointed at the pod. Ben approached the pod and inspected the man inside. He rapped on the thick glass.

"Huh. Nobody home. Oh well. Let's move on, shall we?" Ben started for the door.

"Hang on."

"What?"

"Give me a hand." Juniper slung her rifle over her shoulder and hunted for a handhold.

"You're not seriously considering taking this thing with us, are you?"

"Yes, I am, especially since I wasted two rounds on his bulletproof face. Besides," Juniper said as she squeezed between the pod and the wall, "this 'thing' is a human." She brought her knees up, braced her back squarely on the wall, and pushed with all she had. The pod was immovable.

"You're mental." Ben turned to leave. Juniper stayed behind the pod, grunting and cursing. Ben sighed. "Fine. I'll be right back."

Ben returned a few minutes later with the transport's winch hook in hand. He nudged her out of the small space between wall and pod and pushed the hook through. Juniper took the hook and wound it to the front, placing it back on its own cable. Ben wordlessly left the room.

"CLEAR!" Juniper heard the tinny, echoed shout after an interminable time and moved away from the pod. The cable went taut as Ben activated the winch. The back of the pod caved a little as the cable strained against the anchored machine. The pod itself began to tilt, leaning forward. The bolts holding the bottom of the pod to the concrete began to groan, a few in the back popping free and pinging against the wall.

"HOLD!" Juniper yelled. The cable stopped drawing back and slackened. She moved the cable farther to the bottom and wrapped it around the bottom of the pod where it had begun disengaging. "GO!"

The cable slid underneath the pod and sheared away everything holding it to the floor. The pod went crashing to the floor, sending a loud *CLANG* and sparks flying through the small space.

"HOLD!" Juniper yelled again. "SLACK!" She re-rigged the cable to encompass the pod lengthwise, creating a more stable connection to drag it out of the bunker. "GO!"

Juniper disengaged the cable from the temporary pulleys Ben had installed in the walls as she followed the pod, calling out a halt each time she needed slack to free the cable from the pulleys. The grinding and screeching noise the pod made on the concrete floor was almost too loud to bear in the confines of the bunker. After an interminable amount of time, the screeching behemoth cleared the bunker entrance.

"Now what?" Ben asked. "This damn thing has to weigh a ton, and we're never gonna get him in the back of the truck by ourselves."

"Yeah, I know. I just couldn't leave him there." Juniper paused. "I'm gonna go back, see if I can find anything else."

Juniper had just gone inside again when Ben called to her in a panic.

"JUNIPER! GET OUT HERE!"

Juniper bolted outside. Ben stood with his back to her and his rifle was pointing slightly downward. Juniper looked down at the man in the pod, now sitting up and rubbing his temples.

"Got a wicked headache," he said. "Anyone have an aspirin? Or Tylenol?"

"What's that?" Juniper asked. The man's hands dropped and he looked up at her, squinting against the weak sunlight.

"You're kidding, right?"

"No."

The man stood to his full height, stretching. His muscles rippled beneath his skin as they were extended and fed real air. The tubes and wires connected to his body fell away. Ben held the muzzle of his rifle steady on him. The man slowly raised his arms and stretched his back. Juniper couldn't take her eyes away, for a variety of reasons. The man rolled his neck left and right, loud pops emitting from the vertebrae as he did.

"That's a little better." His eyes were starting to adjust. He felt the cool breeze and looked upward at the tops of the Ponderosa trees. Then he looked down, the only "clothing" on his body being the waste collector around his waist. *No wonder she's staring.* "Either of you got clothes to spare?"

Juniper rummaged in the back of the truck for a minute and found some clothes scavenged at other places around the basin. She tossed the clothes to him. "See if those will fit."

The man winced a little as he pulled three darts out of his skin. He motioned for Juniper to turn around. When she didn't, he started pulling on the waste collector in front of her; that got her attention and she quickly turned, blushing. He did his best to get into the clothes; the trousers were a bit tighter than he would have liked and the shirt was a tad small in the biceps. He fixed the shirt by simply ripping the sleeves off at the seams.

"What's your name?" Ben asked.

"Grayson. Grayson Brooks."

"How'd you end up in there?"

Grayson paused. "Some folks said I was a traitor. They decided I should rest a while for my alleged transgressions." Juniper took a cautious step back. Grayson read the look on her face. "I'm no traitor. I was wrongfully accused."

"Most people say that when they've been judged a traitor," Ben said. He still held the rifle's muzzle steady on Grayson.

"That they do," Grayson said, stepping out of the pod. He turned to Juniper. "You have names? Or should I make some up?"

"I...I'm Juniper. That's Ben."

"Shut up, Juniper. He doesn't need to know anything."

"He still doesn't. Just our first names." Juniper glared at Ben. She turned back to Grayson. "So, before we tell you more about *us*, what's the rest of *your* story?"

Grayson leaned against the truck and pressed the palms of his hands into his eyes. They were sore and gritty. On top of that unpleasantness, his legs felt weak. "What year is it?" Juniper and Ben looked at each other. Ben shook his head.

"It's around 2480, give or take," Juniper said. Grayson's head shot up, his eyes wide.

"2480?!"

"Y-yes." Juniper felt the uneasiness creeping up again. Grayson sat heavily in the duff and put his hands in his head. "How long were you in there?"

"Four hundred years…" Grayson rested his head on the truck's tire. "They really meant life sentence."

Juniper moved closer and knelt next to Grayson. She felt there was no danger. His grief washed over her as Grayson slipped deeper into rumination, remembering the people and places he had known. She hesitated to reach out to him, also feeling the anger underneath. However, she relented, laying a hand on his meaty forearm.

"What can we do?" Juniper whispered.

"Nothing." Grayson closed his eyes briefly, feeling a strange calm and warmth radiate throughout his body. When he opened his eyes he looked straight into Juniper's. "What's there to eat?"

Orange shadows danced on the trunks of the Ponderosas. The fog had lifted from the forest floor and the stars shone brightly. Grayson looked upward through the narrow tunnel created by the trees. It had been a long time since he had seen so many stars, maybe one of his desert deployments. Even while assigned at the bunker, there was no need to go outside at night, so he never got to see the high desert night sky. The food Juniper and Ben prepared had been bland but plentiful; it was settling nicely as they talked beside the fire.

"So," Grayson said, lowering his eyes, "what all has happened in the last four hundred years? Start with why we're in the middle of a forest?"

"It's been forest for as long as I've known it," Juniper said. "The elders speak of a time when this was a dry, lifeless land, but that was long ago. They say a change in the weather happened rapidly after some evil people used tech we don't know of to completely melt the polar ice caps within a few minutes. Coastal villages were swallowed up by the ocean almost immediately when the water rushed in. After a few years, ecosystems around the world changed. Here, the forests creeped down from the foothills and covered this area." Grayson sipped at the warm cider he held, the warmth comforting.

"And what about the people?"

"That's a bit more complicated," Juniper said. Ben stood wordlessly and left the fire. "The evil people that destroyed the ice caps released a virus at the same time to wipe out most of humanity. It was called the *Codagenesis* virus; some doctor had discovered it was responsible for the dinosaur extinction after an asteroid hit the Earth. He was able to re-create and make more of it thanks to samples he found somewhere. The corporation he worked for stored the reproduced samples.

"Unfortunately, one of the evil people was able to get into the secured facility where they were stored and sneaked some out. Almost all the people of Earth died. The remaining ones were unaffected, or they...changed. Entirely."

"I remember when the caps were melted and the virus was released. Ziggurat kept the name to themselves, though. Appropriate name, I suppose."

"What does it mean?"

Grayson drained his cup. "*Coda* is Latin, means 'tail,' and *genesis* is from Ancient Greek and Latin, meaning 'origin' or 'beginning.' Translated literally it would mean 'beginning of the end.'

"Who would release such a thing?" Juniper looked almost hurt by the thought.

"The terrorists—the evil people—were anti-government

extremist nutjobs bent on starting humanity over again. They didn't appreciate the power of the virus, though. They didn't realize it couldn't be controlled and inadvertently wiped themselves out before their 'dream' could even be realized."

Juniper stared at the fire, lost in her own thoughts. The flames popped and crackled as pitch caught fire. Grayson looked up to the sky again, listening to the sigh of the breeze through the pine needles above.

"You're taking this remarkably well, Grayson."

"I've never been one to worry too much about what I can't change."

Juniper smiled. "We should all be so lucky."

"I don't know that I'm lucky. Just a grunt that got injured and sent packin'."

"Grunt?"

"I was a Marine."

"What's that?"

Just like with Tylenol, there were going to be things normal to Grayson that Juniper hadn't encountered in her lifetime. It was going to take time to adjust. "A warrior."

Juniper was pleasantly surprised. That kind of knowledge would be useful back home.

"So, what about you?" Grayson asked. "What are the people like around here?"

"We live in clans. Villages are spread out so we can share the natural resources. We all cooperate with one another mostly, but there are times when conflicts arise. Battles usually last for just a few hours. If there's no clear winner, the leaders come together to discuss how to end the conflict and attempt a compromise.

"My clan is a foraging clan—we don't really grow crops or hunt, though there are a few of us who can. We barter with surrounding villages for food, clothing, and other needs. Ben is my foraging partner."

"Uh huh." Grayson stretched out, his muscles still stiff. "Who are your enemies?" Juniper became still and looked down at the ground.

"What makes you think we have enemies?"

"You live apart from others, and the others may have what you need or want. You also have things others may need or want. They'll take it by force if necessary. Who are your enemies?"

"They call themselves the Keepers. They control the ruins of Bend, where they've set up their encampment. The stories are that they're brutish remnants of the old times, people who were mutated by the virus. They're nothing but thieves and cowards, all of them. When they're not stealing our food and other things, they're stealing our people."

Juniper's eyes misted. She had to take a deep breath. "They took my parents when I was very young. My parents knew things a lot of people don't; how machines worked and how to farm. That made them very valuable to my clan, but very valuable to the Keepers as well. We've never been openly attacked, though, so I suppose we should be grateful. Still, gratefulness for the general peace won't give me my parents back. They're probably long dead."

"It's okay, Juniper, you don't have to go on. I've got a good enough picture."

"Thank you." Juniper stood and wiped her eyes with the back of her hand. Grayson stood with her, a habit of courtesy.

"We...uh, we don't have much room in the truck," Juniper said, "but you're welcome to find a bit to share."

"I'll be okay out here. Do you have a spare blanket I can borrow for the night?"

"That, I do have." Juniper retrieved a blanket from the back of the truck and handed it to Grayson. "If you get hungry again, there's a bit of bread in the pack by the fire."

"Much appreciated." Grayson moved toward the fire and spread out the blanket. Juniper crawled into the back of the truck and lay with her head facing out, watching Grayson by the fire. He sat on the blanket, his shoulders hunched, watching the fire. So much was still a mystery about him. She felt the sadness radiating from him again, and though he tried to hide behind his tough words, he was grieving for the world he had lost. Everything he knew.

Juniper's eyelids soon became heavy. Something about Grayson was very comforting. He was courteous, and though he was a warrior, his eyes were kind and showed a vulnerability that many wouldn't be able to see. Even now, close to sleep, Juniper could feel the warmth radiating from deep within Grayson. As she watched him by the fire, the dance of the flames lulled her to sleep.

THREE

The brisk morning air was astir with a light breeze that caressed Juniper's cheek and woke her. She blinked the sleep from her eyes and looked to where Grayson had been the night before. He was gone. The blanket was folded neatly near the place where he had slept. The fire was still burning and had been stoked throughout the night from the look of it.

Juniper dropped down from the truck and peered around both sides. She took up her rifle and started toward the front of the truck, where Ben's snoring still rattled the cab. Grayson was nowhere to be seen.

"Dammit."

"What's wrong?" Juniper squeaked and spun. Grayson was behind her, carrying a bundle of small logs under his arm.

"You...! Don't do that!" Juniper slapped the shoulder of the arm not carrying wood. "I thought you ran off!"

"No. Didn't know how long we planned on staying, thought I'd get some more wood."

Juniper pushed the hair in her eyes behind one ear. "Thanks. I'll get some breakfast going."

"Sounds good," Grayson said. The bread didn't last very long. Sorry."

Juniper smiled. Ben managed to join them as their breakfast finished cooking, and they ate quickly. Juniper wanted to get back into the bunker to see if they could find anything else of value. Juniper gave Grayson a flashlight, which she shook for a few moments before handing it to him.

"You would've called it a 'shakelight.' It's old tech, an LED powered by a magnet, copper coil, and a capacitor."

"Cool."

Grayson took point, as he was familiar with the bunker. He took them to the left corridor, as they had already explored the other side. He led them into the first lab, where they found first aid supplies and lab coats that could be repurposed into other clothing. The other labs were much the same. Once they reached the end of the corridor, Grayson pulled open the door, though not without some difficulty. Inside was a storeroom of weapons and ammunition in quantities the foragers had never seen.

"This is incredible," Juniper said. "We've been looking for a cache like this for a long time!"

"How did you not find this place sooner?" Grayson asked.

"It's very far south of our village. We've only just begun searching this area."

"But still, four hundred years? You think someone would've found it."

"Um, did you happen to notice that, even with Bend being the largest city in the area, this is *still* the middle of nowhere?"

Grayson smirked. "Fair enough."

Ben and Grayson did the bulk of the hauling, loading up the back of the truck with as much as it could carry, ammunition taking priority. While they were loading, Grayson chose an AR-platform rifle and loaded five magazines. He inserted one in the rifle and stuffed the others in a chest rig he found.

The truck took more than it looked like it would, though there was still a lot left in the weapons store that could be collected later. Still, the amount of fresh ammunition would be enough to keep Juniper's people virtually swimming in brass for a long time. The weapons would be extremely valuable for hunting, protection, and trade. Each one had been inspected by Grayson for rust and corrosion; miraculously, every weapon was in pristine condition.

Grayson took a side trip during one of the runs to check out the cell he had been in. Another pod had been in there with him, though its glass was all over the floor. He looked at the computer console, but it looked as though it had been smashed when his pod was pulled over.

"Damn."

He inspected the pod and thought it odd that all the glass was on the floor outside the pod, and none remained inside. That meant that whoever or whatever had been in the pod had been able to break the shatter-proof glass with little more than three feet of space in which to work. Grayson looked for a label to see if he could identify the former occupant. Just as he was about to give up, he saw a laser-cut metal sticker with a barcode and letters just under where the glass had been.

K. SAGE 20800403

"So you made it out, huh? What'd they do to you?"

When they were finished, the three of them lifted the door, closed it, and scattered the pine needles and duff outside to make it appear as if the bunker had never been opened. They all climbed up in the cab of the truck, weapons between their knees. Ben took the driver's seat.

"Where to?" Grayson asked.

"Our village, Awbreytown." Juniper handed him a map and pointed. "It's here, on top of this hill. It was one of the few places the Bendites didn't gobble up when they started building toward the sky."

Grayson smiled. The map showed that Awbreytown was located on top of Awbrey Butte, overlooking downtown Bend. He was intrigued to find out what his hometown looked like now, even if these "Keepers" had taken control of it. The truck rumbled along the road, groaning in protest along the rolling route. Ben dodged low-hanging branches to preserve the solar panels mounted on top of the cargo box. The trees never seemed to let up, and Grayson kept looking out his window, amazed at how thick the forest was. His thoughts were consumed by the life he had known, a life now many years in the past.

The truck broke through the tree line, and Grayson looked over to see a crumbling skyline which could only be downtown Bend. The dilapidated buildings raked the blue sky with their ragged tops and windowless façades. Some of the skyscrapers had fallen over and now rested on the next building over. Behind them, the Cascade Mountains still stood sentry over the west—there was snow only at the points of the tallest peaks, and none graced the once-thriving winter haven of Mount Bachelor.

"What the—? Juniper, you see that?" Ben pointed through the windshield at several columns of smoke rising from the northwestern part of Bend.

"Yeah, hang on." Juniper retrieved a monocular from the

glovebox and raised it to her eye. "I can't see anything from this far, but it's definitely coming from Awbreytown."

Ben didn't respond other than downshifting and setting the truck going as fast as he could, the electric motors underneath whining. The ride got worse as they plowed over the rough road. Grayson had to steady himself with one hand on the roof of the cab. They began their ascent of Awbrey Butte, the hill for which Juniper's village had been named, and the truck objected to the grade with more whines, groans, and pings as Ben pushed it to its limits. The smoke was rising thicker into the sky.

"Come on, come on," Juniper said under her breath.

The truck broke through a stand of trees. Fire raged throughout the village, some structures having already fallen into themselves. Ben slammed on the brakes. Juniper simply stared out the windshield in shock. A tear trickled down her cheek. Ben threw open the door and jumped out, screaming obscenities at the sky. His face turned purple as he screamed. Juniper collapsed on Grayson's shoulder and sobbed. Grayson tentatively put a hand on her back, unsure of how to console her. Ben finally fell to his knees, gasping and coughing.

Grayson looked out the windshield at the carnage, scanning the area for any movement. He took his hand from Juniper's back and picked up his rifle.

"Stay in the truck." Grayson opened the door and gently lay

the still-sobbing Juniper on the seat. "Ben, get your weapon. Stay behind me." Ben obeyed, falling in.

The two men walked the village. Grayson was grateful to have something familiar in his hands and the ability to do something useful. There was nothing to be salvaged from the village. Everything had been taken or burned. There were no other people hiding. Those that remained in the village were dead and lay about the grounds with savage wounds or were burned beyond recognition. Grayson lowered his rifle.

"Keepers?"

"Must've been." Ben slung his rifle over his shoulder. Hands shaking, he pulled a dented flask from his hip pocket and took a long pull from the spout.

"Anything in underground storage they may not have known about?"

"Yeah, over by my shed." Ben led Grayson to a smoking heap. He tramped about what Grayson believed to be the rear of the ruined shed. A hollow *thump* signaled to Ben what he was looking for. Ben reached down and threw open a dirt-covered trap door.

"I'm gonna go get the truck and check on Juniper," Grayson said. Ben nodded. Grayson jogged back to the truck and climbed in the driver's seat. Juniper was curled up on the right side of the bench seat. She was no longer sobbing. Her breath was ragged. Grayson said nothing. He started up the old truck and drove it to

Ben's position.

Grayson pulled out a couple of boxes from the back of the truck to accommodate items from Ben's store. Among the items were food, clothing, dried tobacco leaves, and jugs of water. Ben was a little upset that they had to leave some of the weapons but was glad that Grayson refused to let go of any ammunition.

Juniper remained in the cab of the truck for the duration of the transfer. She dropped from the cab just as they closed the tailgate. Grayson watched Juniper silently as she took in the scene again. She looked down the hill at Bend. A guttural, primal scream rose from deep in her chest. Her eyes went wide, her mouth drawing open in a gaping O. The sound she emitted was full of anger, sadness, and pain. But what was more astounding to Grayson was the way the soil in front of her leapt up and began blowing away. He swore the trees nearby were bending away from her. The sound abated, but Juniper's mouth remained open in a silent scream. She turned away from Bend, sobbing. Grayson approached and put a hand on her shoulder. Juniper buried her face in his chest, grasping the rig tightly in her hand. Grayson embraced her wordlessly.

"We should get moving," Ben said, breaking the silence. He took another drink from his flask as he spoke. "If anyone made it out, they'll probably be at Ochoco." Juniper pulled away from Grayson and wiped her eyes. She looked up at Grayson and smiled.

"Thank you." Juniper climbed back into the cab of the truck.

"What just happened?" Grayson asked. "How did she do that?"

"Juniper's…er…special." Ben took a moment to find his words. "She was kept in a bunker twenty years ago, kind of like the one where we found you. Only this one was active, run by scientists. Of a sort. They did things to her, things I don't understand. She told you about the Keepers, but did she tell you about the Whitecoats?"

"No."

"The Whitecoats live up in the mountains, doing who-knows-what to people they snatch from around the area. Juniper was taken when she was a little girl and spent a few years being tortured by them. I don't know the specifics, but she was changed. She calls herself an *empath*, whatever that means."

"She has…what's it called…psych…psychokinesis, though."

"Never heard of that. I'll have to take your word for it."

"She can move things without touching them," Grayson stated.

"Yeah. Not all the time, but yeah."

Ben turned and walked to the cab of the truck. Grayson got in on the passenger side. Juniper sat in the center of the bench seat, staring straight ahead, face slack, eyes unseeing. Ben started the truck and headed out of Awbreytown.

The time passed without much talk in the cab. The forest gave way to grassland and the expanse of a huge lake. The truck rumbled on over a well-rutted road paralleling the shoreline. Tendrils of smoke rose ahead of them. These were smaller fires than the ones that had devoured Awbreytown.

"That'll be Ochoco," Ben said. "We'll be there in about five minutes."

They pulled up to a gate in a defensive wall made primarily of Ponderosa logs tightly lashed and sunk vertically deep into the ground. Grayson approximated its height around thirty feet. The front wall ran alongside the shore of the lake for several hundred yards, then banked at a ninety-degree angle and continued into the water, where the logs marched on until disappearing under the surface. A watchtower loomed on the right side of the gate, and in the watchtower was a single sentry with a rifle aimed down at the truck.

Ben turned off the truck and stuck his hands out the window. "Better do the same." Grayson obliged, sticking his hands out his window.

"State your name!" The sentry didn't waver in his aim.

"Ben Cooley, Juniper Scanlon, and Grayson Brooks," Ben called back. The sentry's eyes lifted from the rifle's scope. He yelled something unintelligible over his shoulder to someone on the ground. The gate began opening from the bottom. Soon the gate was open just enough to allow the truck under.

"Pull forward!" Ben did as he was instructed. Just as the back end cleared the wall, the sentry barked, "Halt!" Ben obeyed that command also, and the gate swung closed. Someone yanked open the driver's side door.

"Alex! Holy hell!" Ben jumped out and gave the man a huge bear hug.

"I thought you guys were goners," Alex said.

"We thought the same about you and the others. How many made it?"

"Forty-six of us. The rest were killed or dragged off by those goddamned Keepers."

Grayson exited the truck, stretching his vibration-numbed legs. He surveyed the wall, which was crudely built but would hold off most minor attacks. The town of Ochoco fronted the lakeshore, and a long beach gave lake access to the residents. A watchtower rose from the beach for an unimpeded view of the lake.

"They came so quickly," Alex continued, "that we didn't even see 'em coming. They were on us before we even knew we were being attacked."

"That's not like the Keepers. They've never practiced stealth tactics, let alone attacked in broad daylight."

"Exactly. Those of us who got out were lucky. I've got no idea what the hell is going on with those damned Keepers anymore. This must be Grayson?" Grayson extended his hand. Alex accepted the handshake. "Alex Rockwell."

"Nice town."

"Thanks. Wish we never had to come here, but here we are. We kept it in reserve for just such an occasion."

Juniper climbed down from the truck and surveyed Ochoco. She took a deep breath and sighed. Alex approached her and gave her a gentle hug. She returned it gratefully, happy to see that at least one of her friends had made it out of Awbreytown. Alex turned back to Ben and Grayson.

"We don't have much in the way of shelter, but we'll find sumpin' for ya. Feel free to wander around, I'll find you when I have something worked out. You'll haveta leave your weapons and stuff with the gate tender here." Alex walked off toward the center of the village. He barked toward one building, and a lanky teen boy rushed out, rifle in hand. The boy scurried up the watchtower ladder and assumed the post. The tender drove the truck, and their weapons, to a garage of sorts near the middle of the compound.

"Can I do anything for you, Juniper?" Grayson approached her slowly.

"I'm fine." She paused. "Maybe we could go for a walk?" Grayson nodded and fell in beside her. Juniper walked toward the lake and turned at the shoreline. Small waves lapped gently on the sand. They continued until they reached the wall, where Juniper turned and began walking back along the shoreline.

"I was thirteen when I was taken from my home by the Whitecoats. I used to live with a family in a small village with no name at the base of the mountains, in the thick of the forest. When the Keepers took my parents a few years earlier, I'd been visiting a neighbor. I wasn't going to get lucky twice, I suppose."

Juniper's voice was soft but firm. "They did tests on me, some of them I don't remember, I'm sure. But it was hellish. They put me in sensory deprivation tanks, forced drugs into me with giant needles and bags, made me do things I didn't want to do. Eventually they pushed me to my limit. One night I screamed — really loud — and the room shook. The Whitecoats around me looked like they had all fainted at the same time, but when I got up and looked at them, they were bleeding from their ears, eyes, and mouths. I was so scared.

"I ripped all these wires off me, grabbed a security card off one of the dead Whitecoats, and took off out the door. Every Whitecoat I passed in the corridor was dead, too. I had no idea how I did it. I ran out the front door of their bunker and into the forest. I looked back only once, but no one was following me." Juniper wiped her cheek with the palm of her hand. "I stumbled into Awbreytown a few days later. I didn't tell anyone what had happened to me for months. And then, not even as much as I've just told you." Grayson remained silent as they continued walking.

They stopped at the other side of the wall. Juniper sat in the sand and Grayson took a seat next to her. She looked out over the lake again. The surface shimmered in the setting sun. Only a few killdeers could be seen darting around the shore, their haunting cries echoing through the compound. Grayson closed his eyes and listened to their songs. He felt the weight of Juniper's head press into his shoulder, then shuddering as she began to sob again. He put his arm around her shoulders and let her cry. There was time. They were safe for now.

FOUR

Ember watched as the stranger strolled into the settlement. His every move seemed liquid and confident. He wore strange, mottled clothes that looked like the colors of earth and tree. Ember wanted to be free in the camp too. The stranger's gaze shifted, and his eyes met hers.

Can it be? Ember wondered. *Can he read my thoughts?* No. No, that would be impossible. She scuttled to the back of her cage to save some dignity, or her life at the very least. Looking upon a freeborn without permission was punishable by death, she knew, but this one was so different from the others. Ember felt suddenly ashamed, covered in grime and trapped behind cold metal bars.

But Keona *had* heard her thoughts. He had gone into the settlement to find the tortured soul reaching out. It had taken only a few minutes to locate the row of cages. There were guards stationed at both ends of the row; acting then was out of the question. Keona kept walking.

Ember's heart plummeted. She had put vain hope in that man, hope that he would reach out and free her. She had no reason to believe he would free her, but she had hoped just the same. Ember's emotions went from shame to worthlessness as she turned her back to the road. She huddled against the corner of the cage with her tattered wool blanket, her ragged clothing no match for the cold. She tied a knot in one of the frays. Eight knots, eight days in the cage.

Tomorrow was the Free Market. Devoted to the selling of whatever wares the Keepers wished, and in most cases, it was new slaves. The clan that ran the settlement handled all security for the wares and slaves in return for the Keepers leaving them alone. Ember didn't know with whom she would leave, but she knew how it would begin. She would be stripped naked, doused with cold water, and a collar placed on her neck. After the inhumane cleansing she would be staked outside the clearing, still nude, where the Free Market was being held until it was her turn to go up on the selling block and the Keepers—and the settlement's men— would devour her with their eyes, imagining all the disgusting things they wanted to do to her.

Ember didn't want to think about it anymore. She closed her eyes and thought of the stranger, smiling at the image of being carted away through the dark. She let the pleasant thoughts carry her into a deep sleep.

The tavern was dark, dingy, and smelled of roasted meat and urine. Tables were occupied by burly men who smelled roughly the same as the atmosphere. They eyed Keona as he moved to the bar at the front of the tavern, the backpack drawing their eyes.

"What'll ye have?" The rough-looking woman behind the bar arrived with a swoosh and a smell that matched the rest of the room.

"What've you got?" Keona asked.

"Ale 'n' pig."

"You take trade?"

The woman squinted at Keona. He was very clean, unlike the rest of her patrons.

"I do. What've ye got?

"Socks, a rain suit, some first aid supplies."

"Wha'ss 'firss aid?'"

"Bandages, ointments, things like that."

The woman threw up her left forearm. Keona didn't flinch. The skin was red and raw from wrist to elbow. It looked to Keona like a burn.

"You make this feel better, I'll getcha some ale and a plate."

Keona swung his backpack around and unzipped the front pouch. The sound made the occupants of the tavern jump. He found a tube of burn cream in the first aid kit, holding out hope that being stored in the bunker in near optimal conditions would have preserved it.

Keona squished the tube in his fingers several times, unscrewed the cap, and held his breath. He squeezed some out, dipped two fingers in the ointment, and ran it along the woman's arm. Her eyes widened, and her mouth slowly opened. Keona braced for a loud screech.

The woman barked out a huge laugh that rang through the tavern and even set a number of other patrons laughing. Keona let out his breath.

"SUMBITCH!" The woman shouted. "He done healed me!" She continued cackling as she wandered off and left Keona to stow the ointment and first aid kit in the backpack. The woman came back in short order with a tall mug of ale and a plate of roasted pork and vegetables.

"I'm Brenda," the woman said, though it sounded like *Brennder*. "Welcome. Where ye from?"

"Far away," Keona said. "Just traveling through."

"Well, mister Faraway, enjoy. That burn been buggin' me since I singed it over the pig fire yesterday. Thanks."

"You're welcome. And thank you for the food and drink."

"Ye need more, jus' axe."

Keona downed the meal, though he was certain the kitchen

would've failed inspection in his time. The ale was surprisingly good, slightly sweet, and left his head swimming slightly after he polished it off.

"Thanks again, Brenda," he said.

"Any time, Faraway." Keona smiled as he made his way toward the front door.

"Ain't no one get a free meal in my town." One of the hulking patrons at a table near the door stood and flexed his arms. His two buddies also stood.

"Shit, CAL! Leave'm alone!" Brenda came around the bar and started shaking her finger at him. "He's *my* cuss'mer in *my* tavern. Ye don' like it, ye can eat at Fat Sally's!"

"Fat Sally don't have ale. An' 'sides, I don't like the way this one looks."

"Please move aside—Cal, was it?"

"We ain't friends. You can't call me 'Cal.'"

"Should I try 'stupid?'"

The man roared and swung for Keona, but Keona easily dodged the clumsy fist. Cal's other fist started its arc, and Keona dodged it, too. Roaring again, Cal charged, and Keona stepped forward and jabbed three fingers into Cal's trachea. The muscles in Cal's throat tightened and spasmed, cutting off Cal's air supply. He sank loudly to his knees, gasping. Cal finally toppled over, his wet breathing sounding like a hound dog had fallen asleep on the floor.

The tavern was silent again, and Brenda again shattered the silence with her barking laugh as Cal's buddies looked fearfully once at Keona before dragging Cal out into the street.

"Shit, Faraway, come have another ale!" Brenda kept cackling as she fetched another mug.

The settlement had fallen silent and dark by the time Brenda shooed out the last of her patrons. Keona lingered outside until the others had gone and headed toward the row of cages. A long chain ran along the top of the cages and through metal loops welded on top of the doors, secured by a padlock on one end. The other end terminated on the back of the cages in an eye welded to the frame. Hinges ran the length of the bottom of the cages, but only one rod ran through them. The design was weak, meant only to hold docile slaves.

One guard stood sentry over the cages. He leaned against the wall of Brenda's tavern and was nearly asleep as Keona crept up to him and quickly knocked him out with a sleeper hold. Keona dragged the guard into the nearest alley and searched him. Keona found the padlock key in a small leather pouch around the guard's neck. He returned to the cages and removed the padlock and chain. The doors of each cage fell with a small *thud* as the end of the chain passed through the loops.

The slaves peered cautiously from the cages. They looked for signs that it was a trick, and saw Keona waving them on, then making a running motion with two fingers. The slaves bowed their silent thanks and ran off in every direction. Ember was the last, and she had remained in her cage, blissfully asleep. Keona crept in and pulled her from the cage, hoisting her into his arms. He carried her into the forest as she slept.

Ember's eyes opened briefly. *Just a dream*, she thought, seeing Keona's square jaw and determined eyes from below. She closed her eyes again and nestled into Keona's chest.

Keona pushed on into the forest until nearly dawn. He found a clearing and set Ember on a soft patch of duff. The fog had gathered thickly a few hours previous, and Keona needed water. He spread out his emergency blanket under the low-hanging bough of a young Ponderosa and shook the bough. He placed his canteen at one end of the blanket and carefully rolled and lifted the blanket into a funnel, pouring the water into the canteen. He repeated the technique several times around the clearing until the canteen was full. He took a quenching swallow. *Piney.*

Keona capped the canteen, shook out and stowed the blanket, then stooped to pick up the woman. She was awake, her eyes wide in fear.

"Do you speak English?" Keona asked. The woman nodded. "I'm Keona. I heard you when I was passing the settlement. You're free now."

"I…I'm Ember." She thought her voice sounded raw, raspy. "May I have some water?"

Keona handed the canteen to her. She opened it clumsily and sipped, fearing a long draw would make her choke. She took a few more sips before capping the canteen and handing it back to Keona.

"We're a few hours outside the settlement. Do you know the area at all?" Ember nodded. "Good. Do you know your directions? North, west, east, south?" Ember nodded again but remained silent. "You can speak freely now. I won't harm you. You're no longer a slave and you can leave any time you'd like. But I'd appreciate your help."

Ember stared at Keona. Could it be true? Was she really free? Her legs twitched, the impulse to run very strong. Yet there was such kindness in the man who had rescued her. "What…what do you wish to know?"

"We're about a half hour from a city called Bend. Do you know of it?"

Ember nodded. "Yes. Bad place."

"What can I expect to find there?"

"Keepers. Death."

"Keepers of death?"

"No, no." Ember sat up a little more. "The people. They call themselves Keepers. That man you killed tonight, he was a Keeper slave transporter."

"I didn't kill him, just put him to sleep. Are there any supplies in Bend?"

"Only those you take from others. Bend is dead. That's why the Keepers steal from the clans around them. They have nothing, know nothing. Only fighting and stealing, stealing and fighting. And selling slaves."

Keona nodded. The fog was changing from a steel gray to a lighter pearl and drifting farther upward. The birds of the forest were singing a little more loudly. He stood and offered a hand to Ember. She hesitated. He bent a little lower and took her hand, then assisted her in standing.

"We'll need to move quickly. Do you feel strong enough to walk for a few hours?"

"Yes."

"Then let's go."

FIVE

Grayson woke with the sun and stepped outside the borrowed hut. He stood tall and stretched; his muscles were still tight from four centuries in stasis. The lake remained still, its glassy surface reflecting the slate gray of the morning sky. Grayson reflected on the few hours he had been alive in a new world. He turned to look over the village and saw no gardens, no livestock. Not even a dog. Grayson turned back to the lake and knelt. He dipped his hands in the cold, clear water and splashed some in his face, over his head. At least water was a resource of which they had plenty.

"Good morning," Juniper said, stepping up beside him.

"Mornin'." Juniper wore a long silken robe that clung to her curves in the light morning breeze. Grayson let his eyes linger a moment before looking back over the lake.

"Ben wants to unload the truck this morning. There's a storage shed on the other side of the village."

"Gotcha."

Juniper and Grayson stood silently, listening to the gentle lapping of the water as they had the night before. Before long, a whistle pierced the calm. They both looked over their shoulders and watched Ben waving at them to come over. As Juniper turned, the breeze caught the front of the robe and parted it slightly above the sash. Grayson averted his eyes as quickly as he could. Juniper snatched the robe closed. Both chuckled and blushed as they walked toward Ben. Juniper peeled off at her hut to change.

Unloading the truck took only about twenty minutes. Ben was drenched in sweat, and Grayson had a light sheen about his exposed skin. Grayson had enjoyed the labor. His muscles finally felt elastic again. Ben, on the other hand, was not as pleased.

"How the hell are you so dry?" Ben slumped into the shade.

"Dunno. Good genes, I guess." Ben gave Grayson a middle finger. Grayson smiled and meandered to the bucket full of drinking water nearby. As he dipped a cup, Alex approached him, Juniper by his side.

"Hey, Grayson."

"Mornin', Alex. What can I do for you?"

"Well, the clan and me thought maybe you'd be up to wanderin' over to this other village north of Bend. They're s'posed to have resources there that we might be able to trade for. Lots of our food and medicine got burned up in the raid."

"Any history of fighting between your clans?"

"Nah. We normally left 'em be. They were too far north to trade with on a regular basis. Thing is, I gotta stay behind and help build out some of the village. This place was abandoned a long time ago, too far from most places. We kept it up as best we could from a distance, but there's some things that need tendin' to. The watch said it looks like there's game in the woods, so we might stand a chance. We'll need seed and fertilizer though, if we have hopes of crops."

"I thought your clan stayed away from agriculture?"

"Normally, we do," Juniper said. "But it's different out here. We have to farm if we're going to survive. Some of the older folks knew how to farm. They kinda aged out of it, and we grew comfortable without it."

"Yup," Alex affirmed, "but we can't go on without it now."

Grayson didn't much like the thought of traipsing around acting as an ambassador for a group of people he barely knew. He felt he needed to know more about his new world before he could speak on behalf of one people. Grayson chanced a look at Juniper, who simply smiled as she tucked a windblown tendril of hair behind her ear. Alex shifted his weight anxiously from one foot to the other as he waited for an answer.

"Yeah, I'll go."

"Thanks a ton, Grayson," Alex said. "We appreciate it."

"I'll go too," Juniper offered. "You'll need someone who knows the people and the area." Grayson smiled and nodded at her. Juniper smiled too as she turned to walk away. Grayson couldn't help but watch as she headed toward her hut.

"Careful with that one," Alex said.

"Huh?"

"She's a handful." Alex stuffed the stem of a clay pipe in his teeth and lit the sweet, pungent tobacco in the bowl with a sulfur match. "Juniper's had more'n her share of troubles. Left their marks on her. She gets mad or sad, things happen."

"I saw a bit of that yesterday, just before we left Awbreytown. I'll be careful."

Alex turned a steely gaze on Grayson. "Not you I worry about, son."

Alex turned and ambled back toward the center of Ochoco, leaving Grayson with his thoughts and a half-full cup of water. He put away the thoughts and downed the rest of the water.

Grayson knocked on the wall of Juniper's hut. She moved the entrance flap aside and stepped out.

"What's up?"

"I need to know a few things."

"Like what?"

"That thing that happened yesterday…" Juniper's eyes fell. "Look, I just need to know how. I'm sure you won't use it against me, but…I need to know you can control it." Juniper's icy blue eyes met Grayson's again, piercing the air between them.

"I can. I learned to control it a long time ago. It came about because of what the Whitecoats did. They did horrible things to me, Grayson. I won't ever go into details because I'm trying to forget. It's been years, and I still wake up sweating in the middle of the night sometimes." Anger was rising in her voice. "So don't you stand there and judge me because of something I didn't want. I never asked for this, and I wish that I had never seen the Whitecoats. Ever."

Grayson lowered his voice to the most soothing tone he had. "Juniper, I'm not judging you. Everything here is new to me, and I need to know as much as I can about this place. Including you."

Juniper's breathing slowed, her color returning. "I'm sorry. You're right. I forget that you're not just new to me. Four hundred years is a lot time to be away from what you know."

"It is. On this trip, I'll ask more than a few questions, I'm sure." Both let down their guard a little. Juniper felt an unexpected warmth for this man, whom she had only known for a couple of days. She could feel both tenderness and strength burning under the stoic façade he maintained. There was something more to Grayson. Maybe he wasn't willing to share it, or maybe it was something of which he was unaware.

"I'm sure I'll have answers. Maybe not answers you'll like every time, but answers." She stepped forward and gave Grayson a hug, a gesture that surprised her as much as it surprised him. He tentatively returned the hug, his tenseness relaxing as he held her. His embrace was tender and reserved, as though he yearned for the connection but didn't want to hold on too tightly. She broke the hug and stepped back. Part of his mystery had been solved.

"Mornin'." Ben seemed to appear out of nowhere. "Alex said you were headed out?"

"Yeah," Grayson answered. "As soon as we can." He shuffled over a bit, adding some space between him and Juniper.

"Mind if I tag along? I'm not much for farm stuff and there's nothing around here for miles. Forage-wise that is. I'll get bored damned quick." Juniper laughed.

"Sure," Grayson said. "Get what you need for a couple days and meet us back here in half an hour." Ben nodded and headed off.

Grayson turned again to Juniper. "So, are you two...ah..."

Juniper smiled. "No. Ben is just a dear friend. We actually met through his wife." Her smile left.

"I take it she's no longer around?""

No. She died horribly. She managed to get some variant of *Codagenesis*, but we have no idea how. It took her in just under two weeks."

"That's awful."

"That's why he drinks. It's only been a year." Grayson nodded. If there was anything he could understand, it was loss.

The early afternoon sun was pleasantly warm as Grayson loaded an ancient electric SUV. Grayson had spotted it the day before while he and Ben unloaded the truck. He asked to swap the truck for the smaller, lighter vehicle in the hope that it would make the trip a little quicker. Juniper called the front seat and Grayson would drive. Ben was still a little road-worn from the previous trip and appreciated the opportunity to relax in the back seat. Alex knocked on the driver's window. Grayson rolled it down.

"Be careful out there, son," Alex said, reaching a hand through the window to shake Grayson's.

"We will be. You be careful in here."

"We'll do our best. Surrounded by walls and water."

"Smartass." Grayson smiled and let go of Alex's hand. "And don't worry, I'll bring this thing back in just the same shape." He tapped the steering wheel.

"Couldn't you purty her up just a *little*?" The two men chuckled.

"All right, boys. Let's get this thing going." Juniper settled into her seat, her rifle nestled comfortably in her lap. "It'd be nice to get to Rimrock before nightfall." Grayson nodded and pointed the nose of the eSUV at the gate. He watched in the rearview mirror as the gate swung closed behind them. The forest pressed in on them again.

"Like I promised, here come the first of a few questions." Grayson flipped on the headlights.

"Go ahead." Juniper put her feet up on the dash.

"How many clans are in the area?"

"Including ours, about…five. There are transient groups that come and go, but there are five main clans. And the Whitecoats." Juniper shuddered.

"Do all the clans get along with one another, other than the Keepers and the Whitecoats?"

"I guess. The Keepers are the only clan I know of that actively despises and fights the others. Rimrock, where we're headed, is pretty isolated from the rest of the area. The people there have generally been okay in the past, if a little skittish. The other two villages—Kalama and Basin—are at the outer edges of where I've gone. The Kalama clan is…odd. The Basin clan is okay, if a little rough."

"So, would you say that the clans try to stay independent, forge their own way?"

"That's accurate."

Sunlight faded quickly as the trees grew denser on the sides of the road. Grayson stopped once to stretch and to get his bearings on the faded map Juniper carried in her pack. It was difficult to say where they were exactly, as the map was drawn at least twenty years before and wasn't to scale. A thin, ragged line cut through the forest marked on the map. It looked like it could have been the old Ochoco Highway. If that were the case, he would meet a river in about ten minutes, and from there it should be about ten minutes more to Rimrock. He hoped.

Grayson climbed in and started out again. Juniper had fallen asleep against the window, Ben sprawled across the back seats. As expected, about ten minutes later he came upon a bridge that went over the river. It had been an irrigation canal when Grayson last visited the area. The bridge was a leftover, patched up with logs and gravel over many years. The roadway itself had been grown over many times, but traffic appeared to have remained somewhat constant. Every so often, a faint trace of the yellow paint of the lane divider could still be seen through the mashed-down overgrowth. Grayson pushed on.

The road finally came into an opening and smoothed out. The remnants of warehouses and sheds were on both sides of the road. He reached over and gently shook Juniper's shoulder.

"Hey. I think we're close."

Juniper sat up fully and grasped her rifle. They both scanned the area as Grayson drove on, looking for any threats. The warehouses gave way to old houses, some of which were reduced to their foundations. They passed Roberts International Airport, though it was hard to tell it had ever been Central Oregon's main airport. Ponderosas had taken over the airfield and broken down the perimeter fencing.

They finally entered what had been downtown Redmond. Some of the red brick buildings still stood, their outer walls blackened by age and water stains. Most of the town had fallen and there were no lights shining in any structures.

"Careful through here," Juniper said. "There might be some nomads out there. Or wolves."

"Wolves, huh? Nice to see they made a comeback."

"A comeback? Were they ever in danger of disappearing?"

"They were. They made a slight rise in population around the time I was put under, but not enough to make an impact."

"They're everywhere now. And hungry."

The eSUV's batteries were draining a little too quickly for Grayson's taste. The darkness of the forest hadn't helped in getting the solar panels the energy they needed. Juniper looked down at her map.

"We should be there s—" As they turned a corner, they drove into a clearing and saw a fence rising forty feet into the sky.

Grayson whistled. "Found it."

He drove into the clearing and rolled down his window a bit. He heard the report of a rifle shot and saw a plume of dirt jump up from the road. Grayson hit the brakes.

"Driver, open the door and step out with your hands in the air!" The voice was shaky and broke on the word *hands*; Grayson suspected the sentry in the watchtower was a boy no older than fifteen. Regardless, he did as he was told, keeping his hands in plain view as he exited the eSUV. *"State your business!"*

"We're here from Awbreytown. The village was sacked and burned. We'd like to discuss trade with your clan." Grayson heard the beep of a radio being activated and the kid mumbling. A tinny voice responded. The kid put the radio down.

"Stay where you are! Our leader will be there shortly! Passengers, OUT!"

Juniper stepped out first, mimicking Grayson's movements. Ben groggily got out of the back, stumbling a bit.

"HEY!" The kid was getting agitated. Ben steadied himself and stood upright. Silence fell between the watchtower and the foragers. Grayson watched three figures emerge from the block structure at the end of a large field and cross toward the gate. It seemed to take them forever to reach the gate, but they arrived. Two men with rifles flanked a woman wearing a white lab coat. Juniper felt uncomfortable on seeing the coat, but there was a warmth emanating from the woman that eased her a bit.

"Mr. Brooks, we've been expecting you," the woman said. "And you, Ms. Scanlon and Mr. Cooley." Regardless of the warmth,

Juniper felt immediately uncomfortable again. "Don't be afraid, Ms. Scanlon. I don't wish harm to any in your party. My name is Kylie Easton. Please, come in." A click sounded in the gate and the men guarding Kylie stepped forward to swing it open.

"Juniper, drive in," Grayson said. "Ben, with me." Grayson and Ben walked through the open gate and stopped just inside. Juniper drove the eSUV through the gate.

"Welcome to Rimrock," Kylie said. "I hope you'll find your stay pleasant."

"As do we." Grayson signaled to Juniper to stop. "How is it that you know our names, Ms. Easton?"

"Please, call me Kylie. Well, Mr. Brooks, I happen to be clairvoyant. Very few things can be hidden from those of us with the gift of second sight."

"Call me Grayson, Kylie. It's a pleasure to meet you." Grayson extended his hand and Kylie took it.

"Let's get you some food and rest, shall we? The last two days must have been quite difficult. Please turn your weapons over to the guards. I assure you that we will take care of them and place them in your accommodations."

They handed over their weapons grudgingly. Kylie led the trio toward the cement building, which seemed familiar to Grayson. As they approached, he could see the faded remnants of pigmentation in the sign over the bank of doors. *Redmond High School*. Grayson looked again at the green lawn that swept down from all sides, much as it had so long ago, and immediately visualized how it had looked when he visited for football games. Grayson couldn't believe the structure still stood. There was evidence of spalling and patching in a few areas of the concrete walls, but it seemed largely intact.

The group entered the front doors and into the commons. A young woman approached the three newcomers and gave each a stack of freshly pressed off-white linen clothing. Grayson saw that nearly every member of the clan—other than the guards and Kylie—wore the linens that had just been handed to him. Juniper pressed closer to Grayson.

"This is the commons." Kylie swept her hand across the room as she led the foragers across the open space toward a set of double doors on the other side. "We use it for meals and gatherings. And this," she said, stepping through the double doors, "is the gymnasium. We use it as our 'town hall,' holding important leadership meetings and more formal gatherings."

"Do you still have pep rallies?" Grayson asked.

"I'm afraid not. My people don't know anything of the game *football*." Kylie stopped in front of an opening in the cinder block wall. "This would be the men's shower room. Grayson, Mr. Cooley, you may use the facilities and meet here again in fifteen minutes. Ms. Scanlon, your shower room is just a few more feet that way."

Kylie began leading Juniper toward a similar opening farther down the wall. Juniper shot a glance at Grayson as she was led away. Grayson gave her a nod to reassure her that things would be okay. Juniper gave him a feeble smile in return.

"I don't like it," Ben whispered as they entered the old locker room. "This place gives me the creeps."

"You're not used to it, that's all." Grayson set the linens down on a bench and walked to the shower bay. He turned the handle as far as it would go—the spray that came out was hot.

"That's gonna be welcome."

The men showered and returned to the spot Kylie had indicated. Juniper came out of the women's shower room shortly after their arrival.

"It's eerie how well these clothes fit," Juniper said.

Ben folded his arms as they waited. Kylie was not long in coming. She led them back to the commons and had them sit at one of the tables. A young man brought a tray loaded with fruit, vegetables, bread, and cheese. He placed it on the table in front of the group before sweeping away to the kitchen again.

"Please, eat." Grayson reached first, handing an apple to Juniper. Their hands touched briefly; an electric charge shot up Juniper's arm and made her heart flutter.

"How long has this place been here?" Ben asked, placing a slice of cheese on a piece of bread.

"It was originally built in 1974, though it's had many upgrades since that time. Several took place in the early 2010s, and major upgrades happened just before the terrorists struck in 2080. Some of those improvements included the addition of hermetic sealing on all doors, windows, and ducting in the event of terrorist attack. How glad we are. The seal kept out *Codagenesis* after it was released. The members of this clan are descended from those that sought refuge here.

"We lived for many years without contention, as you can imagine. With so many of the population decimated, we were an island. We accepted people from the outside who were not infected but we had to turn away the ill. We couldn't afford the possibility of mass infection through mutation of the virus. Those we could not accept were told of a settlement to the south set up for last rites, as we didn't have the cure in our stores."

"There was a cure?" Grayson asked.

"There was. It was held in reserve by the company that had patented it, BioGene. The parent corporation, Ziggurat Consolidated, refused to release it except to those employed by Ziggurat and to select allied governments around the world. Nearly all rejected the conditions of its release. The American government tried to strongarm Ziggurat for the cure by freezing their assets and arresting key players, but Ziggurat dug in its heels and went underground. Quite literally, in fact. The descendants of those people are known to the clans here as Whitecoats. I've not been able to see them at all, which is worrisome for our people, since we don't know their intentions. At any rate, the settlement for last rites was destroyed by the Keepers, and all who inhabited it were killed.

"We've been able to sustain ourselves by propagating our own seed in the old agriculture and horticulture wings of this building and converting some of the land northeast of this building into food-producing plots. We've abandoned the practice of eating meat, as the livestock simply were too costly in resources to maintain. However," Kylie said, smiling as she bit into a small square of cheese, "I simply cannot live without a few cows and goats to provide dairy."

"That's pretty remarkable." Grayson looked about the commons at the few people milling around. "And what about defense? Clearly you have perimeter fencing, but what other means do you employ?"

"The fence is electrified, to start. There are watchtowers spaced along the fenceline and are manned at all times. We also maintain battlements in strategic areas along the roofline for any successful breach of the fence. We have rifles, pistols, crossbows, and an armorer to maintain them. Before you ask, no, you can't meet him right now. He's on a reconnaissance mission to find caches of armament to support current stockpiles. We've reused cartridge brass so many times that much of it is in danger of failure."

"What kind of training do you do?" Grayson was impressed by the inventory. More important to him was how they used it. Juniper and Ben listened raptly as the two spoke. Questions about the compound seemed to come easily to Grayson.

"There are suburban ruins beyond the western fenceline that have proven excellent combat training fields. We run exercises for forest combat as well, though our settlement has seen enough of that over the past few centuries that we feel we're well-equipped to repel most attacks. Our expeditionary forces engage enemies or wolves nearly every time they venture out."

Grayson cleared his throat. "On to the matter at hand. The reason we visited…"

"I'm quite aware of the reason you've called, Grayson." Kylie smiled. "We have plenty of reserve seed and fertilizer, and we would be pleased to share it with Ochoco. As a courtesy, we will also provide a small trailer to carry the fertilizer."

"Thank you!" Juniper interjected. Relief coursed through her along with the warmth from Kylie.

"You're quite welcome. I would ask also that Ochoco consider trading some of the ammunition you found at Pine Mountain in return for the seed, fertilizer, and trailer."

"Of course," Grayson said.

Grayson was dismayed that Kylie had ferreted that bit of information out of his mind. He was hoping to keep it close to the vest as an insurance policy. Grayson noted the unwelcome probe.

"If you'll excuse me, it's been a rather long day for me here, and I require some respite." She motioned a young woman over. "Gemma, would you be so kind as to escort our visitors to their rooms?" Gemma nodded.

"Thanks again, Kylie." Grayson extended his hand. Kylie's return handshake was just as firm as the first.

Gemma led them to three rooms in the south wing. What had once been classrooms had been partitioned into many, much smaller quarters. The rooms they were provided with were clearly set up for guests. Gemma gestured to each in turn. They found their belongings inside as promised.

Ben crawled into his bunk and immediately fell asleep. Juniper arranged her things in a way that felt comfortable. Grayson lay awake in his bed for a time. He stared at the ceiling and ran through all information he had obtained in three short days. It felt as though he had woken up on a different planet. *Except everyone speaks English.* He smiled at the ridiculousness of his own thoughts.

As Grayson's eyelids finally grew heavy, a soft knock came at the door. He stood and went to the door, opening it just a crack. Juniper was on the other side, dressed in the flowy silken robe she seemed to favor at night.

"Hi. Can I come in?" Grayson stepped aside and let her in. He left the door ajar, as much for himself as for any passersby.

"You doing okay?" Grayson asked.

"Better. The last couple of days have been hard."

"I can imagine."

"I suppose you can. You must've seen some awful things back in your day."

"I did." Silence fell as they both ruminated for a few moments.

"I just...I wanted to thank you for coming here. You didn't have to, but you did."

"I've gotta find my place here. I've never been one to be idle, and it doesn't look like there's a lot of opportunity for me here other than volunteering for things like this."

"I suppose." Juniper moved for the door. "That's all I wanted to say." Grayson stood at the door as she exited.

"Uh...good night." Grayson couldn't think of anything else to say.

"Good night, Grayson." Juniper swished to her room. Grayson closed his door and sighed. He checked his rifle, dropping the magazine and counting the rounds, inserting the magazine, pulling back and releasing the bolt. He set the safety and placed the rifle next to his bed. He checked the pistol he had taken from the cache in Ochoco in the same way, then placed it under his pillow. Grayson lay down again, closing his eyes, willing himself to sleep.

SIX

Keona became aware of the men following them around midday.

They had walked beyond the outskirts of Bend and successfully escaped being seen. During the walk, Ember had opened a little, speaking of her rather bleak history and the death of her family at the hands of the Keepers. Trust for Keona had blossomed in her, and she felt more comfortable with him each passing hour.

Keona needed her trust at that moment. He had spotted two men behind them and to the right. They had been following Keona and Ember for the better part of thirty minutes, trying to remain covered by the trees and ferns. Keona unslung his backpack and opened it as they kept walking. He reached in and retrieved his pistol, pulled the slide back, released it, and gave it to Ember. She held it gingerly.

"Have you ever fired one before?"

"A long time ago. It was nothing like this." Ember inspected the pistol, holding it a little gingerly. "I wasn't very good then."

"Don't worry. You'll hit what you're aiming at. Just keep a firm grip and point it with straight arms."

Keona handed her an extra magazine. He pointed at a downed tree and motioned for Ember to hide. She did as she was asked. Keona turned in the direction of the two men following and saw them hiding behind ferns. He stared directly at them. They knew their position was compromised.

The first one rushed clumsily, crashing through the foliage directly at Keona. He was immense, standing well over six and a half feet tall and rippling with lean muscle. The face was contorted into a mask of rage, vein and sinew bulging through scraggly hair and beard. His height and width was nothing short of freakish. He wore rudimentary clothing and what looked to be soft leather boots tied with leather strips. Keona stepped aside and let the man tumble to the ground. His companion followed closely, and though he was just as large, he wasn't as clumsy and Keona took him straight on, using the man's weight to counter the charge and throw him to the forest floor. A harsh *whoosh* of air escaped the second man's lungs as he hit. The first roared, approached swiftly from the rear, and wrapped an arm around Keona's throat. Keona dropped quickly to a knee, knocking the man off-balance. He placed his hands on the man's arms at the same moment and used the downward momentum to throw the man over his shoulder. The man landed on the second attacker's body, sending out another grunt from the already winded man.

Keona drew up to his full height and stood silently, waiting for the two men to regroup. They did, hesitantly, and squared off with Keona. One pulled a blade reminiscent of a katana from a scabbard lashed to his back, and the other pulled his fists out of his pockets with two smooth metal rods gripped tightly in his hands. Keona dug in his rear foot.

They rushed him at the same time. Keona stepped left and grabbed the sword-wielding man's wrist. He rotated it at an awkward angle and the man screamed in pain, letting go of the blade. Keona grabbed it as it began falling and thrust the blade deep into the man's belly. The second attacker spun as quickly as he could and swung his weighted fist at Keona's face. Keona swung the limp body of the first attacker to meet the punch and dislodged the blade at the same time. As the first attacker fell, Keona swept the blade up under the second attacker's armpit and slashed, the blade biting deep. Continuing his momentum, Keona landed a deep slash to the second attacker's back. He fell to the earth and struggled to get up, finally giving up as blood gushed from his first—and fatal—

wound.

Ember rose from her hiding spot with the pistol held out stiffly in front of her. Her hands shook, the muzzle trembling slightly. Keona approached her and pushed gently on top of the pistol so that she would lower it.

"It's over. You're okay."

"That was...that was...I've never seen anyone fight like that." Ember was awed at the way Keona had moved, so gracefully and yet so brutally.

Keona returned to the first attacker's body and retrieved the sheath for the blade. He put it on his own belt and slid the blade home. Ember tried to give back the pistol.

"Keep it. We may need it sooner rather than later." He suddenly felt the presence of others in the area. "We need to move." Keona put the backpack on and grabbed Ember's free hand to lead her on.

"I've never seen anyone fight like that." Innes McKenzie was prone in the undergrowth. He watched the man and woman rush off into the forest. Innes was in disbelief, having just watched two Keepers taken down effortlessly in a matter of seconds. One of his scouts began slinking backward, the rustle of leaves betraying the scout's intention. Innes unholstered his pistol and pointed it backward without looking, knowing exactly where the scout would be.

"Stay." The scout did—and promptly wet himself. Innes smelled the urine in the air. "Oh, for fuck's sake." He stood angrily and pulled the scout up by his collar. A third scout jumped up and stood quietly.

"You piss your pants on recon? *Seriously*?!" He shook the scout, making the younger man start weeping. "Move your miserable ass. Back to Rimrock. GO!" He spun the scout and kicked him hard in the backside.

They made their way back to Rimrock quickly. Once through the western gate Innes dismissed the younger scouts. He stalked to Kylie's room and pounded on the door, then barged inside without waiting for invitation.

"Good evening, Innes. So good to see you." Kylie sat back in her chair, knowing what was coming next.

"Goddammit, Kylie! I can't go out there with these green scouts! I'm gonna end up mauled or *dead*! I need at least *one* person with me who doesn't turn white at the hint of a fuckin' shadow!"

"Calm yourself, Innes. I'll work on finding someone who matches your fortitude, though I don't believe it will be easy."

"Fine. But the next one who pisses himself is gettin' left in the forest."

"I understand. Please, go find something to eat, and maybe some ale to steady your constitution."

Innes threw open the door and left, not bothering to close the door behind him. Kylie sighed and stood to meet her next visitors. Grayson and Juniper approached, Juniper looking over her shoulder.

"Sorry," Grayson said. "We were on our way to the commons when we heard the yelling." Juniper stood beside Grayson, her fingers fidgeting together.

"No apology necessary, Grayson. Everything is fine here. Please, continue on your way." Kylie gently closed the door.

Juniper and Grayson did continue to the commons and visited the kitchen. In line, they received a bowl of hearty stew and some bread before finding an open table. They sat across from each other and dug in, eating silently together, both practicing their best table manners.

"What are you thinking about?" Juniper asked, finishing the last of her stew and pushing the empty bowl to the side.

"What happens next." Grayson dabbed his mouth with the cloth napkin that had been provided with the flatware. He also pushed his bowl aside. "Once we get the seed and fertilizer back to Ochoco, I'm not going to be of much use anymore. I don't have any farming skills to speak of, and I've never really gotten along with the idea of a pastoral life."

"We could always use a hunter and a warrior. We've grown pretty weak in those skill sets."

"I suppose." They let the silence descend on them again. Juniper continued to look at him, even as he dipped his eyes. She let the silence continue as she carefully chose her next words.

"I...I'd like it if you stuck around, Grayson," Juniper said finally. He lifted his eyes to meet hers. "In just a few days, you've given hope to my clan. And, by coming to Rimrock, you've granted them a chance at rebuilding their future." Grayson didn't know how to best respond, so he gathered their dishes and carried them to the kitchen. When he returned to the table, Juniper stood and took his hand.

"You've made a difference to me, too. You're the only person I've been around in years who hasn't shown fear when you see me." Grayson squeezed her hand gently. "I've felt like a monster since I came back from the Whitecoat bunker. Everyone has kept their distance for so many years." Juniper wrapped her arms around him, resting her head on his chest. "Please don't leave me behind."

Grayson hesitated briefly before returning the embrace. This was something for which he hadn't trained. The Marines did not generally encourage vulnerability. Something in the way Juniper held him made him fiercely protective, and he knew at that moment what his new path would be.

"I won't."

Juniper looked up at him. Though her eyes were glistening, she smiled. She stood on tiptoe to gently kiss his cheek.

"Thank you."

An air raid siren shocked Grayson awake. Reflexively, he threw on the chest rig, stuffed his pistol in the holster he had installed on the rig, and took up his rifle as he sprinted from his room. Juniper and Ben joined him in the corridor as he raced shirtless and barefoot toward the commons. A ladder ascended from the middle of the commons floor to the roof. All three were acting on instinct as they shimmied up the ladder. Juniper noted that Grayson's body moved in a way that belied his size, quickly and with ease. She felt exhilaration coming from him, and dread from everyone else surrounding her.

The foragers erupted from the porthole into hell. Machine guns were firing from each battlement at which they were installed. People were yelling from every direction. Grayson determined where the bulk of the fire was concentrated and rushed across the roof to the east. He peered over the edge next to one of the battered M60 machine guns. He was stunned.

Awash in the glare of the floodlights were hundreds of thick, muscled men crashing against the electrified fence. They screeched as they hit the fence, recoiled, roared, and charged again. Veins pulsed everywhere their flesh was exposed. Spittle ran from their mouths. Most astonishing, other than their berserker appearance, was that none of them stood less than seven feet tall. Bodies piled up at the foot of the fence. The men kept pressing.

"Keepers!" Juniper shouted. Grayson looked at the barrel of the chattering M60 next to him. It was beginning to glow red.

"Cease fire!" The kid behind the trigger wasn't letting up. His eyes were wide in shock. "I said, stop firing!" Still no response. Grayson let the rifle rest on its sling, got behind the gun, and knocked the kid off the trigger to his butt. The kid looked up at him fearfully. Grayson hopped up on the nest and turned his back to Juniper. He unzipped his pants and unleashed a stream of urine onto the barrel of the M60, which sent back the sounds of hissing and a column of steam. Grayson jumped down and readied his rifle.

"Use burst fire," he said to Juniper. "Don't keep your finger on the trigger longer than five rounds. This thing is gonna fail if it gets any hotter." Juniper nodded. Grayson turned to the edge and lifted his rifle, squeezing off a few rounds into the press of Keepers. Each shot found its mark. With every round fired, one Keeper fell. A fresh burst of fire opened on the west side. *They're flanking us*, Grayson thought.

"I've got this side," Juniper yelled, the M60 barking with a five-round burst. "Head over to the west!" Grayson churned his feet as fast as he could. The gunner on the west parapet was doing much better, letting off five- to ten-round bursts of fire before re-centering the sights on target. The Keepers were also less forward, not as willing to press against the fence. Ben had taken up position next to the gunner. The Keepers' behavior changed as soon as a few of their brethren fell; they started pressing against the fence then as well. *Son of a bitch.* Grayson realized they were using the dead to ground themselves against the electric current. He could tell they were getting shocked, but the resistance through the dead appeared to dull the jolt a bit.

An unearthly roar came from deeper in the forest. The Keepers halted their assault, looking back over their shoulders toward the sound. They crawled down from the fence and began backing slowly into the forest. Grayson pulled away and ran to the east side to meet up with Juniper. The Keepers on that side were retreating as well. The gunfire ceased. Another roar came through the trees, answered by the call of hundreds of Keepers. That sound was worse than all the combined gunfire. It chilled Grayson's blood.

"What just happened?" Juniper asked.

"They were testing the defenses."

"Are they coming back?"

"I don't know. They may be redoubling their attack, but we'll just have to wait and see."

The kid he knocked over was still on his butt. Grayson yanked him up.

"Next time I tell you to *cease fire,* you let go of the trigger. Understand?" The kid nodded profusely. "Good. Find some water to cool that barrel before it warps to uselessness. Go." The kid ran off.

They waited on the roof for an interminable time, but the Keepers never showed again. The Rimrockians descended the ladder and went back to their rooms. The kid poured several buckets of water on the barrel of the M60 he had nearly destroyed until it was cool enough that he could touch the barrel. Several other Rimrockians stayed on the roof to sweep and gather the brass to be reloaded. Grayson and Juniper were the last to descend the ladder into the commons. Kylie was waiting at the bottom.

"You've had your first encounter with our 'friends' from Bend, I see."

"Why didn't anyone tell me they were like...*that*?" Grayson was only *slightly* angry. Awe and a little fear were more prevalent.

"Sometimes, the only way to understand something is to experience it firsthand. Why don't you wash up and get some more rest?" Kylie held out her hand to usher them on.

The foragers did as Kylie suggested, though they were too amped up to rest. Ben decided to go for a walk, while Grayson and Juniper opted to enjoy a beverage in the commons. Grayson heard they raised coffee beans in the greenhouse and roasted them in the kitchen. He was anxious to try it, having missed out on coffee since waking up in his new reality. He had the attendant brew a cup. The smell intrigued Juniper.

"May I try some?" she asked. Grayson reluctantly handed the

cup to her. Juniper squinted at the bitterness. Grayson chuckled at the reaction. He took the cup back and sipped. Heaven. Grayson closed his eyes and smiled. The comfort of something he knew began to melt away some of the anger he still felt.

"I'm not sure I can appreciate it as much as you are." Juniper took a sip of her peppermint tea.

"It was an acquired taste in my time, too. People used to dump milk, sugar, syrup, and whipped cream in it and still tried to call it *coffee*."

"That sounds more pleasant." Juniper wrinkled her nose. Grayson smiled and continued sipping.

"The Keepers surprised me." Grayson paused for a moment. "You didn't tell me they were…uh …"

"Different?" Juniper dropped her eyes for a moment. "No, I didn't. I didn't know how to describe them to you. *Evolved* is the wrong word, so is *mutated*. *Enhanced*, maybe?"

"They've definitely strayed off of the evolutionary path." Grayson finished his cup of coffee and moved on to Juniper's. "Seems like there's new information every hour."

"Is there anything I can do to help?"

"Yes. Don't hold anything back. If I'm gonna make good decisions, I need to have as much information as you can give." Juniper nodded. "Are the Whitecoats similar?"

"No. They've become something else also, but in a different

way. They're much more intelligent than the Keepers and the clanspeople throughout the area. They aren't physically strong, though. They rely on their intelligence to survive. That's why they were experimenting on me. They were trying to find a safe way to induce psychokinesis in their own people."

"It seems counterintuitive to experiment on people who are physiologically different."

"You don't talk like a warrior." Juniper smiled and placed a hand on Grayson's. "It does, you're right. My guess is that we're still similar enough that they believe the experiments should prove fruitful. The Whitecoats have kind of a...a shared mind."

"A hive mind," Grayson said. "That's what we would've called it in my time. But it was a science fiction thing."

"Like bees? That makes sense."

"The worst part is that they take the clanspeoples' children, who aren't as strong, but their minds are still open."

"I assume they don't take Keeper children."

"No. The Keepers' children are freakishly strong and their minds are too weak to accept what the Whitecoats do to them." Juniper was clearly becoming very uncomfortable talking about the Whitecoats.

"Where was the bunker you escaped from?"

"At the base of the mountains west of the old town of Sisters. I couldn't tell you exactly where. They called the facility *Hope*, which

I suppose is as fitting for them as it is ironic for the clanspeople."

"That's the middle Sister."

"What?"

"The mountains, they're called the Three Sisters and are named *Faith*, *Hope*, and *Charity*." Grayson set his cup down and looked at Juniper with deep seriousness. "Did they talk about other facilities, bunkers, anything like that?"

"They did. Never how many though."

"They may have at least two others, if they were naming their facilities after the mountains they were being built near."

"If that's the case, there are many more Whitecoats than we have imagined." Juniper shuddered.

"It looks like the most pressing concern is the Keepers. There's no reason they would have been testing Rimrock's defenses tonight unless they were planning a full attack. It could be days or weeks." Grayson looked around the commons at the people going about their business.

"You're thinking of staying here, aren't you?" Juniper asked, already knowing the answer. She squeezed Grayson's hand.

"We can't leave them in the dust. I watched the way they fought, and I don't think they're ready for a true assault. You see that kid I pushed off the M60? He was scared out of his mind. They need someone to prep them."

"What about Ochoco?"

"You and Ben know the way and how to defend yourselves." Grayson stood and took up the empty coffee cups.

"I'm staying with you," Juniper said. "Remember your promise?"

"I do." Juniper followed as Grayson returned the cups to the kitchen. "We can send Ben on his own, then. I'm sure he'll be okay. *If* there aren't any remaining Keepers in the forest to the east. We can talk to Kylie about sending scouts ahead of Ben, just to make sure the area's clear."

"Sounds good. Thank you."

They knocked on Ben's door. When he answered, Grayson briefed Ben.

"Guess it could be worse," Ben said. "I still don't trust these folks all the way, though. Maybe we can get the scouts to halt just a few miles out. I'm not sure I want any of 'em knowing exactly where Ochoco is."

"Same," Grayson said, "but if they're going to be allies, we'll need to at least feed into their good graces."

Juniper felt concern wafting through the air. She closed her eyes and willed a protective bubble over them. "Boys, we should wrap it up. I think Kylie's 'listening' in."

"That just helps to confirm my unease," Grayson said. "Okay, Ben. We'll do our best to forestall any lengthy push by scouts. Just make sure you get to Ochoco. If we run into any trouble, Juniper and I will be able to take care of ourselves. When you make your way back, if we're not here, something went sideways. All good?"

"Understood," Ben said.

Grayson was suddenly very tired. Juniper felt the wave of exhaustion flood through her own system.

"You should get some rest," Juniper said. "Go lay down."

"Yeah, yeah. I should." Grayson ambled off toward his room. Juniper did the same. It had been a rough morning.

Kylie shook her head in frustration. *Damned girl.* She walked out of her office and to the front doors, looking out over the east lawn. *She's going to be a problem, I can feel it.* Kylie disliked having these interlopers in her settlement, though she saw the value in their skills, particularly Grayson. She further disliked her consciousness being pushed out of the strangers' conversation by images of a girl dancing in a field of flowers. That was Juniper's doing.

The sun had begun rising — gold, purple, and pink fire glowing above the treetops. The day still had promise. Kylie stepped out and breathed deeply of the moist, piney air.

No matter, she thought. *We're going to be okay. It'll all be okay. Grayson will make sure of it.*

SEVEN

Charles Zhang sat atop the facility with his legs crossed and his hands resting on his knees, inhaling the crisp, cool mountain air and exhaling reverently. The field reports had angered him, and he needed solitude to reset himself. A large contingent of Keepers had moved north and attacked the fence at Rimrock—this did not bode well for his people. The Keepers had isolated themselves for nearly fifty years; if the field report was correct, their behavior suggested they were looking for new territory. It would only be a short time before they started scouting in other directions.

A separate worry, though related, was that the humans had defended the compound in a way they never had before, sending pinpoint fire amid their normal undisciplined hail of bullets. Rimrock was not known for having patient, trained shooters.

Both reports pointed to a much bigger problem developing.

Zhang unfolded and stood. The sun had dipped behind the mountains and the air was cooling quickly. He descended into the bunker his ancestors had named *Hope* and hustled to his office to escape being approached with anything more that day. Zhang's plan was dashed, however, when his assistant knocked on the door just after he had taken his seat at his desk.

"Sir, we have the humans ready for inspection."

"Fine, fine. I'll be there shortly." Zhang sighed as the assistant departed. He rubbed his temples in a futile attempt to curb the pounding headache developing. The long, thin fingers of his hands couldn't apply as much pressure as he would have liked. To his forebears, he would have looked sickly thin. His pale skin looked nearly gray. Most noticeable was his large, hairless head which housed large, almond-shaped eyes, a brief spark of color separating the pupil from the dark gray sclera.

All his people shared these features, a product of living underground without much sunlight and the unquenchable thirst for knowledge. Their records showed that their forebears had all been scientists, and that they had been sealed off from the world when a virus called *Codagenesis* had been released among the human population. The scientists had all been inoculated against it, but being in the sunless environs had somehow allowed the dead virus in the vaccine to turn them into what they were within a relatively short evolutionary timeline.

Zhang ran a hand over his smooth head before standing to depart the office. His soft-soled shoes barely made a whisper on the polished floors as he walked to the lab where the humans were being held. Zhang's headache was getting increasingly worse as he approached the lab. His attitude was following suit.

As he entered the lab, the technicians parted to allow him an unobstructed view of the humans inside. The three humans were stripped bare to allow Zhang to appraise their physical features. They were tethered to the floor by lengths of chain, preventing them from moving or even from covering their private parts.

"Sir," a technician said, "we've prepared them for the initial testing."

"Good. And they've been able to withstand the trials without fail?"

"Yes. All three."

Zhang paced before the humans. They were of average build and appeared healthy. Their flesh was unmarred by battle or disease. Two females and one male. The females shamefully hung their heads. Only the male held up his head, hands to his side, wearing a defiant look as they were being scrutinized. Zhang didn't like the male's demeanor.

"What's your name?" Zhang asked him.

"Taylor."

"Is that a first name or a surname?" The male didn't respond.

"I see. Well, *Taylor*, the testing you're about to undergo will not be easy without a mindset of acceptance. I fear you'll have a difficult time of it." Taylor remained silent. He wouldn't break eye contact with Zhang.

"You three will be subjected to experimentation that will ultimately make you valuable assets to my people. You will learn how to control your world with your mind and will learn how to accept orders from me willingly. Resistance will become painful. If you allow the experiments to succeed, I will find a place for you among us. You will no longer call us Whitecoats as outsiders but will learn to call us by our true name, *Jiating*, which means 'family' in my ancestors' language."

One of the females began to weep. Zhang approached her and lifted her chin. She wouldn't meet his eyes. He took time to scour her body with his eyes. Unlike the Jiating females, she was full at the hips and had ample breasts; her stomach was flat, without stretchmarks. She had never borne a child.

"Dear, look at me." Her tear-filled eyes met his. There was no defiance, only fear. "You will be well cared for, should you choose to accept your fate. I promise you that." She nodded almost imperceptibly. Zhang released her chin, and her eyes looked down at the floor again.

"Sir, with your permission, we're ready to begin."

"Proceed."

Zhang departed the lab to the sound of the female audibly sobbing. As he entered his office, he pulled a blank piece of paper from the pile on his desk and lifted the fountain pen that sat in an upright holder. He began writing a brief message to his military commander, General Timothy Staats, at the Faith bunker.

> *General Staats:*
>
> *The Keepers cannot be allowed to continue scouting the territory. Activate your forces to begin an incursion on Bend. Ensure the Keepers are not allowed egress, contain at all costs, then eliminate population. With prejudice.*

He sealed the letter in an envelope and set it aside. An ancient bit of technology that the Jiating had retrofit for communication within their facilities, a telephone, sat at the corner opposite his pile of paper. He lifted the receiver and dialed the extension for the courier's office. Messages of the type contained in the letter were too sensitive for delivery any other way.

"Sir?"

"I have a letter for General Staats. Send a courier for immediate delivery."

"Yes, sir. The courier will be there in three minutes."

Zhang set the receiver in its cradle and again placed his fingers on his throbbing temples, rubbing them ineffectually. War was inevitable.

The courier placed the note in Staats's hand thirty minutes later. The courier's electric dirtbike sat outside nearly overheating from the exertion that had been placed on it through the woods and foothills. Zhang did not tolerate delays. Staats tore open the envelope and waved the courier away. As he read, his lips spread into a grim smile. He had been preparing his army for just such a moment.

Unlike his brethren at the Hope and Charity bunkers, Staats and his soldiers were more muscular and stood nearly a foot taller. They still had the pallid gray skin, elongated heads, and large eyes, but careful breeding and years of physical training had altered their physiques to allow for formidable warriors.

Staats folded the letter and marched to the war room. He used the intercom to summon his advisors and commanders. He took his seat at the head of the long conference table and awaited their arrival. One by one, the seats filled on either side of the table until full. Staats nodded his head to the sergeant at the heavy steel door. The sergeant moved quickly to close it.

"Leader Zhang has asked that we march on Bend to seal the Keepers inside. We are to mobilize at once. Sisemore, do we have what is needed?" Lieutenant General Michael Sisemore nodded.

"We have sufficient supplies to support personnel and

equipment. The technical division has given me assurances that the carriers are fit for extended deployment, and the quartermaster corps has been busy procuring, stockpiling, and rotating provisions in the event such orders were given."

"Excellent. Every member of this staff will be entrusted with leading their companies to victory. This is the moment we've been preparing for. I will join you in the field for strategic support and may be called upon at any time for directives. Should any of you fail, Leader Zhang will likely meet your failure with exile or death. I suggest you do not fail."

The staff stood as Staats waved his dismissal. Staats remained behind to look at the maps his army had developed. He was confident his army would succeed, though this was to be their first engagement in nearly twenty-five years. The last battle fought against the Keepers had ended in the utter defeat of the Jiating, pushing them back to the bunkers in which they had lived and thrived for decades. His army was now better trained, better provisioned, and harbored a mindset of victory above all else.

Staats returned to his office and pulled a bottle of human scotch from his desk. The bottle was new, unsealed, and had been waiting in his desk for just that occasion. The scotch had been bottled in 2020, survived the spread of *Codagenesis* and the fall of humanity, and discovered by his great-great-grandfather in this bunker, then hidden away in a filing cabinet in the storage room, until Staats found it while looking through his great-great-grandfather's effects. He cracked the seal, unstopped the bottle, and poured a finger into a glass. Staats sniffed at the lip of the glass, notes of caramel and oak wafting from the deep amber drink. He sipped and smiled as the drink dribbled over his palate and down his throat.

"To the war," he said, sipping again.

EIGHT

Grayson and Juniper ate breakfast silently. Ben had departed Rimrock an hour earlier with the eSUV and trailer, which Grayson had quickly loaded with the seed and fertilizer. Scouts had been sent ahead of Ben by thirty minutes and were to return by nightfall if the route had been clear; they were to return at once with Ben if Keepers occupied the way. Kylie had assured Ben that she foresaw no danger and that he would arrive at Ochoco safely. The scouts were an extra measure insisted upon by Grayson. The rest of the day would be spent waiting.

Grayson and Juniper spent the rest of the morning walking around the compound, getting to know its layout and the people who lived there. Though quiet, there was a preciseness about the way the Rimrockians went about their lives. Their quarters were immaculately kept, as was the commons, and landscape maintenance was almost meditative for the groundskeepers. Since there was no gasoline, all landscape maintenance equipment was manual; reel lawn mowers, weed whips, hand clippers. The absence of internal-combustion engines had quieted the environment. Grayson reveled in the songs of the birds and the chittering of squirrels, animals which had somehow escaped the ravages of *Codagenesis*.

On return to the main building, they were met with the excited chatter of a cluster of Rimrockians. Grayson held Juniper's hand as they pushed through a crowd that had gathered outside Kylie's office. She stood in the doorway, hands up, palms out, attempting to quiet the crowd.

"Please, *please*. I don't see any reason for panic."

"Who are they? What do they want?" One of the Rimrockians had pressed forward to ask the question, hoping to be heard over the general buzz of the crowd.

"I'm unable to see their intentions," Kylie answered. "They seem to be closed off to me. There are only two, however, and I don't sense anything but calm."

"Where will they be arriving?" Grayson asked. "Which side?"

"They should be arriving in five minutes at the main entrance. They'll be able to bypass the gate."

Grayson gave Juniper's hand a squeeze and dashed off to his room, Juniper close on his heels. Inside, he reached under his pillow, grabbed his pistol, and shoved an extra magazine into the left hip pocket of his pants. He reached for his rifle, then decided that with only two potential hostiles he wouldn't need it. Juniper arrived at his doorway as he was about to exit. Her short rifle was slung on her shoulder.

"I'm coming too."

"I wish you wouldn't."

"I know."

Grayson had no time to argue. He nodded and took off at a jog toward the main entrance. The crowd had shifted from Kylie's room to the commons, a small sea of people milling about in front of the entrance doors.

"Get back! Stay away from the doors!" Grayson's order was followed, albeit reluctantly. Enough of them had seen what Grayson was capable of with a firearm and were quick to defer to his judgment. He and Juniper took up positions on opposite sides of the entrance corridor to allow for clean lines of sight.

The commons fell quiet as the clanspeople waited. Grayson steadied his own breathing, his pistol held ready. Juniper stared calmly at the doors down the barrel of her short rifle. Time felt as if it had slowed to a crawl.

Finally, two silhouettes could be seen. A man and a woman by the looks of them. They approached the doors at a leisurely pace, which Grayson decided was a good sign. They passed into the shadow of the building, which obscured their features as they walked up to the glass doors. The man reached out and rattled one of the locked doors. He took a step back and held out his hand. Grayson heard the lock click and the door opened on its own.

"That's far enough," Grayson barked. The man stopped, and his head cocked to one side.

"Grayson?" The voice cut through the tension and made Grayson's heart skip a beat. He wasn't quite ready to lower the pistol, though.

"Keona?!"

"Yes. How are you, old friend?"

"At the moment, a bit confused. I thought you escaped from Ziggurat."

"As did I. Unfortunately, I was tranqued and dragged back to the bunker. I was tried while unconscious. Unbelievable, eh?" An uncomfortable silence passed between them. "Look, Grayson, I'm sorry. I didn't mean to hurt you in any way. I just couldn't keep getting exposed to the experimentation they were doing on me."

"Experimentation? I was told you'd been sequestered as a patient."

"That's what they told you, huh?" Keona took a few steps farther into the corridor and into the light, but Grayson didn't lower his pistol. "I was the subject of a battery of experiments, Gray. I was dropped in sensory deprivation tanks, given psychoactives, poked, probed, and God knows what else. They turned me into something different. Once they saw what I was capable of, they locked me up."

Juniper lowered her short rifle. A tear streaked down her cheek. She knew precisely of what he was speaking and could feel the pain radiating from Keona as he spoke. Grayson saw her movement from the corner of his eye, but kept his pistol trained on Keona. Grayson wanted to believe what Keona was saying.

"Please, put the gun down. I'm not a threat to you. I've always been your friend."

Grayson made no move to stow his pistol. Suddenly, the gun bucked in his hand and flew the distance between him and Keona. Keona caught it, ejected the magazine, ejected the round in the chamber, and removed the slide—all with remarkable speed— before dropping the weapon in pieces and holding his hands out palms up. The Rimrockians that had been raptly watching gasped or screamed. Juniper stood.

"Calm," she said. The crowd fell quiet again, all of them overcome with a sense of calm that wasn't entirely their own.

"An empath?" Keona looked at Juniper with interest. Juniper spun in surprise.

"Y-yes."

"Grayson, surely you can tell I'm being truthful. I'm your friend. If you don't believe me, maybe trust her?" Juniper turned her head to Grayson and nodded. Grayson reluctantly stood and walked forward. He stooped to pick up the pieces of his pistol before stopping directly in front of Keona.

"Then we have a lot of catching up to do." He stuck out his right hand, which Keona shook firmly.

"Yes, we do."

Kylie stepped forward. "Wonderful." She motioned to Gemma and a male the foragers hadn't met, who rushed forward. "Please escort our newest guests to the facilities and fetch them some clean clothes. They're road weary and would appreciate a soothing shower."

Keona and Ember were led to clean up. Ember was hesitant to leave Keona's side at the shower rooms.

"It's okay, Ember. I'm going to be right here in this room. I'll be able to come quickly if I hear anything strange." Keona smiled and watched her go into the women's shower room, Gemma gently leading her and reassuring her.

Gemma led her over to the shower stalls and showed Ember how to turn the water on and off, and how to control the temperature. She also explained to Ember that the strange cake was used to clean her skin.

"But won't that burn after?"

"No," Gemma said gently. "What you're used to is an abrasive powder made from wood ashes that hurts your skin; this is called 'soap' and it just lifts dirt from your skin and washes it away."

Gemma smiled and stepped away. "I'll be just over by the entrance. Let me know if you need anything else."

Ember marveled at the warm water that seemed endless and came from nowhere. She took off her meager clothing and tentatively stepped into the stream. She instinctively recoiled a bit, remembering the cold, stinging "showers" she was used to. The water that fell from the shower head fell like a warm rain though, and Ember was quickly drawn completely in. The warmth coursed over her body and stripped away the grime; her muscles relaxed with the gentle caress of the light cascade and she was soon reveling in the strange magic of warm water. Ember drew the cake of soap joyfully around her skin, using her hand to scrub away the most stubborn dirt and oil, enjoying the lightly sweet smell of lavender and mint.

After, Ember dried herself off with the fluffy towel Gemma left for her outside the shower stall. She dressed in the soft linen clothing, feeling completely new. Ember couldn't remember a time when she felt so good. She and Gemma walked out of the shower room and met up with Keona just outside. He smiled at her exuberance, happy that she was feeling more human.

Keona and Ember were escorted back to the commons. Keona kept the short sword lashed to his torso. It was an uncommon enough item that he didn't feel comfortable sending it to his room with an unknown attendant.

The four outsiders chose a quiet area in which to talk. Grayson, Juniper, and Keona sat easily, but Ember remained standing. Though clean, Ember still feared that she would somehow taint the chair she was offered. Keona stood, spoke quietly to her, squeezed her hand gently, and helped her into a chair. She squirmed a bit as she settled into the over-soft seat.

"How long have you been out?" Grayson asked.

"About three weeks. You?"

"A week now. How'd you get out?"

"I woke up. Somehow, the power finally failed on my pod. I tried pushing the door open, but it was still mechanically sealed. So, I broke the glass, or whatever it was, to get free. Bastards thought they'd suffocate us with that mechanical fail secure if we ever woke up."

"That sounds like Ziggurat." Grayson shook his head.

"And you? Did your pod fail too?"

"Sort of." Grayson chuckled. "Juniper here and her pal Ben pulled me off the power grid. I guess I should count myself lucky those locks on mine didn't fire."

"Maybe they did." Keona took a sip of water from the glass on the side table next to him. "Did Juniper ever tell you how you got out of the pod?"

As he thought back on it, Grayson couldn't recall exactly how he had come to be sitting up in the pod. He focused and thought back, but he remembered simply pushing the door open. The memory was hazy, as he was still groggy when he had opened the door.

"Ben called me from outside," Juniper said. "He was there when Grayson opened the pod."

"And do you remember anything strange about the pod?"

It was Juniper's turn to focus. She brought the memory up clearly, then paused it. In her mind's eye, she studied every detail of the scene. Nothing looked out of the ordinary. Ben had his rifle pointed at Grayson, Grayson sitting upright in the pod, the pod door standing out—

"Bolts!" Juniper exclaimed. "Grayson, there were bolts coming out of the door. They were bent…" Keona nodded.

"They must've got to you too, brother. When you went under for your leg surgery, they kept you there for a couple of weeks. You probably thought it was a side effect of the pain meds for post-op, but they worked on you. When they told me about it, I flipped out. But your treatment was different from mine. They were trying to turn you into—for lack of a better word—a super-soldier."

"What the fu-…Are you saying that they gave me, what, super-strength?"

"Yes. Have you noticed that physical activity has become very easy?" Grayson thought back to hauling the logs for the fire, loading and unloading the truck at Awbreytown and Ochoco, carrying the seed and fertilizer to the trailer.

"Son of a bitch."

"Yeah," Keona said. "They kind of explained it to me, though I'm still not sure I fully get it. They messed with your myostatin levels and gave you some sort of serum that kept your muscles from getting grotesquely over-defined but many times stronger. They did it with some of the other guards too, but they ended up looking like Schwarzenegger on a steroid binge."

"So here we are. Captain America, Jean Gray, and Doctor Strange." Grayson laughed.

"You always were partial to Marvel."

"Like you weren't. No one liked DC." They both chuckled.

Juniper didn't understand what they were talking about, but she finally sensed the wall between them breaking down. Grayson was letting Keona in. Ember still sat uncomfortably, shifting and fidgeting in the chair. Juniper smiled at Ember and turned to face her. Ember suddenly felt calm running through her. Her body relaxed. She finally felt the cushions on the chair swaddling her.

"Did you happen to catch the date on the computer?" Keona asked. "The one in front of the pods?"

"No. It got smashed when Paul Bunyan here," Grayson motioned to Juniper, "pulled my pod over. All I know is that it's been about four hundred years since we were put in stasis."

"Well, that's a shame. I was able to log in; it was June 12, 2484 when I left. A Monday. So today it would be Sunday, July 2. Four hundred four years."

Grayson slumped back in his chair. Even after a week, it was still almost too much to comprehend. Juniper put her hand on top of his. Keona sipped at his water. Ember had fallen asleep in the chair.

"Well, here's where *we* are." Grayson sat back up, not willing to wallow. "We're in a compound they call Rimrock. Used to be Redmond. This, I'm sure you'll remember, is the old high school. Juniper and Ben lived in a village called Awbreytown before it was burned to the ground by mutants called Keepers, giant dudes that terrorize everyone around Bend. We went to their backup village, Ochoco, where we met the survivors of the Keeper attack. Ochoco is where the viewpoint over Prineville used to be—Prineville's now a huge lake. We sent Ben back this morning with a load of seed and fertilizer so Ochoco can start farming. I came here to facilitate the deal. And now I'm staying, because the Keepers attacked a few days ago and these people have little actual training. They barely held off two waves that could have brought down the fence if they hadn't just been testing the defenses. That about sum it up, Juniper?" Juniper nodded.

"Well, it seems that I came at the right time." Keona finished the water in his glass. "You'll need help getting everyone ready for the next dance."

"That I will. It'll be good having you here. Innes, the armorer, won't be so happy about it. He's the one who trained them all to begin with."

"I seem to remember an old Marine that hated others training his people."

"Yeah, well, it's because I'm the best."

"Not that this hasn't been fun, brah, but I'm beat. Two weeks in the bush is rough on anyone." Keona looked at Ember, sleeping peacefully in the chair. "Clearly."

"You got it," Grayson said. "We can go over details starting tomorrow. Rest."

The three outsiders stood. Keona bent to pick up Ember and carried her to her room. Grayson and Juniper walked silently hand-in-hand to their rooms, and silently parted outside Grayson's door. They wordlessly said goodnight, Juniper feeling that warmth coming from him that was only there when she was around. She smiled and entered her room.

Grayson closed his door and sat on the bed. *Super soldier, huh?* He stared at the wall for some time. This new ability would have to be tested. He needed to know what he was capable of doing, how far he could push it, and, most importantly, know how to control it. He got ready for bed and lay on the slightly squishy mattress. He closed his eyes and mentally prepared for the next day.

Grayson awoke to a gentle brush on his arm. He blinked a few times in the dark and started at the silhouette in his room.

"Sorry," Juniper whispered. "I...I just didn't want to be alone." She stood awkwardly by Grayson's bed. He was uncertain of the protocol for this kind of encounter. It wasn't anything for which he was trained. He opted for scooting toward the wall, leaving space for her at the edge of the bed. She sat gingerly and folded her hands in her lap. She, too, was in unfamiliar territory.

"Anything in particular keeping you up?" Grayson asked.

"Everything and nothing. It's hard to believe it's all gone. I mean, I knew we had Ochoco, but Awbreytown was my home."

"I know what you mean."

They fell silent, not knowing what else to say to each other. Juniper lay down next to Grayson and curled up with her head under his chin. She shuddered as she began to sob silently. Grayson wrapped his arms around her, the silken robe she wore slippery under his fingers. Soon, Juniper's shuddering stopped, and her breathing became slow and deep. The rhythm of her breathing calmed Grayson, his eyelids grew heavy, and he, too, slipped off into a deep sleep.

NINE

Staats watched tensely through night-vision binoculars as the first wave crept silently toward the ruins. Two companies, roughly one hundred fifty soldiers, were moving under the cover of darkness toward the main Keeper encampment. From the scout reports, there were guards posted at the main entrance, but none at any other point around the camp. The second wave was being held in reserve. Staats smiled.

The first wave struck quickly, overwhelming the forces inside with stealth. There was no alarm raised within the camp. The second wave was sent in and attacked from the opposite side. The Keepers made it easy, as they slept out in the open and with lots of space between them.

"Excellent." Staats smiled and lowered his binoculars. The rest of the battalion sat safely a quarter of a mile away; clearly they would not be needed here. The field reports suggested there were some other minor camps scattered throughout the forest, but the Keepers here, roughly two hundred, had been completely wiped out by the first assault. The human slaves of the Keepers were not spared if they were in the way. Staats conferred with Sisemore on the next move.

"The recon patrol reported a secondary camp twenty-one clicks north, just shy of Rimrock. The Keepers have an estimated five hundred foot there. That would explain the report of the attack. They lost approximately two hundred in their initial assault, from which they retreated."

"Do we know of their leadership structure?" Staats asked.

"Unconfirmed, but it looks as though they have a single commander. His name is…" Sisemore riffled through his notes. "Hamby. The secondary leader for their away team outside of Rimrock is called Neff."

"Good. Send in Greenwood's team. Hamby is the target. I want a precision kill, leave the Keeper force in confusion. We know they're too stupid to do anything without a leader, and if they have only one, let's end him. Once it's done, they'll need to call it in, and we'll move on the Keepers."

"Copy that, sir."

Sisemore hustled off. Staats lifted his binoculars again to see the carnage his soldiers had wrought.

"Beautiful."

Hamby rested on the ground, staring up at the sky. He had always liked the stars, though they held no particular meaning for him. Hamby was, by all accounts, simple; few words ever escaped his lips, and those he spoke were limited to terse commands or needs to be met. His life had been one mostly of simplicity, and he enjoyed the rush he got from stealing people or supplies. He liked having slaves.

The slaves he elected to keep in this camp were his favorites. Hamby looked over at the nude human female next to him, remembering her earlier service fondly. He decided he wanted that again. He rolled over and slapped her face to wake her up. She was instantly awake, and Hamby crudely motioned to her what he wanted. The woman rose to mount him, but skittered away backward, her eyes wide in terror.

Hamby was about to yell at her as a blade severed his trachea. Blood coursed down his front. A Jiating soldier caught the woman and clapped a hand over her mouth to keep her from screaming. Pristine humans like this one were to be kept, if possible, for the scientists at the Hope bunker. The soldier whisked her out of the camp. The other three soldiers dashed behind.

"Target is down," the sergeant whispered into a throat microphone. "Repeat, target is down."

Staats reacted to the radio call with silent jubilation. The antiquated technology was proving helpful, even with the necessary delays caused by use of relay positions.

In just a few hours, the battalion had moved west of the secondary camp south of Rimrock and took up positions. Two fresh companies were on standby for the call.

"Execute," came Staats's single-word order.

The first and second waves moved in on the sleeping Keepers. With frightening efficiency, Staats's soldiers killed all as they slept under the starry sky.

Neff nearly ruined the surprise, waking as his throat was cut. He jumped to his feet, wide-eyed, one hand around his throat and the other raking wildly in the air at the three Jiating nearby. They attacked swiftly, the final slice nearly severing Neff's head completely. Two Jiating lowered the body to the ground so as not to make a loud *thud* that might awaken nearby Keepers.

By the end of the second assault, whatever Keepers were left in the world would never have a central home again. The gravest mistake the Keepers of Bend had made was keeping their population numbers low to dissuade attrition and challenges to their leadership. Staats was ecstatic at this developing territorial superiority. He hoped Leader Zhang would be just as proud.

"Clear."

Staats and Sisemore grinned, shaking hands at the call. They retreated to Staats's private tent, where he produced his bottle of scotch and poured two glasses. They silently toasted each other, sipped, and sat.

"We have the area." Staats leaned back in his chair, letting the scotch warm his insides. "We have finally conquered the Keepers, and I'm confident the humans will submit. This is indeed a glorious day for the Jiating."

"Now that we hold the area, what should our next move be?" Sisemore sipped at the scotch, which was a tad more bitter than he would have liked, but tasty otherwise.

"That's not for us to decide. Leader Zhang will issue his orders in due time."

"May I make a recommendation, if that is not too presumptuous?"

Staats sat up and leaned forward. "What is it you have in mind?"

"Rimrock. They are the most advanced humans in the central region. We may only be able to maintain our supremacy if they are defeated."

"Hold on a moment. It would be best if no other ears were present for the remainder. Hallie, please take your leave."

The human stewardess, who stood in the far corner unnoticed by Sisemore, nodded her assent and left the tent. Sisemore shifted uncomfortably in his seat.

"I don't see why you keep her around," Sisemore said, swirling the scotch. "She's too quiet, even for a human."

"She has been a good and loyal servant for over a year now. Her initial resistance was troublesome, true, but she has proven useful. And I like the way she smells."

"That's disgusting." Sisemore remembered quickly to whom he was speaking. "...Sir." After a brief pause, Staats laughed, to Sisemore's relief.

"As I was saying," Sisemore continued, "the humans at Rimrock should be eradicated. They are said to have advanced technology hidden within their compound, beyond that of simple solar panels and batteries. Our assets have reported a wing of their building in which there is a blue glow at night, which would suggest they may have computer monitors. If that is the case, they may have other technology that could prove dangerous."

"It may also mean they have nothing but entertainment technology, like the 'movies' of our ancestors. Have the scouts confirmed the equipment?"

"No, sir. The reports currently only mention the blue glow; it would be an error to ascribe it to anything at the moment. It's just— best guesses."

"Precisely my point." Staats sipped at his scotch. "However, I'm inclined to agree with you, if only because I dislike having competition. How many humans live in the compound?"

"Estimated numbers are between fifteen hundred and two thousand. Our full battalion would be outnumbered nearly two to one, but we should be able to overcome them if we attack silently, at night, as we have done here."

"What are their defenses like?"

Sisemore went to the map of the region and pointed to Rimrock. "The main defense is the electrified fence that surrounds the compound. The fence is a half mile long on each side. It's supported by solar energy collection stored in batteries, which are housed within the perimeter, in this outbuilding." Sisemore pointed to a square structure on the west side of the main building. "There are large, open areas surrounding the main building, which provides no cover. This is problematic, as they have mounted machine guns at intervals along the parapet. The building is closest to the perimeter fencing at the southern end; but there's still five hundred feet of nothing but grass between the fence and the building. That would be our surest entry point."

"After disabling the fence."

"Yes, after disabling the fence. However, just to make things more difficult, they also have an outer perimeter alarm system that senses movement two hundred feet into the woods beyond the treeline. All efforts at stealth would be lost, and we would have to cross approximately seven hundred feet in a matter of seconds.

That, I'm afraid, is impossible. We would need to disable that alarm system before any real efforts at incursion could take place."

Staats nodded his agreement. He studied the map, looking for easier options. There didn't appear to be any. Sisemore had done well in his assessment. Sisemore waited for as long as he could for the solution he had held close.

"There is *one* other option sir, and it does carry inherent risk."

"Let me hear it." Staats smiled.

"The humans run combat exercises every so often in the old housing area west of the compound, and to do so they must disengage the western perimeter alarms. They also leave the gate open for emergency retreat. If we placed a company at the west to engage the humans during combat practice, we can be reasonably certain that they would be caught off guard and we could destroy the battery house, thereby disabling the entirety of the fence. We would then be able to take the compound from any side we wished, though the south is still the most advantageous."

Staats smiled broadly. "Excellent work, Michael. I'll present your full assessment to Leader Zhang as soon as possible." He shook Sisemore's hand and poured an extra measure of scotch.

"Sir, that's far too much for me to consume without losing my senses."

"It's only for one night, and well-deserved for your work."

Sisemore waived caution. "Thank you, sir!"

*   *   *

Hallie Wyeth peeled her ear away from the tent. She had heard enough. Rising from her hiding place between supply boxes and the tent, she scanned the area for patrols. None appeared present, as the Jiating were celebrating their victory and settling in for the night. This was her moment.

Hallie sprinted into the darkness, her bare feet making virtually no sound as she ran across the pine duff. She had made sure to make use of the Jiating dislike of delay in her favor, keeping her running legs in shape as she attended to Staats's demands daily for over a year. Her quietude, agility, and servile demeanor had won her Staats's confidence, allowing her access to areas and conversations she never would have otherwise. Thanks to the Jiating offensive, Hallie was closer to Rimrock than she could have dreamed possible even a month ago.

At her flat-out speed, she approached the eastern gate in less than two hours, having paused only twice to listen for sounds of pursuit. The guard in the watchtower watched her approach through the trees.

"*Halt!* State your name and your business!"

Hallie stopped in her tracks. "Hallie Wyeth!" Her name came out as one word while she tried to catch her breath. The gate opened immediately. All guards had been given her name in the event she arrived unexpectedly. That had been two years ago.

Hallie raced in and went straight to Kylie's office. She knocked hard on the door. Kylie opened it immediately and embraced Hallie.

"So good to see you, Hallie! I was beginning to worry when I lost sight of you two years ago!"

"Thank you, it's good to see you too. I was captured by the Whitecoats while I was on mission. That's why you couldn't see me."

"Of course. Please, come in. What did you learn in your time with the Whitecoats?" Hallie entered. She placed her hands on top of her head and took deep, slow breaths to get her wind back.

"They call themselves the *Jiating*. It means 'family' in old Chinese, apparently. They have three bunkers in the mountains, each one beneath one of the Sisters mountains; they call the bunkers Faith, Hope, and Charity, after the mountain they lie under." Hallie breathed again. "That's not our biggest problem. Tonight, they killed the last of the Keepers, who were camped just south of here. They're planning to attack Rimrock."

"I thought it was odd that the Keepers simply disappeared from my sight." Kylie sighed. "When do they plan on attacking?"

"General Staats didn't say. His second-in-command, Lieutenant General Sisemore, suggested a stealth attack when the Rimrockians are in urban combat training. They would enter while the perimeter alarm system was disarmed and attack the battery house through the open gate."

Kylie nodded. They had clearly become lax about security during training exercises, though how the Jiating had gotten so close as to be aware of this was unsettling. She was frustrated by not being able to see the Jiating in their daily activities. Hallie's report was evidence that they were indeed a threat in the area, though she couldn't have imagined that her people were so close to annihilation.

"Go get yourself cleaned up and meet me here in fifteen minutes." Hallie nodded and jogged through the door to the showers. Kylie strode away to Grayson's room, rapping firmly on the door. Grayson answered in nothing more than the light underwear he had been issued.

"Everything okay, Kylie?" Grayson's eyes squinted against the light of the corridor outside.

"No. Would you please meet me at my quarters in fourteen minutes? Rouse Juniper as well."

"Sure thing." Grayson left the door open as he turned to dress. Juniper met him at her door in the same way he had greeted Kylie, groggy and dressed only in her underwear. She nodded her assent and dressed quickly as Grayson waited outside. They walked together to Kylie's room, where Innes and a woman they didn't know were already conferring.

"Dammit, Kylie, I knew something like this was going to happen. Did they give any indication as to when they plan on moving on us?" Innes was red-faced and trying desperately to keep his anger at bay. He was failing.

"No." Kylie looked up at Grayson and Juniper as they approached. "Thank you for arriving so quickly. This is Hallie Wyeth." The woman nodded her head at them. "She has given us distressing news. The Jiating, who we have called Whitecoats for many years, have eliminated the Keepers."

Juniper recoiled. *The Keepers are gone?!* She was unable to process that information immediately. There had been so many of them. At least, there had seemed to be.

"They intend on breaching our compound via the west when we are training and disabling the battery system that powers our fence, then mounting a full assault at the south."

The group stood silently in the room in an attempt to fully absorb the news. Nothing could have prepared any of them for it. Grayson was the first to speak.

"Then we cease training to the west. If we have no city in which to fight, then we have no use for urban training right now. All combat training should be conducted here, at the compound, to ensure each person knows how to repel an attack inside the fence."

"I agree." Kylie turned to Innes. "Do you have any objections?"

"No," Innes said simply.

"Good. I trust you will also be willing to hand over the training to Grayson and Keona?" Grayson had been thinking he would tap

Keona for assistance; he kept forgetting that Kylie could read his thoughts. *I'll have to work on letting my mind be so open.*

"Yes." Innes ground his teeth and his face turned red. Grayson didn't need to read his mind to understand that Innes wasn't happy with this decision.

"Preparations begin now."

TEN

Staats kept his fury in check, though barely. Zhang was not a subordinate.

"While I applaud your defeat of the Keepers and the astuteness of Lieutenant General Sisemore's proposal, I have no pressing urgency to eliminate the human threat just yet."

"But sir, we have reason to believe…"

Zhang raised his hand but spoke softly. "Enough. I will not tolerate rebuttals without permission. I will consider your proposal for future implementation. In the meantime, I insist that your army continue their training. The humans will not be as easy to overcome as the Keepers, I assure you. You may go."

Staats rose and stalked out of Zhang's office. He kept it together until he got into the electric transport outside. He slammed the steering wheel with his hands and roared. His decision to travel alone on this outing was of benefit; Sisemore shouldn't see his top commander losing his temper. Staats started the transport and peeled away.

Zhang watched the transport speed away toward Faith from his office window. He shook his head at Staats's outburst manifested in the dirt spraying from the tires. Hopefully Staats would direct that energy at more worthwhile pursuits. Zhang knew the plan had merit, but it posed significant risk. The humans were not likely to be as careless as the Keepers had been, and Rimrock was better organized and armed than any other clan near them. It would behoove the Jiating to eradicate the less sophisticated clans throughout the region first to eliminate potential allies with whom Rimrock could align and would leave them as an island to be defended on all sides. Zhang felt this was a critical oversight that Staats should have caught in his assessment, especially given his position.

Zhang decided to visit the labs three levels below. As he entered, the technicians turned and bowed shallowly, their customary greeting. Zhang paced in front of the sensory deprivation tanks and gazed at the humans inside. One of the females, the one with whom he had spoken a week prior, twitched in her apparent sleep. He stopped to watch. She twitched a few more times.

"She's responding very well." A technician had placed himself next to Zhang. "There are indications that she's making contact beyond the bunker."

"With whom?"

"With her sister in the eastern territory, well beyond the boundaries of our region. She has reported that she has not told her sister of the bunkers, instead telling her that she is safe and asking after other family."

"You do know that humans lie, yes?"

"Yes. We sever the deprivation when her brain becomes too active, according to protocol. I believe we can now try to have her contact a Jiating volunteer."

"Please do. The less contact she has with her kind the better. And the others?" Zhang indicated the remaining four tanks. "Are they progressing?"

"No, sir."

"Be rid of them, then. Replace them as soon as possible."

"Yes, sir." Zhang watched as the tanks were drained, the blindfolds, respirators, and earmuffs removed. The humans all appeared dazed, including his favored female. In a gesture uncharacteristic of Zhang, he selected a towel and draped it over her shoulders. She pulled it around her body gratefully.

"How are you feeling?"

"Cold." She shivered as she said it.

"What is your name, girl?"

"Trinity."

"I hear you are doing well, Trinity." The technicians, all but the one assigned to Trinity, were ushering the others through doors in the back of the lab, to what the technicians surreptitiously called the *Kill Room*. "I hope that you will find comfort in your new position." Zhang led Trinity into the shower room, her assigned technician following nervously behind. Zhang gently removed the towel and gave Trinity a gentle push toward a shower stall. Trinity moved clunkily into the stall. The technician thought that Zhang's interest in the female was odd. He had never shown this behavior before.

In the Kill Room, the technicians were leading their charges into a row of shower stalls. In their stupor, they didn't realize that the stalls were not the ones they regularly visited after a deprivation session.

"Enter." The humans did as they were told, in unison. "Shower." As they turned the handles of their individual showers, a pneumatic piston shot from the shower head and penetrated their skulls. The technicians—with difficulty due to their lack of physical strength—dragged the limp bodies to a chute in the rear corner, loaded the remains onto a hydraulic table, and sent them sliding down to the oven room. The technicians hosed out the shower stalls, washed their hands, and left the lab to get lunch in the cafeteria.

Staats's office was a ruin when Sisemore answered the

summons. His foot crunched on glass as he stepped into the office. Staats sat at his desk with his back to the door, looking out his window at the Cascades.

"Sir?"

"Things did not go as we hoped."

"As I inferred from the state of your office. What were Leader Zhang's wishes?" Staats turned in his chair and glared at Sisemore.

"We are to stand down, train, and await Leader Zhang's orders."

"I see."

"*I don't!*" Staats roared. "This directive is short-sighted, do you not agree? We should be in the field making use of our warriors!"

"Yes, sir." Sisemore said no more, fearing that anything other than utter agreement would further anger his commander. Staats stood, placed his hands behind his back, and paced in front of the window. His gaze was directed downward.

"As I see it, we have two options. One, we stay at Faith and practice at killing. We sharpen our already-honed skills, perfect our techniques beyond their current perfection, and while away our free time with hot meals and comfortable beds in which we toss and turn. Two, we defy a direct order and mount the attack on our own, without support from Hope and Charity." Staats looked up at Sisemore, clearly expecting a response.

"Sir, with all due respect, I don't believe the latter is advisable.

We may risk death or exile."

"*BY WHOM*?" Staats thundered. "A cowardly leader who wishes nothing more than to exercise his power over his minions?! A weak faction of scientists and historians who can barely hold up their books, let alone another Jiating? I *ask* you, Sisemore, do you wish to serve that kind of Jiating for the rest of your life?"

"I...sir, it..."

"Spit it out, goddamn you!"

"No, sir, I don't. But I also don't wish to run the risk of death."

"You fucking coward." Staats stomped to Sisemore and placed his hands around his throat. Sisemore clasped his hands on Staats's wrists, trying to pry away the hands that were choking the life out of him. He tried to speak, to plead, but it seemed as though Staats's hands were only getting tighter. The black walls of a tunnel were forming in Sisemore's vision, narrowing in on Staats's crazed face.

Staats suddenly looked surprised. His hands loosened, his arms dropped to his sides. Blood filled the sclera of his eyes, spilled out of his nose and ears. His tongue flopped out of his mouth. Without warning, Staats's face turned completely around and a sickening *crunch* emanated from his neck. Sisemore slumped against the wall, clutching at his throat, as Staats fell to the floor. The phone on the desk began ringing. Sisemore struggled to his feet and staggered to the desk, picking up the receiver on the fifth ring.

"Congratulations on your promotion, General Sisemore."

Zhang's voice was low and calm on the other side. "I do hope that you will be more respectful than your predecessor. You are commended for your faithful service in the face of great bodily harm."

"Y-yes, Leader Zhang." Sisemore's voice croaked as he spoke.

"I will be sending stewards to clean up your office momentarily. Do have a pleasant afternoon."

"Thank you, sir."

At the mention of the word *steward*, Sisemore wondered where Staats's stewardess had been. He hadn't seen her since the night of the Keepers' eradication. It struck him then; she must have run off to Rimrock when they were only a short distance away, after the eradication of the Keepers. If she had been eavesdropping before her disappearance…That would have explained Staats's sudden erratic behavior. Sisemore knew immediately that they had lost the element of surprise.

"Dammit, sir."

ELEVEN

Two weeks of hard training had been good for the Rimrockians. They felt more confident in their ability to defend their home and spoke endless praise for the trainers. Kylie was very pleased with the progress her people had made in such a short time.

"All right, people. Enough for today!" Grayson yelled over the din to be heard. Most of the Rimrockians were smiling as they stopped the pursuit drill, though they were covered in grit and sweat glistening in the late afternoon sun. The radio on Grayson's belt came on.

"Visitor at the gate. Ben Cooley."

Grayson mashed the push-to-talk button. "Let him in!" Grayson was elated. Ben's return meant a fresh supply of ammunition. Grayson jogged to the east gate. Ben was climbing down from the cargo truck as he approached. "Good to see you,

Ben! We were getting worried."

"Yeah, sorry it took so long. Alex was having a hell of a time with some of the rebuilding and I stayed back for a bit. The scouts get back okay?"

"They did. Come on in! Get some food and rest up. I'll take care of the truck."

"Much appreciated."

Grayson pulled the truck into the loading bay between the agriculture wing and the auditorium. A couple of the clanspeople came out to help as Grayson started unloading the cargo. Some of the boxes held new weapons as well. An unexpected but welcome gift; they could start phasing out some of the older weapons from the Rimrock armory.

Juniper came out to the bay with a glass of water for Grayson. He gulped it down happily, then wrapped Juniper up in his arms and gave her a wet kiss.

"Ugh, get off! You're so gross!" Juniper laughed despite her words and kissed back. Grayson was dirty, though he still hadn't broken what he would have considered a sweat. *I'll do it tonight,* he thought.

Since Keona's revelation about what had been done to him, Grayson couldn't bring himself to try out his theorized abilities. It was the only thing he could think of that had scared him since he was a boy. His father had drilled into him that fear was for the weak, and he had disallowed fear in his life ever since. However, if he were to test the limits of his newfound abilities, he needed to do it sooner rather than later, regardless of the fear he felt. Grayson didn't know how his newfound strength might affect his new peers, or, more importantly, Juniper.

Juniper swayed happily in his arms. She had grown to love Grayson in the short time they had known each other. Since the night Juniper had gone to Grayson's room two weeks earlier, they had been nearly inseparable. They ate together, they walked together, and they fell asleep together. She had no reason to trust him so implicitly, no reason to feel the way she did about him, but the earnestness and warmth that radiated from him was all for her. Juniper could sense it. Even more, she could see it when she looked into his eyes—he saw nothing but Juniper when he held her. He accepted her for who she was and never sought for her to change. Grayson was a gift from the universe.

Grayson released her and closed the cargo truck. "That's that. I'll go get cleaned up. See you for dinner?"

"Of course. Once *I* change. Ew!" Juniper shook stray dirt from her shirt and stamped it from her pantlegs, laughing as she did so. Grayson laughed as he rounded the corner and headed inside. Juniper looked out at the forest beyond the fence. The trees were peaceful, dancing and uttering a long *shhh* as the breeze coursed through their boughs. Juniper smiled at the quiet scene. Every day held the possibility that the peacefulness would end, so Juniper took in any moment she could enjoy.

Juniper went to her room and changed for dinner. She knocked on Grayson's door when she was ready, and they walked arm-in-arm to the commons. Ben sat at a table, clearly in the middle of his meal. He waved as they approached.

"Evenin'." Grayson extended his hand and Ben stood to shake.

"Howdy, Grayson. How's things been?"

"Tell you all about it when I get some food. Skipped lunch for training today. You want anything special, Juniper?"

"No, I'll have whatever they're serving up."

Grayson departed for the kitchen and Juniper sat. Ben looked a little skinnier since the last time she had seen him.

"You been okay?" Juniper asked.

"Yeah. Been workin' hard is all." Grayson arrived with two trays and placed one in front of Juniper. "Alex ran into some issues with some of the structures in Ochoco. Being so close to the water, a few were rotting out. We retrofitted all the watchtowers and parts of the fence that ran into the water. He said he could handle the rest. That's why it took so long to get back."

"Glad you were able to help out. How were the seed and fertilizer received?"

"Well, they got way more than they were expecting, so they decided to pay it forward with those extra guns you unloaded."

"Merry Christmas to us," Grayson chuckled. The other two smiled, but clearly didn't get the joke. "Ah. Right. Christmas was a holiday I used to celebrate. It was a season of kindness and goodwill."

"I like the sound of that," Juniper said. Grayson smiled at the dribble of mashed potato on her chin and wiped it off with his thumb.

"Your turn," Ben said, the gesture not escaping his notice.

Grayson recounted the story of the Keepers' demise, the Jiating, Hallie's flight and report, the arrival of Keona and Ember, and the training he was running. Ben nodded and chewed.

"Sounds like you've got it mostly figured out here." Ben wiped his mouth with the back of his hand.

"Mostly. We're still smoothing out the rough spots, but we're getting there." Juniper had finished her meal in the time Grayson had been talking. Grayson wolfed his down and took all three trays back to the kitchen.

"Anything around here I can do?" Ben asked on Grayson's return.

"I'm sure the maintenance crew could use some help on patching the spalling around the building. I'm amazed this place still stands. Must be held together with bailing wire and duct tape by now." Ben and Juniper gave him polite smiles but didn't ask what *spalling, bailing wire* or *duct tape* were.

Grayson kissed Juniper and waved goodbye to Ben after dinner and made his way to the firing range. Keona was the only person on the line. The rhythmic *pop pop pop* of Keona's pistol was pleasant in the still air, the staccato beat reminiscent of electronic dance music of the turn of the millennium. Keona ejected the magazine and inspected the barrel to ensure the gun was empty, then started tinkering with the rear sight.

"Trouble?" Grayson asked.

"It's shooting to the left." Keona adjusted the sight, inserted a half-loaded magazine, and sent all five rounds downrange. Keona nodded in satisfaction and began cleaning the pistol.

"I'm starting to get a little stir crazy here, brah." Keona had been born and raised in Honolulu, and he hadn't quite lost all the island vocabulary, at least with Grayson. "It's been great being of use, but I'm starting to be concerned about what might be out there while we rest and train."

"I know, Keona, I know. Kylie feels that patrols are still too dangerous right now. The Rimrockians are still undertrained. She doesn't have confidence that they would be able to adequately defend themselves if they came under attack, especially since she can't see them."

"All the same, I'd rather be out there checking the area for signs of surveillance. The fact that they knew what they did about the alarms, fence, and battery house...Rimrock's been watched for some time. They're still watching, for all we know." Keona resisted the urge to send bullets into the forest beyond the twenty-five-yard berm. Grayson picked up a semiauto similar to the one Keona was cleaning. He punched it out to arm's length and looked along the top of the slide. He liked the way it felt in his hand, the grip molding to his palm nicely.

"Can I take this one?"

"Be my guest. I'll let Innes know." Keona stowed the newly cleaned and smithed pistol into a box of eight others and closed the lid. He turned to face Grayson. "Brah, I've gotta go out there. Something doesn't feel right."

"You go out there, you're gonna set off the alarms. I don't think Kylie would be pleased." Grayson loaded five extra magazines for the pistol he selected. "I'd hate to think you'd get sent away for something like that, but these folks are a little skittish and don't react well to danger."

"No time like the present to learn."

"I'll float it by Kylie. Go get rest, I'll clean up."

Keona clapped Grayson on the shoulder as he departed for the main building. Grayson looked around to make sure he was alone. He walked to the cartridge bins at the end of the line and looked inside. Three bins, each about four feet on each side, all full of spent brass. Innes's team must have been slacking on the reloads. Grayson reached out and grabbed the rim of a bin. He closed his eyes and sighed. His grip tightened, he lifted; his arm was straight out, but it felt like he held a small dumbbell in his hand. Grayson opened one eye and looked along the length of his arm.

"Son of a bitch." The full bin was steady in his outstretched hand. He set it down and switched hands. Same result. He lifted one in each hand at the same time, then sandwiched the third between the two and lifted. Same result each time; he lifted with barely any weight registering to his system.

Grayson set the bins down and looked at his hands in wonder. He had loved Captain America as a kid. It looked like Keona was dead-on in his assessment. Curious, he looked down the strip of grass that ran from the practice range to the south fenceline. He figured it was close to one hundred yards from where he stood. He turned, set the balls of his feet into a sprinting position, and took off, counting one-one thousand, two-one thousand. Pushing harder than he did while training the clanspeople, he reached the fence in about three seconds.

"Impossible."

He turned and sprinted back to his starting position with the same result. He laughed gleefully. Grayson felt ready for anything.

TWELVE

Days, then weeks passed without incident. The training continued well, and the weather was pleasant. The August heat was tolerable with the forest blocking so much of the sunlight during the day. Every trainee was now proficient with firearms and basic hand-to-hand combat.

Still, Grayson felt tense. The unassessed threat of the Jiating loomed over them daily. Kylie could be of no assistance since their minds were closed off to her. It was for that reason that Keona had finally persuaded Kylie to allow patrols beyond the gates. He had led the training and took the first patrol group out the night before. The next group was scheduled to go in just a few hours. Grayson was invited, but he elected to stay behind and review maps of the area. He sat at a table in the commons, reviewing the crude maps drawn by previous generations. It was frustrating, trying to decipher current territory with old maps.

"Hello, Grayson." Kylie walked up to the table and glanced at the maps. "Ah, yes. Innes's maps. I'm afraid they're not of much use anymore."

"You can say that again. I've been looking at these things for hours, and I'm not finding much beyond the year 2250."

"I believe I can help with that. Come, follow me."

Kylie began walking toward the corridor adjacent to the kitchen. Two guards were always posted there, and Grayson had never felt the compulsion to explore that wing of the building. He followed now, curious. Kylie spoke briefly to the guards, who allowed both she and Grayson into the corridor.

"Very few people are allowed in this wing. It's important that you do not share your observations and experiences with anyone beyond Juniper and Keona. We are safest if most people don't know of what we house in here. However, since you and Keona are leading the training, I believe it's time you have more resources with which to continue."

Kylie led Grayson to a door with a proximity card reader. It was the only one of its kind Grayson had seen in the building. Kylie produced a fob from her coat and swiped it in front of the reader. She led Grayson into a dark room and turned a dimmer switch to give the room some light. All windows had been permanently covered with large pieces of linen cloth to dissuade prying eyes. In the center of the room was a large, round desk. On it—computers.

"Well, that's great, Kylie. Are they of much use without connectivity, though?"

"Oh, but they are connected, Grayson." Kylie booted up one of the machines and opened an email program. She logged in and showed Grayson the screen.

"I've spoken with a clan of contemporaries in the eastern territory regarding our circumstances. They have advanced technology and manufacturing that we simply don't have here. Their climate remains semi-arid and is far more conducive to the production and maintenance of electronics and other machines. They've launched a few satellites to communicate with several clans as well as satellites for other purposes. One of their technicians taught me how to use and maintain this computer system during a visit several years ago."

"How many of your people know of this?"

"Only Innes knows, though he refuses to trust anything the computers show him. Which is a shame." Kylie opened a web browser and typed in an IP address. The screen immediately populated with a map program that had overlays for satellite imagery and terrain.

"In their travels, they saved some old servers from a building in some place called Mountain View, far south of here. They found some excellent computer code and rebuilt it. After replicating the hardware, they retooled the code and began producing this map program, which now shows more current conditions on Earth after many passes by the satellites previously mentioned."

Grayson smiled widely as he took over, using the old mouse to navigate the screen. "This is awesome, Kylie! Are the satellite overlays up to date?"

"Mostly. The most recent satellite imagery was automatically integrated two months ago. Unfortunately, I have had limited time with which to dedicate my attention. Maybe it would be of much more use to you and Keona?"

"Definitely! Thank you so very much, Kylie."

"And please, be sure to read the communications to Vale. They may be illuminating."

"Thanks again, Kylie." Kylie smiled and nodded as she departed the room.

Grayson dug in hungrily, first scanning the immediate area and then points where he had been. Everything was clicking in his mind, and he was updating his memory as he went to ensure he knew how to navigate the area. He then chose to scour the mountain range for signs of the facilities Juniper mentioned. As he zoomed in at the base of the Middle Sister, he saw it. The smallest hint of white among the trees. There was a network of trails leading out from the bunker and one road that ran north and south, presumably to connect the facilities. Grayson felt like he had hit the mother lode. He would go back to the maps, but he needed to go through the emails, as Kylie had suggested. Through them, Grayson was able to piece together Vale's history.

Vale had been a haven in the days after *Codagenesis*, much like Rimrock. As the world around them collapsed, the residents banded together to keep outsiders away from the town and were able to save most of the population. Travelers attempting to escape to the interior of the country were routed around the north side of town and toward Boise, Idaho. Others trying to flee west were turned away at a roadblock east of town and sent north of Vale as well. Anyone who tried to sneak in once they had been re-routed were shot on sight. The bodies were burned in an open field well away from the main water source, the Malheur River, and the cremains hauled into the hills south of town by autonomous solar vehicles. The surviving soldiers of the National Guard in Ontario, Oregon had disobeyed both the Governor of Oregon and the President of the United States and withdrew to Vale, where they were eagerly accepted. There, they aided in the maintenance and development of technology for future generations.

Over the last two centuries, Vale had become the sentry against eastern infiltration to the Oregon territory by nomadic groups and individual vagabonds that crossed over the Snake River from the east. They launched new satellites using small orbital rockets and had made slow progress toward rebuilding a new society. As it stood, they had an estimated population creeping toward twelve thousand, all descended from the original survivors and select refugees.

As for the rest of the state, Oregon no longer existed as Grayson remembered it. The land was divided into territories marked by natural boundaries. The western territory encompassed everything on the western side of the Cascade Mountains from the Columbia River to Ashland, except for the coastal cities that were swallowed by the ocean after the terrorist destruction of the polar ice caps. The central territory was east of the Cascades from The Dalles to the swollen Klamath Lake. The eastern territory comprised of everything else between Prineville and the Snake River. Most scouting parties had confirmed the eastern territory was unpopulated other than Vale.

Washington and Idaho had ceded to Canada in the uproar after *Codagenesis* ravaged the land. California's population centers along the coast had also been decimated by the Pacific Ocean; it was now home to the west coast's largest bay, stretching between the former cities of Chico and Fresno.

Grayson sat back, running his hands through his hair and staring at that magnificent machine. They had a direct line of communication to allies and intel on the geopolitical makeup of the region. That development would aid significantly in the event they learned of imminent attack, as well as for future planning.

Grayson turned off the monitor. He had some plans to make. He rushed out the door and through the hallways to Keona's room, a new energy coursing through his veins.

Keona answered the door bleary-eyed, having just gone to bed a short time before. Grayson stepped into the room and closed the door.

"Dude, seriously good news." He told Keona about the computer in the guarded wing, and of Vale. Keona was instantly awake.

"With that, then, do you wanna have an impromptu strategy meeting?" Keona was already pulling on his boots.

Grayson asked Kylie to let both he and Keona into the computer room, to which she agreed. They dove back into the map program, then opened an old word processing application to begin documenting their strategy. They first tracked the known bunkers using the trails Grayson had discovered. Using their knowledge of the bunker from which they had escaped, they determined the Jiating bunkers likely had extra levels to accommodate labs, training areas, and living quarters. Capping their estimate at two extra levels each, they figured the Jiating could comfortably house approximately 1,500 to each bunker. Had they not learned of Vale, those figures would have been disheartening.

"According to Hallie's brief, though, only the contingent at the

Faith bunker have military training." Grayson rubbed his eyes. The adrenaline was wearing off. "That'll definitely give us superiority in numbers, if just barely."

"Yeah, but we also don't have a decent understanding of the experimentation they're doing. They may be trying to accelerate the same telepathic and telekinetic potential in the noncombatants to bolster their fighting force." Keona swiveled back and forth in his chair. "If that's the case, we'll be outnumbered two-and-a-half to one." They soon concluded that they were going to need to scout the twenty-four-mile area between Rimrock and the mountain bunkers—or roughly 260 square miles of forest—and that they were going to need assistance from Vale to keep Rimrock from falling.

Sisemore read the latest report from the trainers. All soldiers were well within training guidelines and deemed battle-ready. Unfortunately, Leader Zhang had sent further directive that all fighting forces were to remain on standby until he determined the time for mobilization. Sisemore continually voiced his concern about the loss of tactical advantage after the steward's escape, but Zhang seemed perfectly content with the current situation. Sisemore compromised by finishing Staats's bottle of scotch.

He stood to look out the window, much like Staats had in years previous. A new appreciation of the beauty outside the bunker had blossomed in Sisemore, especially with the considerable weight now pressing upon him.

"May I enter?"

Sisemore spun at the familiar voice. "Of course, Leader Zhang, please. May I get you anything to eat or drink?"

"No, thank you." Zhang sat in the plush visitor's chair and gazed out the window. "I fear I may have kept you in the dark too long concerning my plans. Staats of course knew, but he was sworn to secrecy. I expect the same from you."

"Of course, sir." Zhang gestured for Sisemore to sit. "Over the past decade, we have been perfecting certain skills and traits within our race. The Hope scientists have been working tirelessly to, er, *rewrite* certain code within our DNA to make possible things that *I* have been able to do since I was born."

Zhang looked at the empty bottle of scotch on the desk. Sisemore thought that Zhang was displeased with the ancient human liquor having been consumed; but the bottle slowly rose into the air and traveled to Zhang's hand, where he grasped it in the air gently and brought the neck to his nose. He sniffed, smiled at the scent, and sent the bottle back to its location on the desk.

"Of course, manipulating matter is no easy thing to accomplish for the uninitiated, and I thought at a young age that it was odd that no one else around me could complete such a simple task. As I grew, I realized that I was the *only* Jiating that could do the things I was doing. Over time, I became able to manipulate items from a distance, much like causing the unfortunate early retirement of former General Staats."

Sisemore listened raptly, though uncomfortable with the prospect of such abilities. The implications stunned him, however. If they had a core group of these enhanced Jiating, they would likely be able to have a slim advantage over the humans in combat.

"It saddens me that our program has not been able to produce the results I wished. It is of great importance to our survival to strengthen our people. *All* our people. Not all wish to be trained into the fighters you oversee, and that is, while disappointing, their wish. Human trials have shown that they are far more capable of accepting treatments, and that is where we have succeeded. We have a compliment to add to your fighting forces when the time comes—a group of ten humans that may be utilized in this way. Is this agreeable?"

"Sir, this is more than we could have dreamed possible. The humans are ready to lay down their lives for you?"

"Quite. They have seen what I am capable of doing to those who defy me." Sisemore recalled the last moments of Staats's life.

"Thank you, sir. We are very eager to receive your next directive."

"We have a little extra work to complete, but I will give you an update in no longer than two weeks." Zhang rose from his seat, and Sisemore mirrored him. "I will leave you with your planning."

Zhang left the office, and Sisemore turned to look out the window once again. His smile reflected the relief he finally felt.

We will arrive tomorrow.

Grayson could hardly believe his eyes. *Tomorrow*? In this world where it took half a day to travel the same distance that took thirty minutes in Grayson's time, he couldn't immediately fathom how they were going to move a full fighting force from Vale to Rimrock in a day.

Unless they can fly.

That was it. They clearly had a way to fly. Regardless, Grayson was very pleased at the response to his request for assistance. He briefed Kylie and Keona on the short email he received from Vale. All training in the north field was to cease in the event that the visitors, as Grayson hoped, would need a clear landing zone.

Keona was in the bush with Innes on a reconnaissance patrol and wasn't expected until evening. The scouts had mapped a narrow swath between Rimrock to just below the base of Faith. They lit out three days earlier with hope they might get some visual confirmation of military activity.

Juniper joined Grayson for dinner that night outside. Grayson continually looked to the sky, enjoying the sight of so many stars, even through the ambient light of the floodlights that washed over the perimeter. She pushed her tray aside and set her head on his shoulder.

"What do you think the Jiating are really like? I mean, I only have the vague memories of being experimented on and my escape. They can't all be that...cruel?"

"They sound like the extraterrestrials I used to read about when I was a kid." Grayson closed his eyes. "I remember the artists' representations of those things were terrifying. Big, black voids for eyes, skinny bodies, huge heads. That's how Hallie described them."

"Their appearance *is* terrifying. But I meant, what do you think, I don't know, their *personalities* are like?"

"Their personalities are more frightening." Juniper and Grayson swiveled their heads. Hallie had moved soundlessly across the grass and was standing behind them.

"Jesus, Hallie, a little noise next time." Grayson put a hand over his heart, which had started beating rapidly.

"Sorry, guys. Kylie wanted me to let you know that she can see partial visions of our guests from Vale bedding down east of here on a broad plain."

"Did she mention what they're riding on?" Grayson asked.

"No, she doesn't routinely see objects from so far away. She did note that they wore matching black uniforms and helmets."

"Thanks." Juniper shifted to speak directly to Hallie.

"So...what *are* they like? The Jiating?"

Hallie's eyes glassed over a bit. "Manipulative. Uninterested in human thoughts or the physical pain they cause us. We're nothing more than laboratory animals, and they treat us as such when we're captured. Among themselves, they're like us. Warm toward their children and romantic partners, maintain friendships, fight among themselves every so often. They all seem very absorbed in self most of the time, though. The Hope and Charity groups spend a lot of their time reading or listening to oral histories. The Faith group is always preparing for battle. And I mean *always*."

Juniper nodded. She could feel the discomfort thrumming from Hallie. Grayson placed a hand at the small of Juniper's back and held it there. He, too, was uncomfortable. The descriptors reminded him a little of some soldiers he had encountered in the field, people so driven by the act of survival and killing the enemy that they lost sight of humanity. Hallie looked down at them again, her eyes clearing.

"I'm glad to be away from them. The last two years were very difficult, trying to maintain a front for all of them to see, especially General Staats. Working around him was intolerable. But I did it. I made it." A single tear streaked down her cheek. She swiped it away angrily. "Whatever happens, if—when—we go to war, do *not* get caught. Do whatever you can to stay free. If it comes to choosing between capture and death…end yourself."

Hallie turned and walked away. Grayson and Juniper watched

her retreat until she was inside the main building again. Juniper turned to Grayson and they silently looked into each other's eyes. No words were needed. They kissed and held each other on the lawn until it became too cold and damp to stay outside any longer.

Grayson escorted Juniper back to her room. He continued to the commons to drop off the dinner dishes and was about to go back to his room, but he was too on edge to rest. Grayson decided to stay in the commons to wait for Keona's return. The wait wasn't long. The reconnaissance group staggered into the commons shortly after he took a seat at a table. They were ragged and dirty from a hard three days. Most went straight to the showers; Keona opted to sit with Grayson.

"How'd it go?"

"Rough." Gemma, the girl who always seemed to be in the commons, brought Keona a pitcher of water and a glass. He accepted it gratefully. "We got to Faith just before sunset on the first day. We got to see the Jiating soldiers in action. They're definitely well-prepared. I've never seen anything like them. Even when they're training, they're completely silent. No grunting, no war whoops, nothing. Just the sound of flesh on flesh when they strike. They're not as physically strong as we are, but they use their bodies efficiently."

"What about weaponry?"

"Mostly variations on what we have, modified a bit to reduce weight. That was the only time we heard noise, when they fired their weapons." Keona paused as he drank a full glass of water and refilled it. "We're in for a helluva fight, brah. That's for certain. Considering the penchant they have for attacking at night, when their enemy's guard is down, we'll have to ensure that our night guard is constantly vigilant."

"Roger." Grayson noted the slouch of Keona's shoulders. "None of that explains why you're so wrecked."

"Well, yesterday we were spotted. We ended up having to rush south to avoid further detection and swung back up through Bend. They had patrols there sweeping for any Keepers that may have survived. Once we were outside their perimeter, we shot straight here. Not before having a run-in with a short pack of wolves near the old Petersen Rock Garden; which, by the way, is a total shambles and I *don't* recommend a visit." Keona downed the rest of the water. "Now if you'll excuse me, I smell like a farm animal. Later, Gray." He stood and went straight to the showers.

Grayson returned the pitcher and glass to the kitchen before retiring to his room. He flopped down on his mattress, exhausted. There seemed to be so much more to plan, yet the Jiating were ready. He closed his eyes.

At some point in the night, he was awoken by Juniper's weight shifting the mattress. He slid over as he always did, though still half-asleep. She curled into her space in his arms. The two now fit together like puzzle pieces. They both sighed heavily before drifting away.

The battlefield was scented with the sharp tang of expended gunpowder and blood. Screams rent the air and bounced throughout the trees as combatant met combatant, or as bullets rent flesh and shattered bone. Grayson was in the middle of hell. A grenade exploded to his left, and he took off running toward the next available bit of cover, his corporal hot on his heels. As he ran, he felt searing heat, tearing pain, and was on his back in a matter of seconds. As he roared, he rolled and saw Corporal Jones next to him, eyes wide open. His legs were gone, and a bloody, ragged hole had been punched through his chest. Grayson closed his eyes and rolled the other way, trying to get up. His leg wouldn't accept any weight. He looked down to see that much of the muscle had been shredded, bone glistening white below his grisly wound. He howled at the sight.

"...*Wake up...*" The calm female voice brought Grayson slowly out of sleep. As he jerked awake, Juniper was waiting for him. Her hand was on his cheek. She smiled at him to ease the shock of the nightmare. Grayson caught his breath and his body relaxed.

"Sorry."

"No need to be sorry, Grayson. Was it the war?" Grayson

nodded. Juniper took up his hand and pressed it to her chest. He could feel her heart beating steadily. The sensation was calming, and soon he was breathing regularly. Juniper lay down next to him, wrapping herself around him. Her warmth and sweet scent eased the tension throughout his body. Grayson was able to drift off again into a calm, dreamless sleep.

THIRTEEN

Morning chores began as they did every day. The business of the day lacked urgency, as there was plenty of time within every day to get things done.

Grayson was the first to hear it. A low, sibilant sound. He looked around, trying to determine from where it was coming. It began getting louder, and others around him started looking around.

Soon, nearly everyone was outside, looking for the source of the strange sound. There was no wind, the trees were still, but there was an unmistakable *whooshing* noise that seemed to come from everywhere at once. Keona scrambled up a watchtower ladder, then hauled himself to the peak of the watchtower. He could barely see over the first line of trees, but the older pines stood too tall to see over. He looked down at Grayson and shook his head. Grayson jogged over to Kylie.

"We need to get everyone inside. Keona and I will stay here, see if we can't figure out what's going on."

"Thank you, Grayson. I wish I could tell you what it was, but my sight's so cloudy right now." Kylie cupped her hands over her mouth, "*Everyone, inside! To the commons!*" The clanspeople were quick to respond and left the outdoors quickly. Kylie followed.

"Can't see a thing beyond the perimeter." Keona leapt from the ladder and put his hands on his hips. "You think it could be trouble?"

"I hope not. The clanspeople are doing really well, but I don't think they're ready for a full-on assault."

"It's close."

Grayson and Keona fell silent to listen to the mysterious noise. It slowly got louder. When it seemed that it was right on top of them, it abruptly disappeared.

"What the hell?" Grayson swiveled where he stood but saw nothing. Suddenly, a giant hull burst through the southern tree line and headed for the north field. Across the front of the aircraft were black letters: *Aviatrix*. Grayson pumped his fist in the air and sprinted toward the field. Keona was close behind him. When Grayson looked back, beaming, he realized Keona's legs weren't moving—he was *gliding* across the lawn.

"Cheater!" He pumped his legs faster. Two more airships

followed *Aviatrix*, each impossibly large aircraft headed for the north fields. As soon as the airship landed, Grayson was able to estimate it at five hundred feet in length. The underside was flat and covered with a propulsion system Grayson didn't comprehend. The highest part of the ship was about one hundred feet in the air. Grayson and Keona stopped below the front of the airship and awaited contact. A door opened in the sleek surface on the side of the airship. A woman emerged and began making her way to them. Her tightly-ponytailed blonde hair flowed behind her as she walked, contrasted sharply by the snugly-fitted black uniform she wore.

"Gentlemen, I'm Echo Larkwood, Commander of the Valerian Defense Corps. I take it one of you sent the request?"

"I did, yes." Grayson extended his hand. Echo shook firmly. "Thank you for coming."

"You're quite welcome. I'm afraid Vale could only spare four thousand and five hundred personnel for this mission. I hope this won't prove an issue."

"All help is welcome, Echo. Thank you. I'm Grayson Brooks, this is Keona Sage." Keona shook Echo's hand.

"Pleased to meet you both." Echo turned to walk back toward *Aviatrix*. "Let me give you a tour."

They stepped through the door into a bright corridor. Echo led them to an elevator door and pressed a button marked *B*. Their eyes were already full, taking in the gleaming white surfaces and polished floors. They embarked the elevator when it arrived and were whisked upward, stopping after a few seconds. When the doors opened, Grayson and Keona stifled the urge to whistle at the bridge. Consoles bearing imagery of propulsion systems, weapons systems, and engineering functions were manned throughout.

"Welcome to the bridge," Echo said. "Every system on an airship of this size is interconnected and must be monitored at all times to ensure absolute efficiency. Luckily, our AI can monitor all functions while the ship is at rest. *Dismissed!*" All personnel rose from their stations and left the bridge, each saluting Echo as they passed.

"This is incredible." Grayson moved to the windows, which faced the main building, and looked out over the roof of the building. The sentries had all clumped together and were looking up at the airship. He couldn't blame them for staring. "What other miracles have you brought with you?"

"Each airship has several fast-attack vehicles, two personnel carriers, two landing craft, two heavy trail-clearing rigs, two unmanned aerial recon vehicles, and finally, a weapon for every person on board. Plus sleeping quarters, food, water, and the ability to act as high-altitude overwatch. Is that satisfactory?" Echo smiled; Grayson laughed.

"Very."

"I'm glad you approve. Now, if you'd be so kind as to brief me on what we're up against."

Grayson, Keona, Kylie, Juniper, and Innes held a round table with Echo well into the evening. Ember had silently joined just to be closer to the only person she really knew. Ben hung back also, happy to hear of the plans but not much use as far as strategy. They ate together, discussed current intelligence, capabilities of personnel, strengths, weaknesses, and technology. Keona was very taken with the advances the people of Vale had made in the past two centuries.

At the end of the round table, the group had settled on a cooperative training strategy that would allow the Valerians and the people of Rimrock to merge into one cohesive unit. With the right weapons training and air supremacy, Grayson felt they had a decisive advantage over the Jiating and would await their offensive on their home turf.

"We'll send two high-altitude drones to monitor the Jiating bunkers when I return to the ship." Echo stood and smoothed her uniform. "I'll report back in the morning." The men stood as Echo took her leave and took their places again after she had gone.

"This is certainly a tactic I hadn't considered, Grayson, though it makes absolutely perfect sense." Kylie looked embarrassed. "We have been self-sufficient for so long, I suppose my ego had gotten the better of me."

"Don't worry too much about it, Kylie. You haven't seen this much activity from the Keepers and Jiating in many years. I'm positive you would have come to the same conclusion were we not here."

"Thank you for your confidence."

"You're welcome. My turn to tell you to go rest. It looks like we did a number on you."

"I *am* tired. I spent much of the time vetting Echo. She's very determined, thinks *very* fast. It's my estimation that she is honest in her pursuits of protecting Rimrock and her people."

"I believe so too. Now, *go*." Kylie chortled and went off to her room.

"Reminds me a little of the old days, brah." Keona had slouched in one of the puffy chairs. Ember was watching them all quietly. She rarely spoke to anyone, and when she did, she did so softly.

"How do you mean?" Juniper asked.

"He means, we used to plan defenses against attacks from people looking to get into our facilities. After *Codagenesis*, people panicked and tried to get into every Ziggurat facility by force. Here in the United States, which was a large grouping of fifty-two territories, many of those people were armed, and it was our job to…uh…"

"Eliminate the threat." Keona spoke flatly. Ember picked up his sadness and lay a hand in his forearm. He smiled wanly.

"You killed 'em." Innes continued to prove that he had no verbal filter.

"Yes, we did." Grayson's eyes went dark, and Juniper could see the shame in them. "And we did it to keep them from getting a cure."

"Yeah, but this time we're planning against a real threat." Keona sat up straighter. "We're planning the defense of our real home, something neither of us really had back then. And we're not the men we were. We're no longer weak-willed, just trying to get by on what we could earn as former military. We have a true cause."

"I hear that." Grayson smiled at his friend.

"I hope so. He's sittin' right there." Innes's obliviousness to the past colloquialism made the old friends laugh. "The hell's so damn funny?"

Echo returned the following morning with the drone reports. They confirmed movement consistent with combat training outside the Faith facility, confirming Keona's earlier reports. The reports also noted the movement of several Jiating personnel to and from what appeared to be an office in the Hope bunker, presumably the office of Charles Zhang. The period of time between arrival and departure suggested there had been a long meeting. Neither

Grayson nor Keona felt great about long meetings held while soldiers were training.

"That's all from last night. I'll have more for you in the early afternoon." Echo stood and turned off her tablet. "Gentlemen."

"Bump up the regimen," Grayson told Keona. "We need to have our people battle-ready in no more than two days. If the Jiating are escalating, we need to be able to meet the timeline."

"You got it." Keona jogged outside to meet with the training command group. Grayson rubbed his throbbing temples and sat heavily at the table. He had little confidence that the Rimrock clanspeople would be able to meet the threat head-on and succeed. The Valerians might, but that was due to technology and years of training. There was no reason they shouldn't pull up stakes and leave the clan to fend for themselves. If the Jiating recovered any of the Valerian tech, they could easily mobilize against the remaining humans and decimate what was left.

Grayson pounded a fist on the table. It splintered, cracked, and collapsed.

"Ah, shit."

He picked up the two halves and hauled them outside to a wood pile, where he battered them into pieces usable for a fire. He rent and twisted the steel legs and supports into a ball. Having no use for it, he chucked it as hard as he could. It cleared the fence and landed with a *clang* somewhere in the forest beyond.

"Trouble?"

Juniper seemed to appear out of nowhere. Grayson flushed and looked away in embarrassment. He never wanted her to see his temper, and there it was.

"Frustrated."

Juniper wrapped him up in a hug and put her head on his chest. The effect on Grayson was immediate, as always. He returned the embrace.

"Sorry."

"They were just things. Things can be replaced." Juniper looked up into his eyes. "What's going on?"

"I'm having doubts about mounting a defense here. The clanspeople aren't ready, and I don't know that we can make them ready."

"They've done a great deal in a short time. Don't let doubt cloud your faith. They will surprise you."

"I certainly hope so." Juniper stood on her toes to kiss him. She left to join the static defense training session to brush up on her skills. Grayson followed, his own training scheduled to begin shortly. He kept reminding himself to breathe on the way. *In. Out. In. Out.* By the time he reached the waiting group of trainees, he had his headache and heart rate under control.

Grayson paced in front of the trainees, all of whom were standing perfectly at attention. Searching their faces, he could find no person with a wavering constitution. All seemed ready to meet anything they might see in the field. A small contingent of Valerian assistants stood to one side of the group at ease.

"I will be tough on you today. The Valerians will be tough on you today. The Jiating have shown us that they are a viable threat to our very existence. We will convince you that you are a fighter. You will not puke. You will not cry. You will not beg to be taken off the field for any reason. You will not leave the field until I command it. Are we clear?"

"*Yes, sir!*" came the reply in unison.

"Good. We don't have time for those who won't learn, who won't pull their own weight. To your right are your Valerian trainers. There will be ten of you to one Valerian trainer. I will be observing. Dismissed."

The Valerian trainers began barking commands to their groups of ten, who moved swiftly and confidently. The Valerians queued the groups in their training ranks and began handing out melee weapons. All the trainees had been given extensive firearms combat training, and the time had come to teach them advanced hand-to-hand and close-quarters combat. Shortswords and batons were handed out and each trainee paired with someone bearing the same weapon. Training began in earnest, the Valerians calling out their commands, the trainees following to the best of their ability. Where the trainee failed, the trainer stepped in and walked them through the strike or defense that should have happened.

Grayson folded his arms and continued watching throughout the afternoon, pleasantly surprised by the results in the training field. The clanspeople pushed their way through the heat of the afternoon sun, the seemingly tireless Valerians keeping them moving. Even the Valerians were showing some subtle signs of respect for their trainees.

As the sun began dipping beyond the trees, the welcome coolness of the evening began settling on Rimrock, helped along by a soft breeze. Grayson stood and stretched.

"Trainees, halt!" All trainees froze in their tracks. "Assemble!" The trainees and the Valerians all trotted back to their starting points. All the trainees stood still but breathed heavily. "I'm very proud of your work today. Each and every one of you are to be commended for your fortitude. I know you're all hungry and tired. So...go eat and rest. Great work. Dismissed." To Grayson's surprise and delight, the trainees all lined up so that they could shake his hand and say their thanks before trotting to the commons.

"Hell of a group you've got here." One of the Valerian trainers, Logan Hawley, stepped up to Grayson as the rest of the Valerians departed for their airships.

"They are."

"They're not as ready as I'd like, but they'll do."

"Agreed." Logan fell silent for a moment. Grayson could see

that he was on planning his next statement carefully.

"What's your contingency plan, Grayson?"

"I haven't given thought to making one. This is their home, now *my* home. I have to take measures to defend it at all costs."

"I see." Logan searched Grayson's face. "The time will come when you'll have to choose between Rimrock or your people. It won't be an easy choice, but that time will come as we are all engaged in the fight. Here." Logan handed Grayson a large, folded piece of paper. It was heavyweight paper and had been coated with something to waterproof it.

"What is this?"

Logan's eyes were pained. He looked like he wanted to tell Grayson something. His eyes then steeled. "Begin building your contingency plan, Grayson."

Logan turned and left for his airship, leaving Grayson alone at the edge of the training field. Grayson opened the paper and looked at the contents. It was a map, with hand-drawn safe routes between Rimrock and Vale. On the other side were instructions on how to approach the western gate of the main complex at the center of town. Grayson dropped the map to his side and he pinched the bridge of his nose with his other hand. His headache was returning.

FOURTEEN

"Thank you all for coming." Zhang looked around the table at the leadership he had assembled. Nine councilors watched Zhang expectantly, having been called at short notice. Never had such a fine group of Jiating congregated. "As you well know, the humans have become a viable threat to us. No longer are they simply a nuisance that must be tolerated. General Sisemore has been preparing our soldiers for the fight they've been waiting for their entire lives. General?"

"Thank you, sir." Sisemore stood. "Our soldiers have trained night and day for weeks and are ready to enter the battlefield. More than ready. Each company has been given their assignments and I have confidence that they will crush the humans where they stand. Rimrock is the only settlement within at least a seventy-five-mile radius that poses our people any threat.

"It should be noted, however, that our scouts reported the arrival of three large airborne ships as of a week ago. They state there are several thousand humans aboard, which will increase the difficulty of the mission. The companies have been briefed and plans altered to meet the new numbers we'll face. Stealth will be of utmost importance during the initial wave, and all offense that follows will be conducted with absolute prejudice."

"General," a quiet voice said at the end of the table, "would you like to brief the war council on our purpose?"

Sisemore smiled. "I wouldn't think to impose upon you, Trinity. Please, you brief the council."

Trinity stood, holding her head high and straight. Sisemore took a step back to give Trinity the floor. Zhang leaned back in his chair and smiled at his new subordinate. She didn't notice.

"I am leader of the Siren Squad. We are composed solely of humans, all female, who possess gifts given to us by Leader Zhang that will ensure the survival of the Jiating. We will be part of the second wave. We have all sworn to serve Leader Zhang, come what may. That is all I'm authorized to say at this time. Rest assured, we believe the Jiating will emerge victorious." Trinity sat. She willed herself to remain calm. Inside, she was screaming.

"Thank you ever so much." Zhang smiled at her again and turned to face the war council. "You have all lent careful advisement to me and to our military. For that, I thank you all. To further thank you, I have prepared documents for each of you, which you will find in the sealed envelopes before you. Please, open them."

The sound of ripping and rustling paper filled Zhang's office. Each Jiating councilor read their document quietly, brows raising upward in pleasant surprise, smiles that couldn't be contained spreading widely across their faces. Sisemore read his with absolute excitement.

> *General Sisemore:*
>
> *In thanks for your service, Leader Charles Zhang grants you the Barony of Rimrock and all titles and rights thereof on this 21st day of August in the calendar year 2484. This gift is given with the expectation that you will be victorious in the coming fight. Should you fail, the Barony will be defaulted to your second-in-command, Lieutenant General Reed Newberry, who will bear the title of General after your elevation.*
>
> *Congratulations, and good fortune.*
> *–His Grace Charles Zhang*

Sisemore set the letter down and looked around the table. The other councilors would have received the same notice, though for different plots of land. Zhang was creating a new political structure among the Jiating, one that called him *king*. Each of the councilors would be considered lords under Zhang and expected to hold their lands against all enemies. The rekindling of the feudal system granted Sisemore powers he could never have enjoyed under the former oligarchy, and he was absolutely reveling.

"As you will see, you have received a gift of lands to hold. It is the expectation that you will defend those lands, and you will also have peoples to populate those lands and to serve you. Be generous to your people, and they will serve you loyally. By extension, *I* will be served loyally. No doubt you are all well-schooled in the former political system by which I intend to lead, so I will spare you the legalities and courtesies expected of you, my lords."

Sisemore placed his letter back into the envelope and stood to address Zhang. "Thank you, Your Majesty."

Zhang smiled and clapped his hands. "Ah, now there's a true lord! You are quite welcome, Lord Sisemore. Please, all of you, let's celebrate!"

A stream of human servants entered the room and set the table. Each lord was poured a glass of marionberry wine and ladled a bowl of soup to start. The lords bubbled with conversation as they drank the wine and sipped the soup. A main course of roast pheasant and vegetables followed, then a dessert of wild strawberries and cream.

Afterward, Zhang stood, clasping his hands in front of him.

Each of the councilors sat up straighter. "You all have enjoyed a meal that befits the titles you now hold. Tomorrow, I expect that your military will deploy and do your baronies honor in battle. Lord Sisemore, you will give the command as soon as you leave this office. I have no doubt you will serve your people well. Good night, all." The councilors all stood for Zhang's exit and sat as he departed.

"I don't know how he expects me to sleep tonight." Royce Jewell, head of the Science Division, was practically buzzing in his seat. He reached for more wine. "This news will keep me up until dawn!"

"Agreed." Lucius Knott, an engineer that led the Facilities Division, leaned back and patted his stomach. "Though I think the food will help waylay the adrenaline shortly." All at the table laughed.

"Gentlemen, I believe this is where we should take our leave and prepare for the morning." Sisemore stood and began leaving the room. "I wish you all good fortune." The remaining lords raised their glasses to him as he departed.

Sisemore nearly ran back to his quarters but restrained himself. On arrival, he picked up his phone and dialed Reed Newberry's extension.

"Hello?"

"Reed, meet me in my quarters. Quickly."

"On my way." Newberry was in the room in a few short

minutes. He was taken aback by the smile that Sisemore wore—it was unlike Sisemore and a little eerie.

"Please, have a seat." Newberry sat opposite Sisemore's desk as instructed. "I have the pleasure of letting you know that you have been promoted to General in my stead." Now it was Newberry's turn to smile. Sisemore briefed Newberry on the council meeting and let him chew on it for a few moments.

"The troops will be glad to hear of it. They've been chomping at the bit to get into action."

"I know. We're going to need to take everything we can, Reed. Otherwise, Zhang will be unlikely to favor anyone who fails. The lands I intend to grant you in my barony will be at risk of being rescinded by Zhang."

"I understand. One question."

"What is it?"

"You don't expect me to call you *Lord* in private, do you?" Newberry smiled.

"As long as you don't expect me to call you *General*." They both chuckled, stood, and shook hands.

"I won't let you down, Mike."

"I have no doubts, Reed. Rest well. We move out at dawn. Alert the troops."

FIFTEEN

Grayson was startled awake by Juniper touching his shoulder. She sat gently on the edge of his bed.

"Something's wrong," she whispered.

"What do you mean?"

"I don't know. The air—it just feels...wrong."

Grayson didn't take Juniper's feelings lightly. He reached under his pillow for his pistol. Juniper stood and slung her rifle over her shoulder, Grayson grabbing his on their way out. They made their way to the commons and whistled up to the roof for the ladder.

On the roof they met up with Innes, who had drawn guard duty for the night along with five others.

"'Mornin', Innes," Grayson said. "Anything happening?"

"Naw. Nothin'. Everything's quiet out there tonight."

Juniper was looking at the treeline intently. Her silence made

Grayson uneasy.

"You wanna take a look through the binos?" Innes held his binoculars out to Juniper. She took them and started scanning the trees. Juniper could feel the disruption in the energy around her, she just couldn't *place* it.

"Dammit," she whispered.

"Don't worry," Innes said. "Nothin's gettin' by the perimeter alarms without a whole helluva lot o' noise."

Juniper nodded and handed the binoculars back to Innes. Grayson placed a hand on her shoulder.

"Maybe we should wake up Kylie," Grayson said.

"I think so. She should be able to tap into whatever this is."

"I have." Kylie's voice startled them. She walked toward them, eyes on the treeline. "Someone's there. Considering I can't see what's there, it can only be the Jiating."

"Why is it that you can't see them?" Grayson asked.

"I fear they've found a way to block intrusion from outside influences. Or, their brains are now operating on a frequency that I simply can't receive. Either way, their energy fields are still disrupting the natural frequencies around them, which is why Juniper can still feel them."

Grayson was now on high alert. If Juniper was picking up on the energy disruption, the enemy was certainly nearby.

"It's time, then. Kylie, please wake and brief Echo. I'll get our forces moving."

"Certainly, Grayson," Kylie said. "Thank you."

"You're welcome. We'll need to be fast and quiet. They're expecting to take us by surprise."

Kylie nodded and descended the ladder. Grayson turned to survey the treeline himself. It was then he noticed the stillness — normally the air was filled with the sound of frogs and crickets in the darkness, but there was no sound but the wind in the trees. He didn't need extrasensory perception to know that attack was imminent.

Grayson placed an arm around Juniper's shoulder. She set her head on his chest and took several deep breaths. Grayson held her quietly for a moment.

"Let's go," Juniper said.

"Best estimates are around a thousand, based on the average body mass described by Hallie," Echo said. The screen on the tablet she held showed a large infrared blob of low heat concentrated in the woods just west of Rimrock. The high-altitude drone imagery was live, so there was no longer any doubt of the threat posed by the Jiating.

"Looks like they're still counting on getting to the battery facility to disable the fences," Grayson said.

"That would be in their best interest, yes." Echo pointed at a smaller, hotter spot just inside the edge of the cooler mass. "This is the anomaly that bothers me," she said.

"That may be the Siren Squad," Hallie said.

"And that would be what, Hallie?" Echo placed her hands on her hips, clearly irritated she didn't have this piece of intelligence.

"The Siren Squad was a secret project that Zhang was working on, I shouldn't even know of it. But when I heard about it, it wasn't anything official. It's a group of human women that have been conditioned to use their minds as weapons; psychokinesis, clairvoyance, mind control. I—I'm sorry I didn't mention it before, it just didn't occur to me that they would have been successful."

Echo crossed her arms and shook her head. "Well, we know now. Kylie, what kind of defense can you mount against that?"

"Well, we can assume their power is relatively weak, considering it's not been practiced for a lifetime. I'm disappointed that I didn't see them; the Jiating must be shielding them somehow." Kylie shook her head in irritation. "Given that they're human, I may have a chance of repelling anything they'll use. I'll need help from Juniper, though."

Juniper nodded. "I'll do my best. I'll be working double-duty though, so don't be surprised if the send is muddy."

"Understood," Kylie said. She turned to Echo. "Do your airships or drones have the ability to emit ULF waves?"

"They do," Echo said.

"Excellent! We'll need to keep that in reserve, since it will disrupt Juniper and I as well."

"What's ULF?" Juniper asked.

"Ultra-low frequency. It will act as kind of a wall for psychokinesis. It will be very inconvenient for us."

"Great." Juniper pursed her lips.

"All right, everyone, we know what to do," Grayson said. "Let's get to work."

Rimrock's best warriors assembled in the commons with a contingent of Vale's command led by Echo. Grayson stood on the platform at the front of the commons with Keona at his side.

"Today's the day. We don't know when the attack is going to come, but we know for certain that the Jiating are here. We've all trained for this, so let's do our best to maintain discipline."

The commons was silent. There was no applause, no whooping. The Rimrock fighters were all nervous and afraid. Juniper sensed it and sent out waves of calm. The group eased almost immediately and began feeling more confident.

Grayson felt it too. He smiled and nodded and Juniper.

"I expect each of you will act according to your training. You've done well in your preparations. This is your home. Defend it. The enemy will not relent. Repel them. Do everything you can to keep it from falling." Grayson took a deep breath and exhaled. "All right, everyone. Report to your stations."

Grayson stepped down from the platform and shook the hands of a few nervous fighters before they trotted off to take their places.

"They're placing a lot of trust in you," Juniper said.

"They are. I hope I don't disappoint them."

Juniper kissed him and gently placed a hand on his cheek. "It's up to them now. You've done what you can."

They prepped their weapons in silence. Keona, Ember, and Ben worked alongside them, the final sounds of pistol slides and rifle bolts bringing the preparations to an end. They stood in a semi-circle and looked around at one another. Grayson shook Keona's hand.

"Good luck out there, 'Ona," he said.

Keona nodded. "To you as well."

They parted, Keona jogging out the front doors. Juniper and Ember scrambled to the roof. Grayson surveyed the empty corridors surrounding the commons and took another deep breath.

"Here we go."

"Wolf, this is Eagle Eye, how copy, over?"

Grayson steadied his eye on the treeline and pressed the receiver in his ear.

"Loud 'n' clear, Eagle Eye. What've you got for me, over?"

Echo hovered over the screen on the bridge of *Aviatrix*. The mass they discovered was burning a little brighter on the infrared, which likely meant they were getting amped up for attack.

"Get ready for contact. I'll let you know when they start moving, over."

"Copy, taking position, over."

Grayson crept silently along the battery house wall, concealed by the tall grass that the Rimrockians had allowed to grow next to with the hope that it would look like a forgotten outbuilding to enemies. Grayson stopped at the front of the battery house, just shy of entering the clearing beyond, and peered through his rifle's scope. It was just an old semi-automatic hunting rifle that had been in Innes's stores, but the optics mounted on it were excellent and well-suited for his mission.

"Negative visual, Eagle Eye. Approximate position of leading edge, over?"

"A hair over two hundred feet, just beyond the reach of the motion sensors."

Silence extended over the net; Grayson waited for more until it was clear there wouldn't be anything else said. "Don't forget to say over, over."

Echo rolled her eyes. "Sorry. Been awhile since we've needed tac comms, over."

Grayson smiled a little as he adjusted the knobs for windage and elevation on his rifle's scope, then set the crosshairs back into the forest. He took in a deep breath and held it for a few moments to steady his aim. Nothing in the area he aimed at. He panned left a few degrees and held his breath again. Nothing. Once more.

There.

Just the merest movement, in the duff below a massive Ponderosa.

"Wolf to Eagle Eye, tango sighted, over."

"Tango?"

"Target. Enemy in sight, hiding under the pine duff, over."

"Copy, Wolf, standby one, over." Echo turned to Kylie. "You're up."

Kylie nodded. She sat in the captain's chair and closed her eyes, visualizing the area beyond the treeline. She saw the pine duff. Briefly, she thought of Grayson and was looking through his rifle scope at the hint of sleeve visible through the pine needles, then she was back above. Steadying her thoughts, Kylie seized hold of the loudest alarm she could think of, then let the thought go over the visualized area.

Immediately, a good number of the Jiating were on their feet, their hands clamped uselessly over the auditory meatuses where their ears would have been a couple hundred years prior.

"Fire, fire, fire!" Grayson yelled. The roofline exploded in gunfire, razing the standing Jiating. Those remaining under the duff recoiled from the rain of lead and copper, but many succumbed. The quick-thinking among them grabbed their fallen compatriots and pulled them close to absorb the incoming bullets.

A wave of Valerians erupted from concealed defensive fighting positions just beyond the fenceline. The firing ceased abruptly on the roof as the Valerians crossed into the line of fire. The Valerians began hunting their targets as the front line of Jiating scurried in retreat. More Valerians ran at a sprint across the west lawn and poured through the west gate and into the forest behind the first wave. Shots rang through the trees as the Valerians cut down any Jiating they encountered.

The gunfire died off gradually as the Jiating were eliminated. The area eventually became silent. He looked through the rifle scope again and saw bloodied pine duff but no movement. He knew they couldn't have hosed them all. He jumped up from his hiding spot, slung the rifle on his back, and started walking toward the west gate.

The thought passed quickly between the three Jiating.

Kill him.

Zhang's voice enthralled the assassins, who rushed Grayson from his left flank. Grayson, startled, dropped to one knee, and sent the first sprawling under their own speed. The second he caught by the throat and gave a gentle squeeze that ruptured their windpipe. Grayson dropped that one and squared up against the last.

Grayson took measure of the Jiating's fighting posture. The

stance wasn't wholly unlike a human, but there were subtle differences. *Probably because of the weight distribution and musculature,* Grayson thought. Then the Jiating sped forward, soundlessly and with shocking speed. Grayson brought in his arms and struck out quickly with a right jab that the Jiating dodged and countered with a stinging left cross, then right, then left again, before bringing up a fast knee to Grayson's nose.

There should have been a crunch, but Grayson's head only snapped back for a moment. The Jiating assassin landed in a kneel, looking up defiantly. Grayson shook his head, then dropped his guard. He stared icily at the Jiating.

"Bring it."

This time, the Jiating assassin snarled and roared as they ran forward, pulled out a nasty-looking hooked fighting blade, and put all their weight behind the run. Grayson let the distance close, quickly calculated the Jiating's trajectory, then feinted at the last moment, snagged the Jiating's arm as they went by, and brutally dislocated their shoulder as he pulled the Jiating back in and rammed the blade into their solar plexus.

The Jiating gasped in shock as they were dropped to the ground, watching their life spill onto the dirt and dust of the clearing.

The first Jiating, the one who had charged, regained their footing, and sprinted at Grayson. They leapt into the air, intending to connect a flying kick. Instead, the Jiating's eyes widened in terror as Grayson caught them by the leg, gripped their neck, and brought them down swiftly over his knee. The Jiating's body went limp as their spinal cord and vertebrae were ruthlessly destroyed. They couldn't scream as their body whistled hundreds of yards through the air, Grayson having hurled them as hard as he could in his fury.

"Who's next?!" Grayson roared, his blood-spattered face twisted with rage.

There was no immediate answer. Silence again filled the clearing.

"Cowards!" Grayson yelled. He spat into the dirt and began walking back toward the doors into Rimrock.

"We are not," a pleasant female lilt said. Grayson stopped and turned. There was no one behind him, but he could have sworn that's where the voice had been.

"I'm not there," the voice said again, then a giggle.

"Where are you?" Grayson asked the air.

"I'm *here*."

"Eagle Eye to Wolf, eight o'clock!" Echo's startled voice caught Grayson's attention and he spun left, just in time to have a human hand strike quickly to his carotid artery and another strike follow to his knee. The sudden dip and spike in blood pressure caused his eyesight to flare and he lost sight of his attacker as he stumbled.

"Get up, there are nine more!" Echo watched as the Sirens

began surrounding Grayson.

Grayson was quickly on both feet again. He shook the stars from his eyes and spun in place, looking for his assailant.

"Right here," the voice said, behind him and to the left. He turned quickly in that direction.

"*No Wolf, other way, OTHER…!*" Echo's voice came through his ear again. He changed direction only to be met with another neck strike and a hard jab to his solar plexus.

Had Grayson been an ordinary man, he would have crumpled. Instead, he caught Trinity by her ponytail and yanked, eliciting a startled screech. Several other women descended on him.

Above him, Juniper watched as the Sirens pushed Grayson back toward the battery house and through the door. She muttered under her breath and scrambled down the ladder into the commons, then burst out the back door.

"*Hey!*" She yelled. The Sirens stopped and swiveled their heads in unison. Juniper planted her right foot and opened her mouth.

And nothing happened.

The Sirens laughed as they slammed the door shut. Juniper was confused. She clutched at the base of her throat, but no sound would come out. A searing pain overrode her senses, and she dropped to her knees.

Zhang floated out from the forest, looking regal as he hovered over the ground.

"You're being quite foolish, girl," he told Juniper, dropping gently beside her. Kneeling, he cupped her chin in his slender hand and lifted her eyes to meet his. Juniper was terrified by the bright, black voids staring back at her. Searing pain rocked her again, but she couldn't scream or call out. Zhang turned her face so that she had to focus on the door to the battery house.

"My little pets are going to make today *very* difficult for you all."

The hum inside the battery house died.

"*Now.*"

The single word went through the mind of every hiding Jiating that had survived, and the forest floor erupted with lithe, silent warriors intent on taking over the compound. The first wave scrambled up the fence and began climbing down the other side.

Bright sparks cascaded over the clearing and the screams of Jiating rang out, echoing off the walls of Rimrock.

"*You didn't think we'd give up* that *easily, did you Zhang?*" The strange feminine voice invaded every fiber of Zhang's poor brain. "*This is* my *home.*"

This time, it was Zhang who felt the searing pain bouncing around his skull. He cried out, hands cupping his cranium as he fell to the ground and crumpled.

"What...?"

Jiating beyond the fence stood in confusion. They began falling silently as their throats were slashed, or their bellies opened and spilled their guts on the ground, or their heads simply took leave of their necks.

Those in possession of their heads and senses made a hasty and silent retreat into the woods. Gunfire again rang out as the Valerian contingent on their way back to Rimrock engaged the retreating Jiating. Grayson and the Sirens walked out of the battery house and stood in the clearing, watching the befuddled Jiating leader try and figure out what was happening around him.

Kylie invaded every corner of his mind, pummeling him with frequencies that no mind, no matter how strong, could endure. Zhang fell to his knees, screaming in agony. His eyes began to turn an opaque white, then a deep red as his skull filled with blood. Keona emerged on the other side of the fence wiping down his blade, the steel coated with the blood of fallen Jiating.

"*How?! HOW...*" Zhang fell to his side, silent.

Trinity and the rest of the Sirens burst into tears, overjoyed to be free from the clutches of Zhang. The people of Rimrock began to converge on Zhang's limp form. *Aviatrix* landed in the fields, and Echo and Kylie disembarked to join the crowd gathering.

Grayson looked down at the slender Jiating leader, worry creasing his forehead. Something about the way things had unfolded made him uneasy. Like the offensive undertaken by the

Keepers, this fight felt too easy.

"Trinity, come here." Trinity smiled and bounced over to him. "Take a good look at him. I need you to be sure that this is Zhang."

Confusion flashed across Trinity's face, then fear. She looked down at the crumpled form and squinted a bit. Trinity looked up at Grayson. She didn't like what the big man was implying.

"It...it *has* to be him." Grayson put a hand on her shoulder. She had shown amazing determination when she rattled off Zhang's plan to him in the battery house. Trinity was willing to do anything to escape him. That meant Grayson needed to make sure *she* knew this was Zhang. She, as leader of the Sirens, would know better than any of his minions.

Trinity took a tentative step forward, then another. The skin was right. The clothes were right.

Her face froze.

"It's not him." Trinity's voice quavered. "It's not *him*." She stood up quickly and began looking around desperately. All the Sirens became tense and huddled together.

Grayson looked out beyond the fenceline.

"You win this round."

SIXTEEN

"Interesting," Zhang said, stroking his chin. "Very interesting."

Sisemore felt uneasy watching Zhang process his field report. The mission seemed to him a failure, but Zhang's slight smile told him that it may have been a small win. Three hundred Jiating had fallen, and the Sirens had turned, but Zhang seemed unperturbed.

"May I ask your thoughts, my king?"

Zhang smiled. "You may, and I'll tell you. This was a test of not only their defenses, but also of their personnel. The large man, he was a problem in hand-to-hand combat, yes?"

"Very much so. He was better trained and stronger than any human I've ever seen."

"Yes. And the girl that rushed out to save him as the Sirens were doing their work, did you notice anything strange about her?"

"I found it odd that she planted herself rather than attacking."

"She's an empath, but an empath whose abilities have broadened into full psychokinesis. I believe she was of the first order of Sirens. The one who escaped."

Sisemore's eyes widened.

"Juniper Scanlon…"

"Correct, Lord Sisemore. Now, there was the third anomaly, the one who was among us in the wooded area and took initiative during our warriors' daze and began hacking us down like so many trees. He eliminated how many in that short span of time?"

"Approximately thirty."

"Thirty. Slain by one man in a matter of seconds." Zhang shook his head. "This anomaly is of the greatest interest to me. We must find him."

"Of course, my liege."

Zhang stood and walked to the small dry bar next to his window. He poured a small measure of the Jiating spirit in the decanter. His people created it with fermented, distilled rye and infused with marionberries. He took a sip and savored the slightly sweet drink. Zhang cast an eye toward Sisemore, who stood rooted to his spot.

"I did not realize there was more to be said." Sisemore bowed his head slightly and rushed from Zhang's chamber. Zhang took another sip of his drink as he looked out on the expanse of

Ponderosas.

The ruse to send one of his brethren as an avatar was one of his better ideas, he thought. Poor soul.

Oh well. The price of progress.

The opportunity to see into the compound had been of utmost importance. Zhang needed to understand the enemy, and threading his mind through several strategically stationed Jiating in the miles leading to the compound was the only way to do it without compromising his own safety. He had intentionally kept Sisemore out of the loop to ensure the success of his plan. The strength of the sight through and the control he had over his subordinate was exciting. Zhang drained the last of his drink, the smile on his face widening as he thought of the possibilities.

The new Rimrockians sat at a long table in the commons, Grayson and Keona downing coffee, Ember and Juniper electing for plain water.

"They were testing us, brah," Keona said, draining the last of his coffee. Gemma rushed in with a fresh cup.

"Yep." Grayson twirled his cup absentmindedly on the table. "And they got what they came for."

"What do you mean?" Juniper asked.

"They know about the three of us. The 'super-powered' outsiders. They've probably been watching Rimrock for some time."

"Oh."

"Yeah." Gemma replaced Grayson's empty coffee cup with a full one and rushed away. Grayson chuckled. "Heh. Always on the move, that one."

That's when the thought struck him. He turned and watched her as she delivered his cup to the dishwasher's window next to the cafeteria. Her lips moved as a hand retrieved the cup, and she looked over her shoulder. Gemma flushed and her lips stopped moving.

Grayson turned to Keona, who simply nodded and hurried off in the direction Gemma had gone. Grayson stood calmly and walked over to the dishwasher's window. He bent over and saw the kitchen porter hurriedly washing the dishes in the sink, setting them to dry, then hanging his apron.

Grayson stood, turned, and flattened himself against the wall outside the window. Hearing the kitchen door around the corner close, Grayson peeled away from the wall and looked around the corner. The kitchen porter, a wiry, anxious-looking kid, was double-timing it toward the agriculture wing.

Grayson followed at a distance. The kid was clearly used to being unnoticed, as he didn't look over his shoulder while he strode to the old loading dock. Grayson again pressed himself to the wall as the kid turned and produced a set of keys from his pocket. Afraid he would lose the kid, Grayson stepped forward.

"Hey." The kid's eyes shot wide and he dropped the keys. "Where ya off to in such a hurry?"

"N-n-nowhere," the kid stammered. "J-just the laundry, for s-some clean...ah ..."

"Uh huh."

Grayson walked over and picked up the keys. There were only a few, and he chose the one that was cleaner on the business end than the others. The kid was stepping away, but Grayson reached out and grabbed him by the shirt, stuffing him into the room as the door swung open.

The laundry room was big, and hot, with very little room to move around the machinery. Grayson studied the layout for a moment and began moving through the room, headed toward the back wall.

"W-where are you taking me?" the kid asked.

"The place you wanted to go," Grayson said. He stopped in front of a door with sticky black marks around the knob. Well-used, rarely cleaned. Grayson jangled the keys.

"Which one?"

"I...I ..."

"Which. One?"

"The r-round one. Stamped with the number 675."

Grayson spun to the correct key, inserted in the lock, and

twisted the knob. A different, dry heat rushed back at him as he stepped through the door. A short corridor beyond terminated at another door with a proxy card reader.

"Son of a…" Grayson trailed off and yanked the kid in front of him. "Give me the proxy key."

"The what?"

"The proxy key. The little card or fob that opens this door."

"I-I d-don't have one!"

"How do you get in that door?"

"I don't! I u-usually just stand right here, and…"

"Ah, hello! I wasn't expecting you!"

Keona caught up to Gemma easily and cornered her. She slunk into the corner, shaking her head, tears streaming down her face. Keona stopped moving forward and motioned for her to stand up.

"Who forced you to do this?" Keona asked.

"Leader Zhang," Gemma said.

"Follow me. If you don't, I'll be dragging you. Do you understand?"

Gemma nodded and stood, straightening her linens. She wiped away the tears with the back of her hand and began walking with Keona back to the commons.

Grayson wasn't near the table when Keona returned with Gemma. He gestured for Gemma to sit next to Juniper, which she did wordlessly.

"Grayson hasn't come back yet?"

"No," Ember said. "He followed the kitchen boy that way." She pointed toward the agriculture wing corridor.

"Keep an eye on Gemma. Don't let her go anywhere. Juniper, maybe work on her?"

"Okay." Juniper stood and helped Gemma to sit, infusing her with calm using a light touch to her hand.

Keona went quickly down the corridor, on the lookout for anything unusual.

"What is it you want?" Grayson asked the bodiless voice.

"Why, Rimrock, of course. But you knew that. Why else would I let so many of my brethren die if not to gather intelligence?"

"Terror."

The kid began squirming in Grayson's grip. Grayson gave him a withering glare, and the kid stopped trying to break free of Grayson's hand.

"Well, yes, of course, there is that. But to what end? They're already afraid of me."

"Tactical paralysis."

"Oh my, you are quite well-versed in strategy. Bravo." A low, intense ache started to build at the front of Grayson's brain. He squeezed his eyes shut, willing it to go away. "No, I'm afraid this is *where* I *excel.*" The pain suddenly flared, causing Grayson to fall to his knees. He clasped his free hand over his eyes.

"Back off, Zhang!"

The pain ceased immediately. Grayson shot a look at the kid, who was still hanging helplessly in Grayson's hand.

"What did you do?" Grayson asked.

"N-nothing. I *can't* do anything."

"Oh! Hello, Kylie!" Zhang actually sounded pleased. *"How wonderful to finally hear from you!"*

"The feeling is not *mutual,"* Kylie said.

Grayson was frustrated. The kid hardly moved. He just hung in Grayson's hand, limp as a fish, watching Grayson stare at the wall.

Okay, you two, wrap it up, Grayson thought.

"Gladly," said Zhang's voice. *"I look forward to speaking with you both in the future."*

Silence.

Grayson looked at the kid. The kid stared back. Grayson slowly released the kid, letting his feet hit the floor.

"I'll be keeping these," Grayson said, stuffing the keys into his pocket. "And if I so much as sniff a fart from this area from here on out, I'll be hunting for you. Got me?"

The kid tried to answer; his lips moved, but his throat was too dry to make sound. Instead, he nodded vigorously.

"Good. Go to your room."

The kid hustled off through the laundry room and took off down the corridor toward the south wing. Grayson closed the door behind him, then bent the knob as for as it would go before breaking. He tested the mechanism, and it was sufficiently stuck. Grayson weaved through the machinery and exited the laundry room, where he found Keona and Kayleigh awaiting him.

"I'm glad I ran into Keona," Kylie said. "What happened?"

"It seems as though Gemma has been feeding intel to Zhang though the kitchen porter," Keona said. "That sound about right, brah?"

Grayson nodded. "It does. That's probably how he knew about the battery house. How long has Gemma been a part of the Rimrock compound?"

"Just a few months," Kylie said. "She said she escaped the Keepers and ran north. We took her in as a refugee."

"How did she get by you?" Grayson asked. Kylie flushed a little and straightened.

"Pardon me, Mr. Brooks, but I am *not* perfect, and I *do* still have a heart. Gemma was in genuine fear; I simply didn't push beyond what was presented to me."

"I meant no offense, Kylie."

"Too late. Now, if you'll excuse me, I've suddenly become quite ill-tempered and would like to be alone." Kylie turned and walked quickly back to her room.

"Oops."

"Way to be subtle, brah."

They walked together to the table in the commons. Juniper and Ember were huddled around Gemma, who was drinking what remained of Ember's water. She looked up as the men approached, shrinking a little. Juniper willed Gemma to relax, and Gemma's body immediately responded.

"All right, Gemma," Grayson said gently, taking a seat opposite her. "Let's start with where you came from."

"I came from Bend—"

"Wrong," Grayson said. "We know you were sent by Zhang. Which facility were you released from?"

Gemma's eyes went wide, and she looked between the two men, who were not menacing, but were simply intimidating. She took another sip of water. Tears were coming again.

"Charity," Gemma said weakly.

"When?"

"About two, three months ago, I'm not sure…"

"What did Zhang tell you to do?" Keona asked. His voice didn't seem to grate on her the way the big man's did.

"He told me to give short messages to the boy in the kitchen. Things like where stuff was outside, or how many people were around."

"Did he ask for numbers of people outside?"

"Mm-hm." Gemma nodded, took another sip of water.

"What were you going to get in return?"

Gemma's eyes widened, and she started gagging. Juniper became alarmed and stood, placing a hand on Gemma's back. She couldn't be choking.

"*Ah, Miss Scanlon,* so good to see you…"

The sound of Zhang's voice echoing in her mind was too much. Her mind clouded with rage, heat rising from the center of her body and bubbling up until it felt like she was going to catch fire.

Grayson stood and started toward Juniper. Keona jumped in front of him and put a hand on his chest.

"Don't, brah. It'll be okay. She's just angry."

Grayson watched helplessly as Juniper's face burned bright red, her features contorting in a way he'd never seen. Just as he was about to shove Keona out of the way, light poured from her eyes, her ears, and her mouth, filling the commons. There was a pulse in the light, and a wave of energy rolled through the commons and shot through the forest. Gemma sucked in a ragged breath.

"Are you okay?" Juniper asked, breathing heavily herself.

"Y-yes." Gemma blinked rapidly.

"What *was* that?" Grayson asked, holding Juniper's arms. He held her out for a moment, checking over any exposed skin. Juniper was perfectly fine. He pulled her into him. Juniper wrapped her arms around him and set her head on his chest.

"*That*," Kylie said, walking gingerly toward them, "may be our greatest chance of survival."

SEVENTEEN

Grayson and Keona stalked the underbrush, moving as silently as they could. Juniper and Ben were just a few feet behind. Grayson looked over his shoulder at Juniper, whose eyes were scanning the forest. She met his eyes and shook her head.

Two solid weeks had passed without a whisper from the Jiating. Patrols had discovered no new signs of surveillance or movement through the areas surrounding the compound. The Rimrockians were becoming exhausted from being in a state of high alert without any release.

After the last communication from Zhang, Kylie had deduced that Zhang must have been using a conduit, or several individuals placed throughout the forest in a sort of chain, to reach inside the compound. The distance from the Hope bunker would have been too far for him to "travel" alone.

Grayson understood the concept and likened it to a radio relay system from his time. He and Keona volunteered to enter the woods and find the Jiating who may be hiding throughout. So far, they had come up with nothing.

"I really don't think there's anyone here," Juniper said. "There's no...energy here. Nothing."

"I don't think so, either," Grayson said. "We've been at this too long to not have seen *something*." He pressed the push-to-talk button on his throat mic. "Wolf to Eagle Eye, over."

"Go, over."

"Anything showing on the thermals, over?"

"Negative, Wolf. Normal terrestrial static, over." Meaning there were only the regular forest dwellers roaming the forest; deer, squirrels, birds.

"Copy. Out."

They all turned and started heading back toward the compound. When they returned, they answered the challenge at the gate and entered. The first order of business was a hot shower and food.

The recon group met at a table in the commons, famished and tired. Innes and three of his scouts galumphed over and joined them.

"Anything to the west?" Innes asked.

"Nope," Grayson said. "South?"

"Nope."

"Awesome sauce."

"A little bland, actually," Innes said, swirling some of the brown gravy on his plate with his fork. Grayson chuckled.

"Uh, no…that's just something we said back in my day. When something *wasn't* particularly awesome."

"Uh huh. You're a real poet, Grayson," Innes scoffed, returning to the mashed potatoes on his plate.

Zhang lay in his bed, cold sweat pouring off his body and into the sheets. Whatever that witch Juniper had done was wreaking havoc throughout his entire nervous system. The Jiating that had acted as his conduit to Rimrock had all been driven mad and had run off to points unknown before returning to Hope, haggard and nearly starved.

Zhang carefully sat up and reached for the glass of water next to his bed, promptly knocking it to the floor. He roared in rage.

His steward rushed in with towels, having heard the glass hit the floor and the following bellow. The glass remained intact, and the steward mopped up the mess as quickly as possible.

"How?" Zhang raged. "*How* could she have done this?!"

Zhang rose and went to the telephone in his study. He picked up the receiver and dialed the guest room in which Sisemore was staying.

"Yes, my liege?"

"Come to my quarters immediately."

Sisemore arrived within minutes. Zhang motioned for him to sit and proceeded to pace in front of the chair.

"What are our capabilities at the moment?" he asked brusquely.

"Eight hundred ninety fully battle-ready."

Zhang shook his head. "That's not enough."

"We have another fifty contingent on training, but no, you're correct, sire."

Zhang's pacing picked up. The sweat was rolling off his head and exposed skin, drenching his clothing. Agitated, he stopped and ripped his shirt off, mopped himself, and threw the ruined garment as far as he could.

"We need to activate the psyops teams."

"Sire, I don't think that they're ready, yet. Their effectiveness hasn't been field tested, and—"

"I DID NOT STUTTER, SISEMORE! YOU WILL ACTIVATE THE PSYOPS TEAMS AT ONCE! WE WILL TAKE RIMROCK AT ANY COST! DO YOU HEAR ME?! *ANY COST!*"

Sisemore was recoiling in his chair. He had never seen Zhang lose all control, and was frankly afraid of what he might do. Zhang was breathing heavily, his nostrils were flared, his eyes bulging, and his thorax was heaving like a wounded beast's.

"Y-yes, my liege. Of course. I'll connect with Charity and begin preparations."

The battlements had all been reinforced to Grayson's specifications, and extra ammunition placed in water-resistant storage near the rifles. The Rimrockians were killing time by practicing hand-to-hand combat and constantly cleaning the weapons. The watchtowers were manned two-deep and rotated every two hours to reduce boredom and eye fatigue. The compound was in order.

Grayson and Keona walked the perimeter. The forest was alive with the sounds of wildlife, the sun was shining, and the air was cool. The scent of vanilla and damp earth floated on the breeze. Nothing was moving beyond the fence. They were getting frustrated with the lack of action. Not because they were itching to fight, but because the enemy's silence was making them jumpy.

"Brah, I should be running out there to find out what's going on."

"It's too dangerous to run solo, 'Ona. You'd get snuffed for sure if they've rallied."

Keona squinted against the sun. "Yeah, well...It's what I was trained for. It's what I do. Hanging around this—" he gestured around "—is great, but I've never been one to *chill*."

They continued their walk, less for security and more for

movement. Grayson surveyed the watchtowers as they went, taking pride in the Rimrockians' new abilities to protect their home.

They ended their walk and headed inside. Ember greeted Keona with a light hug and a kiss at the door, then dragged him away for the evening. Grayson shouldered his rifle and headed for the kitchen, where a new girl was serving the coffee and a new kitchen porter was doing the dishes.

"I can feel it too."

"Jesus, Kylie!" Grayson started, then chuckled. He was likely never going to get used to Kylie sneaking up on him. "What are you feeling?"

"The change in the air. There's something new happening out there. I just wish I could get a read on it."

"Have you talked to Echo?"

"I have, and she's not seeing anything with the drones."

Grayson nodded and started walking to the tables. He chose a seat and sat heavily, the stress weighing him down. Kylie sat across from him with a steaming cup of tea.

"I suggest you and Juniper start working together, then." Grayson sipped at the coffee. "You two have a better chance of finding out what's going on out there than all the fancy electronic equipment in the world."

"Likely. I've not felt the same lately, though. As if my clairvoyance was...I don't know...fading? I guess that's the right word. My failure with Gemma was the only confirmation I needed."

"Juniper might be able to boost your signal. Like an amplifier."

"Possibly. She's an extraordinary person." Kylie stared at Grayson as she sipped at her tea. Juniper arrived a few moments later and sat next to Grayson, threading her arm through his.

"Talking about me again?"

"We were, actually," Kylie said, smiling. "Tell me, Juniper, what all do you know about your powers?"

"Well, they come out at exactly the right time or exactly the wrong time, and I have to be careful about how I aim them."

"That's very nice and wonderfully broad. How about specifics?"

"…I can calm entire crowds of people by willing it, I can control a person's emotions with the lightest touch…I can explode a brain inside someone's skull merely by screaming, I can send someone through the air by wishing it, and apparently I can withstand telepathic attacks from horrifying mutant humans. That about covers it."

"Tomorrow, let's run some tests, shall we?"

Juniper sighed heavily. "Sure. Don't have much in the way of plans." Kylie smiled and walked away.

"Well," Grayson said, "*I* have an idea."

"Oh do you? Lemme guess. It has to do with our room?"

"Some of it."

Juniper stood and pulled on Grayson's arm. "Don't keep me waiting. Let's get going."

EIGHTEEN

Kylie met Juniper early at the north fields, where there was plenty of room to conduct the testing Kylie had devised. The low clouds hung just above the field, creating an eerie ceiling under which they would work. Kylie was dressed warmly to fight off the humid morning chill.

"All right, Juniper." Kylie stuffed her hands in the pockets of her oversized cardigan. "First, let's see what you can control. Over there are three logs. Let's start with the smallest and move our way up to the largest. I want you to try to move them just by…"

Before Kylie had finished speaking, all three logs zipped away toward the end of the field.

"Well." Kylie cleared her throat. "Let's move along, then, shall we?"

Kylie ran Juniper through a short battery of psychokinetic

testing, all of which Juniper easily passed. The amount of control she exhibited over her powers excited Kylie. Never before had she met anyone with abilities like her own, let alone someone with powers that appeared far beyond.

"This next part is going to be uncomfortable. For the both of us." Kylie took off the sweater and set it on the ground. She sat on it, and invited Juniper to sit in front of her. Juniper did so, slightly unnerved.

"We're going to attempt to invade Hope. I don't know what I expect to see, if anything, but if Grayson's assessment is correct, and I can tap into your field like plugging in an antenna, we will have a valuable resource with which we can plan ahead."

"O-okay."

Kylie placed a hand on Juniper's. "You'll be fine. Now, what I want you to do is picture the happiest thing you've experienced. Once you have that picture, nod your head, and I'll, er, 'plug in.'"

Juniper closed her eyes and let her mind wander for a moment. Then she thought clearly of Grayson. She smiled broadly, enjoying the sense of warmth and safety that crept over her, and nodded.

Kylie closed her eyes. Colors of every kind swirled in her vision. Juniper began to feel slightly sick to her stomach, and the vision of Grayson was fading.

"*Concentrate*," Kylie's voice said through the fog. Juniper sat up straighter and relaxed her body, concentrating on the feelings she first had at the beginning of the trial. Grayson came back into sharp relief, and the sickness faded out.

Kylie suddenly burst through the colors and was in a bright room. Zhang paced at a desk, sweating profusely. On the opposite side sat another Jiating, this one nervous.

"Eight hundred ninety fully battle-ready." The voice was shaky and sounded as though it were in a tunnel.

"That's not enough," Zhang's voice said.

"We have another fifty contingent on training, but no, you're correct, sire."

The pause unsettled Kylie. Zhang ripped off his shirt, dried himself, and flung the shirt away.

"We need to activate the psyops teams."

"Sire, I don't think that they're ready, yet. Their effectiveness hasn't been field tested, and —"

"I DID NOT STUTTER, SISEMORE! YOU WILL ACTIVATE THE PSYOPS TEAMS AT ONCE! WE WILL TAKE RIMROCK AT ANY COST! DO YOU HEAR ME?! *ANY COST!*"

The sudden explosion of anger startled Kylie out of the connection, and Juniper's eyes popped open as she felt sudden compression on her chest like she had been punched.

"What was *that?"* Juniper asked, clutching her heart. It felt like it was going to beat out of her chest.

"That was Zhang planning to activate a secret weapon," Kylie said, brushing a sweaty wisp of hair from her eyes. "From the sound of it, it's going to be something involving powers like ours."

"Not good," Juniper muttered.

"No. No, it isn't."

They hustled off the field and to the commons.

Grayson felt an insistent presence in the room with him, followed by Kylie's voice.

"To the commons, please, Mr. Brooks."

"That's new," Grayson said aloud. He hustled down the corridor to the commons, where he met the defense team. Innes was looking extra grouchy.

"Why the hell'd'ja drag us all in here?" Innes asked, scratching deeply through his puffy beard.

"Juniper and I have discovered something that we urgently need to tell you."

Echo studied the maps on the screen in the bridge aboard *Aviatrix*, Grayson leading her along. The thermal imaging from the high-altitude drones was exactly what they needed for this mission. He pointed out the areas for the Faith, Hope, and Charity bunkers; squares slightly warmer than the environment around them.

Grayson was also able to identify thin lines that looked like they may be trails used as communication routes between the bunkers, since they were too narrow for supply lines and cut over the natural features of the land rather than running with them. That meant that there likely would be no hardline comms between the bunkers, which, when the Rimrockians led an offensive, would work in their favor.

"What kind of ordnance do you have aboard the drones?" Grayson asked.

"None, unfortunately." Echo stood. "We never anticipated using them for offense, only surveillance. We *could* modify them at the underbelly, but we don't have any kind of precision ordnance."

"Bummer." Grayson leaned on the console. "How does the ULF-thingy work?"

Echo smiled. "We can transmit high-intensity infrasound through the hulls of the drones or the airships. We can focus the transmission to encompass a maximum of one quarter of a square mile."

"That should be plenty." Grayson turned to Kylie. "So, what should this do? If we were to use it?"

"It should disrupt the frequencies the psychokinetics use to communicate to one another and invade our thoughts."

"Have there been any precedents for this?" Keona asked."

"Sadly, no," Kylie said. "It's only theory."

"Any chance you'd be up for a test?" Grayson asked.

Kylie shifted nervously. "I suppose. Tests done with high-intensity infrasound in the 21st century showed no long-lasting ill effects." Still, Kylie wrung her hands anxiously.

"We have to assume Zhang is planning an offensive. It'll be in our best interest to strike first. We have the numbers, so we should see whether or not an ULF attack would work."

"I'll do it," Juniper said. Grayson frowned. "Don't look at me like that. I can do this."

"The fact that Kylie's nervous as hell doesn't give me all the confidence in the world," Grayson said. "Plus, it's her theory, she should be the one to test it."

"That's fair," Kylie interjected, "but I'm also not as powerful as Zhang or Juniper. I'll gladly do it. Juniper should connect with me, and Echo can run the transmitter. Again, there should be no long-lasting effects. The frequency should only disrupt the pathway between minds, like cutting a string. Nothing more."

Grayson huffed but nodded. Juniper sent him calm, and Grayson felt her warmth in his core.

"Not fair," he said, smiling.

Echo re-routed one of the high-altitude drones to hover over Rimrock. Juniper and Kylie disembarked *Aviatrix* and took positions in the field facing one another. Echo panned a hull camera to capture them and zoomed out. She pressed a button on the console.

"Give me a thumbs-up when you're ready."

Kylie and Juniper nodded. They stilled themselves and closed

their eyes. After a few moments, Juniper threw a thumbs-up. Echo
pushed a virtual slider on the console to *8 Hz* and tapped a square
marked *Deploy*. Juniper threw the thumbs-up again.

"Must not have done anything," Echo said. "She's still
waiting." Echo bumped the slider to *10 Hz* and pressed the square
again. This time, Kylie and Juniper looked up at the airship.

"Anything?" Echo asked over the loudspeaker. Juniper
brought up a flattened hand and wiggled it in the air. *Kind of.*
"Wanna go again?" Kylie and Juniper nodded, then reset. Echo
bumped the slider to *14 Hz* and pushed the square.

Nothing. No hand signal of any kind. Then, Juniper looked
excitedly up at the airship and gave two thumbs-up. She and Kylie
went back aboard the airship and up to the bridge.

"It was weird," Juniper said. "It was like someone clapped
loudly in front of my face, and I was immediately back in my own
mind. I couldn't re-establish the connection."

"I had the same sensation," Kylie said.

"Good. Will that same frequency work for the Jiating? Do you
think their brainwaves will run around the same frequency as
ours?"

"Mr. Brooks, that's a very astute question. Even if I'm unable
to tap into their collective waves on my own, we can assume that,
given their evolution—or devolution, depending upon how we look
at it—is only around the century mark, their brains still function at

or near the same frequencies as ours."

"What would you say the likelihood is?"

"Reasonably certain. Eighty percent."

"We'll roll with it, then."

NINETEEN

Zhang's breathing and nervous system had finally reset. Three weeks was a stunning loss of time, for which the inhabitants of Rimrock would pay dearly. He resumed leading his people with dignity and ease, the way he had always run his kingdom. The psyops teams were ready to deploy, and Sisemore's fighting Jiating were ready to avenge their fallen. The taking of Rimrock would be a secondary joy to them.

He sat calmly in the chair at his desk and opened his mind. Soon, he saw the Jiating assembled at each facility, rows and rows of fighting and telewarfare assets ready to be pointed at their enemy.

"My subjects," he crooned, "welcome to the new dawn! Today is the beginning of a glorious reign of all the surrounding lands. You will all have more than you can imagine, in wealth and in space. No more will we live confined to the darkened hallways of our ancestors! No more will we have to hide from the wretched human race. We will rule this land, we will dictate our survival, we will determine who shall and shall not live among us.

"WE ARE JIATING!"

A chorus of silent cheering erupted in the air, all Jiating rejoicing in the glory of their kind. Zhang reveled in seeing his subjects cheering their king, even as their bodies stood stock-still and tensed for a fight.

A bright white light and a loud *snap* awoke Zhang, and he was suddenly alone. He attempted to reconnect to his subjects, but he wasn't able to find a soul. Zhang snatched up the telephone receiver and dialed for his steward. There was no answer. In the silence, he heard the first scream.

Keona's blade bit deep into the thirtieth warrior as he sped through the rows of fighters. They were still standing confused as he began his campaign of death. As their comrades fell, several finally regained their senses and attempted to engage Keona.

A wave of fighters rushed Keona from all sides. The first line fell to his lightning-quick sword. Pushing his body up from the floor, he directed a pulse of energy downward. The ground disbursed it through the horde, throwing Jiating away from the epicenter as Keona landed. Necks and limbs broke as they were flung violently against the concrete walls, ceiling, and floor.

Keona rose with sword at the ready. Hesitant Jiating fighters began a slow push forward, not eager to be opened by Keona's blade. They began a slow dance, some pushing in to lure a strike, but Keona was disciplined.

The first screamed and rushed from his right, dodging Keona's first slash. The Jiating misjudged their counter and watched in horror as their arm separated at the elbow. The shock barely registered before their head separated from their neck.

Keona was now turning in a circle with the crowd, awaiting the next challenger. A muscular Jiating stepped forward, crouching in anticipation.

"This will be your final battle, human," Sisemore said.

"Then I'd better make it a fair fight." Keona sheathed his blade, placing his hands at ready.

Sisemore charged, and Keona easily used Sisemore's momentum to throw him against the wall of Jiating opposite. Using their collective energy, Sisemore was thrust back into the circle toward Keona and managed three glancing blows on Keona's chest and face. Sisemore disengaged to assess the effectiveness of his attack.

Keona smiled.

Sisemore felt the human's punch throughout his entire body, though Keona had landed only a single punch at Sisemore's diaphragm. Sisemore suddenly couldn't breathe, stars dancing in front of his vision. He fell to a knee. Pain rippled throughout his chest and abdomen. Keona swiftly brought his leg up and down in an axe kick. Sisemore's head met the concrete floor at fatal speed.

The mob stirred.

Grayson's rifle thundered in the bunker. Jiating collapsed silently on the floor. The daze eventually wore off and the Jiating turned to find a wall of humans armed with all manner of projectile weapons.

As the Jiating turned, the rest of the humans opened up in a barrage of relentless gunfire. The Jiating first attempted to attack, then pulled back when they realized these weapons weren't running out of ammunition. They turned again and tried to claw their way out of the bunker. The doorway simply jammed with so many bodies trying to go through at once.

When the gunfire died down, a mountain of death was piled in front of the interior door.

"Okay everyone, go light." Grayson slung his own compact rifle on his back, drew his pistol, and racked the slide. "We're on a hunt now; move in teams of two and clear the bunker like you've been trained."

Juniper stepped forward and cleared the doorway, shifting the bodies like so much firewood. She and Grayson stepped through the portal first, pistols up.

Innes roared before he pulled the trigger, the noise ringing through the chamber an equal measure of man and gun. As with the first two bunkers, the Jiating were dazed after the sudden loss of communication with Zhang. This group of Jiating weren't nearly as well-trained as their counterparts at Faith, and they fell apart as the first shot rang out. None appeared to have escaped the bunker.

"Clear it!" Innes shouted, shouldering his short rifle. His group jogged toward the door and began clearing the facility.

Zhang was shocked. Why couldn't he reach any of his subjects? What was that scream? Why was everything silent after that? He attempted one more time, futilely, to connect with even one subject.

Fearing the worst, he gently opened his door. The corridor outside was silent. Zhang stepped through and swiveled his head both ways. Nothing was in sight. The fear mounting, he took off at a run for the nearest exit.

Keona stepped through the door, spattered in the blood of Zhang's subjects.

"It's time we settled this," Keona said, floating effortlessly above the polished floor, the tip of his sword leaving a trail of blood droplets behind him.

Zhang's feet tangled beneath him. He collapsed in a heap at Keona's feet. Zhang's large, black eyes looked up at Keona, whose own eyes bore down on him with a fury Zhang had never seen in a human.

"Stand up and fight." The words were cold, emotionless. For the first time in his life, Zhang felt raw terror. He was helpless.

"That's what I thought." Keona landed lightly, reached down, and hauled up Zhang by his shirt. Staring into the blank, black eyes, Keona saw his own enraged face reflecting back. He willed himself off the floor and floated back toward the main chamber and outside, Zhang dangling from his fist.

Echo and Kylie stepped out of a landing craft to meet Keona at the mouth of the Hope facility. Zhang hung limply from Keona's hand, utterly defeated.

"The Jiating are no more," Kylie said, for the first time letting her rage crack her calm features. "This was not what we wanted. Surely you know that?"

Zhang remained silent.

"No matter," Kylie said. "You will not be harming anyone ever again." She tilted her head toward the Jiating leader. Echo produced a set of wrist cuffs and placed them on Zhang before hauling him into the landing craft, Kylie and Keona a few steps behind.

TWENTY

The Valerians departed the morning after the battle, taking Zhang with them for further interrogation and study. Several remaining Jiating at the mountain facilities had surrendered and had been placed in the brigs aboard each airship. Rimrockian volunteers stayed behind at the facilities to clear the dead and to begin occupation.

Grayson and Keona took comfort in their coffees, sitting on the same side of the table so they could watch the main entrance. Rimrock was safe from her enemies and the community could finally live in peace, though their old habits couldn't be turned off. Keona was still on edge.

"I don't know, brah. I still feel like there's more to this place." He drank the last of his coffee and pushed the cup aside. Grayson did the same.

"It's a brave new world, 'Ona. The population is markedly decreased, so there's no reason to expect that we should've failed."

"I know. But still, there's just something nagging at me. Zhang took over the Keepers with minimal effort, then we did the same with the Jiating." He swept an arm around the commons. "And now here we are, calmly drinking coffee in the commons while the bulk of Rimrock is asleep."

"Enjoy it, 'Ona."

"I'm trying, but like I said…"

"Good evening, gentlemen. Mind if I join you?" Kylie sat next to Keona without awaiting an answer. "I sensed some discomfort over here, thought I might see if I could be of some help."

"Maybe," Grayson said. "Keona here is bemoaning his easy win."

"Not what I said."

Kylie chuckled. "No, I imagine not. I can appreciate the apprehension. It must not be easy waking up to a new reality so far removed from your own. Then, of course, to win a battle so handily. My."

The soft click of safeties being released echoed in the commons.

"I really must thank you for handing over the central territories to us. We couldn't have taken it without you. We are finally free to reign supreme."

Grayson knew the muzzle trained on his head was only a few

feet behind him. Same for the muzzle pointed at Keona. The rage began to build in him, but he spoke softly.

"You bitch." Kylie chuckled.

"Poor, simple Grayson."

"Why?" Keona asked.

"Survival, Mr. Sage," Kylie said, standing and smoothing her linen clothing. "The Keepers were a useless, thug race, and the Jiating threatened all life in the basin. Between them, Rimrock would have been crushed into nonexistence. But, thanks to you, we'll no longer have them lording their fear over us.

"We were at a crossroads at the time you arrived. We could attempt to coexist with the Keepers and the Jiating, but the resources here, though seemingly vast, are not enough to support us as well as ravagers such as the Keepers. The Jiating were simply a threat to our existence, and we couldn't tolerate that, either. You gave us the skills and discipline necessary to eradicate these threats, and for that, we thank you.

"However, we can't allow men such as yourselves to roam free among us. Your barbaric pasts and training have been useful to this point, but it also threatens our peace and way of life. I'm afraid I can't allow outsiders possessing your skills to live."

As if on cue, three men half-dragged Juniper, Ember, and Trinity into the commons by their arms, cloth gags strung through their mouths, their hands bound behind them. Each captor held a pistol in their off hand. Ben was suspended between another two men, barely conscious, blood trickling from his nose and mouth and onto his linen shirt. Juniper and Ember wore nothing but their underclothes, which meant that they had been pulled straight out of bed. Grayson's fury threatened to overcome his common sense, but Juniper's tears as she struggled held him in check. He felt Keona tensing next to him as well.

"Please, now, no hero antics," Kylie said. "I can see what you're thinking, and rest assured, you've trained our people well— you know what you can expect if you resist. Trinity's Sirens found out the hard way."

The muzzle behind Grayson finally met the base of his skull. He took this as the order to stand and prepare to march. He and Keona rose at the same time.

"Take one step backward," a gruff voice said. Grayson instantly hated Innes. He took a step back, as did Keona. The women took two different approaches to being captive. Juniper and Trinity struggled mightily, but Ember was pliable.

"Walk toward the west doors." Grayson and Keona complied, walking in step. Juniper and Ember were push-dragged behind them. They opened the doors into a brisk, moonlit night. The Ponderosas swayed and creaked in the wind brushing their tops. The scent of pine and vanilla was on the wind.

"I wish we'd met in a different lifetime, Mr. Brooks," Kylie called from the threshold. "Things would have been different." She closed the door as the four outsiders were led into the west field.

They kept quiet as they were marched to the gate.

"Halt," Innes commanded. They did. Innes had the sentry behind Keona watch both of them as he unlocked the gate. They went through, and Innes again had them halt as he locked the gate. The outsiders were led beyond the treeline into the darkness of the forest, where the moonbeams couldn't penetrate the canopy to the forest floor below. At a small clearing, Innes halted them once more.

"Down."

Grayson's body didn't want to comply. His muscles strained against his will as he knelt. He wasn't going down without a fight. He looked at Juniper, tears sparkling in the moonlight, she and Trinity obviously drugged to weaken her abilities, or this whole mess would've been done and over. The fire leapt in his chest, and —

Seven shots rang out in quick succession, the flashing and the noise momentarily disorienting Grayson. When his senses returned, the Rimrockian sentries all lay dead around the outsiders. Smoke rolled up from the muzzle of Innes's pistol.

"Never could stand those fuckers. Whiny." Innes holstered the smoking pistol. "Let's get the hell outta here."

Grayson hurried to Juniper and untied her, slinging her arm over his shoulders so he could bear her weight. Ember had become alert, and Keona quickly released her bonds before hauling Ben to his feet. Innes released Trinity before taking off at a light jog.

The group trotted and stumbled through the forest, taking game trails to avoid making too much noise. The cold began leaching through the linen clothing they wore, but they didn't dare stop. Keona took up the rear and whisked forest floor debris and pine duff over their tracks to obscure their route.

After forty minutes Innes signaled a stop. They rested on the pine duff, breathing heavily. Ben had cleared up halfway there and took on his own weight again. Trinity and Juniper, however, were still woozy.

"Why are you helping us?" Grayson asked.

"After all you did for us, I couldn't just turn my back on you. When I learned what Kylie had planned, I made my own."

Innes moved a pile of debris a few yards away from the game trail and hauled over two large canvas bags. He undid the ties and pulled out the clothes they had surrendered at the time they arrived, except Ember's rags. For her, Innes had packed overclothes to fend off brush and the cold. In the other bag were compact rifles, pistols, and ammunition, along with Keona's favored blade.

"How did you haul all of this up here by yourself?" Keona asked, happy to see his sword nestled among the weapons.

"He didn't." Hallie's voice startled them all as she stepped into their midst.

"Thank you both," Grayson said.

Hallie pulled a tightly rolled paper from a drop bag on her leg and handed it to Grayson.

"I believe this is where we need to go."

Grayson unfurled it. It was the map to Vale. Hallie pulled a syringe from the same drop bag and injected it into Juniper's arm. Grayson immediately tensed.

"Relax," Hallie said. "It's flumazenil. Kylie used benzodiazepine to suppress her abilities. This will help her recover."

Juniper indeed started showing signs of recovery quickly.

"Ach...what a headache..." Juniper stood shakily and got into her clothing.

Hallie gave Trinity the same injection. Trinity could finally mourn the nine other Sirens, weeping quietly as she dressed.

"What about the truck?" Keona asked. "They might use that to get ahead of us."

"Nah. I cut the solar panel wires and shorted the batteries." Hallie smirked. "It's not going anywhere until they can repair and charge it. Which won't be for a while, considering the batteries are lithium-ion and will have to be replaced."

Rested and hydrated, they lit out on the trail again. Ben muttered under his breath as they marched onward. The rest of the group remained silent.

*   *   *

At daybreak, they reached the outer perimeter of Ochoco. They circled the north end to scout for any activity. Nothing looked out of the ordinary, but they had no way of knowing if the alarm had been sounded at Rimrock, or how long ago.

"I'll go in, take a look," Keona said. "Back in a few."

Keona slunk off through the brush. The rest of the group hunkered down. The watchtower seemed empty, but they were a good distance away and the top of the tower was against the sun. There was no smoke beyond the wall, but it was still early in the day and any fires from the night before would be long cold.

Keona made his way back to the group as silently as he had departed.

"Tower's manned. Everything seems normal." He turned to Juniper. "How's your read?"

"Everything feels okay," she said. "There doesn't seem to be tension or fear of any kind inside."

"Then we go," Grayson said. "I'll take point."

As he rose, the rest of the group stood and followed. He put his hands in the air and walked toward the main gate with purpose. A glint flashed across the clearing.

"Halt!" came the command. The column did as ordered. "State your name!"

"Grayson Brooks and seven others." Muffled shouting could be heard as the sentry relayed the name down the other side of the wall. The sentry turned back to the column.

"Approach. Keep your hands in the air as you do so."

The gate creaked open and Alex hustled out to greet them.

"What happened?!" he asked. "Where's the truck?"

"What you see is what you get, Alex," Grayson said. "We were double-crossed at Rimrock."

"Sonuva…Okay, in, get in!"

"Alex, they need to check their weapons—"

"No, they don't," Alex said, cutting off the gate tender. "They're keepin' 'em. I'll shoot 'em myself if they cause any trouble."

The group walked briskly to the main building, a lodge of sorts that they hadn't entered on their previous visit. Inside, Alex had them sit at a long table and snapped his fingers at the attendant. Quickly, water and food were brought to the table by several people.

"What happened?" Alex asked.

"Fuckers were gonna kill us." Ben chewed his bread noisily and spoke around his mouthful. "We trained 'em, showed 'em how to use their stuff, and they were gonna *kill us*."

"Figgers." Alex shook his head slowly. "What's your plan?"

"We're pushing east," Grayson said. "It's not safe for us here any longer. Or for Ochoco."

"Aw, hell, we can't go anywheres. Most of us are too old or too stupid." Alex pulled out his clay pipe and lit it. "I know *I'm* pretty damn tired. 'Sides, I don't think they'll cause us much fuss. Now that we'll be trading partners and all."

"You'd still trade with them?!" Juniper's eyes widened in horror.

"Well, accors! Yer gonna need allies to feed you info wherever you land, wouldn't ya? I can't imagine you'd let them slide on this breach o' trust. Somethin's brewin' upstairs, I can see it."

Grayson chuckled. "You really aren't as dumb as you look, are you, old man?"

"I wouldn't go that far," Alex said, the pipe clamped in his smiling mouth. "I look pretty damn dumb."

"What do you mean? They escaped?"

Kylie was actually having a difficult time processing what she had just been told.

"Not exactly. We think...we think Innes and Hallie have gone with them." The sentry fidgeted as he spoke. "The guards are...ah...the guards are all...dead."

Kylie felt the blood warming her neck and face. This was unacceptable. She had taken *every* precaution. Or thought she had. Clearly, Innes was more skilled at hiding his thoughts than he let on. Sneaky man. While the scenario playing out had been improbable, she should have lent more appreciation to the abilities of the outsiders and the people she led.

"Send scout teams of four in every direction. They *must* be found."

The sentry hurried off to fulfill Kylie's command. Kylie pounded her fist on her desk and screeched madly.

Reed Newberry was exhausted. He pulled himself closer to the stream, willing the water to enter his mouth. Instead, he cupped his shaking hand and dipped it into the clear, cool water. He gingerly lifted it to his cracked lips and sipped. There was no reason to expect to live much longer, but he kept trying.

After drinking what he could, Newberry gathered some of the wild onions growing next to the stream bank and found several Ponderosa pinecones ready for harvest. He reached into his pocket and removed the fire piston he had made as a boy and had carried with him ever since. He inserted bits of a dry pine needle and slammed the piston, creating a small coal. Newberry dumped the coal on dry tinder and soon had a small fire. As it began to burn hotter, he put the pinecones near the heat. As the pinecones began to open, he reflected on how his father had told him the fire piston was a fun toy, but useless in the Jiating world.

How wrong you were, father.

Once the pinecones had fully opened, Newberry moved them off the fire to cool. He munched on the onions as he waited. Once done, he tapped the pinecones lightly on a nearby rock and gathered the nuts as they fell out.

Newberry didn't know where he was going to go. He kept warm by his small fire and crunched away at the pine nuts as he tried to think of friendly territory. Then he laughed quietly. The Jiating had no allies. There were no other Jiating settlements. His people had just been effectively eradicated from the face of the planet, for all he knew. The bitter laughter turned to sudden sadness and he sobbed.

Angry at himself for allowing this weakness, he fell asleep next to his fire, curled up in a fetal position.

"Wakey, wakey." Newberry was being prodded. Bleary, he squinted against the morning sun. A human. *Perfect.*

"Good morning," Newberry said cheerfully. "I suppose breakfast is out of the question?" A boot sailed into his chest, knocking the wind out of him and roiling his already weak stomach.

"Funny guy, huh?" Rough hands hauled Newberry up. "Tenny, take this back to Rimrock. I'm sure Kylie has some questions for it."

The sentry began pulling Newberry along. It was going to be a very long day.

REVELATION

TWENTY-ONE

Grayson scanned the water to aft as he pumped the long-shafted oars, making sure they weren't being followed. Keona took watch at the bow, and every now and then called out corrections to their heading. Grayson would pull on the opposite side oar until Keona called "ahead," at which time Grayson would pull on both oars equally again. No other person would have been able to make the heavy pontoon boat skim across the lake so quickly. They had been lucky thus far, but he wasn't counting out being bested again. Kylie had successfully hidden her true agenda from them for months; it wouldn't shock him to find that she had other tricks up her sleeve. Grayson hoped for the best case scenario and that the Rimrockians couldn't catch up before they reached Vale. Leaving before dawn that morning felt like the sensible thing to do.

Logan's map was tucked safely in Grayson's backpack, though

he had memorized the route they were on now. After Logan had given it to him, he studied it obsessively until he knew every viable route by heart. Something about Logan's warning set off alarm bells, and Grayson was glad he had listened to his instincts. He only regretted not taking action to leave sooner; but he truly had believed they could make Rimrock their home.

The hull of their boat scraped against the eastern shore of the lake. Grayson hauled in the oars and set them on the deck as the group disembarked the craft quickly. Grayson pulled the rickety pontoon boat the rest of the way onto the beach. At roughly 2,200 pounds, the boat wasn't going anywhere without lots of muscle or a machine.

The group readied their weapons and set out on their way, ready to traipse as far as they could before sunset. They opted out of taking their old truck, as it was too easy to spot from a distance. It would make travel far slower, but the trade-off was a higher likelihood of success, something they sorely needed.

After a thankfully uneventful day, the group slogged into the site of an old, abandoned mine. Grayson estimated they had traveled thirty miles, not a bad head start. Confident that they weren't being followed, they built a fire ring and a small fire before settling down.

The group remained mostly quiet, weary from a long day of

travel and the events of the past two days. Juniper pressed into Grayson, watching the fire pop and crackle. Ember was fast asleep by full dark, as were most of the refugees.

"Shitty times, brah." Keona poked at the coals of the fire as they let it begin to die down.

"Yeah."

"I feel like we're trapped in an episode of that old TV show. *The Twilight Zone*. You ever catch that series?"

"Nah. Never did like those old shows much."

"Yeah, well...Time travel and the future was a recurring theme. There was one, had the same guy that played the trainer in *Rocky*, you remember him?"

"Vaguely."

"Anyway, this dude is put on trial for being a librarian and believing in God, two things that are considered obsolete and therefore illegal by the totalitarian state, and he's sentenced to death."

"Grim."

"Yeah, but he tricks the dude who sentenced him into being in the same room with the bomb he made to kill himself. After the sentencer begs to be let go *'in the name of God,'* the accused relents just before the bomb goes off."

"Heh. Nice. Figures the coward would get off."

Keona chuckled. "Not quite. Since they were broadcasting the execution, everyone saw that the dude who sentenced the accused was a God-believer, so his second-in-command had him beat to death."

"And this was a true story?" Juniper asked.

"No, it was a fictional story," Keona said. "Made up for entertainment."

"Sounds like your people had an awful view of the future."

"Well, we're kinda living it." Keona poked at the fire.

"I suppose we are," Juniper said. Grayson pulled her closer.

They watched the fire a little while longer before bedding down for the night. Juniper was troubled by the parallels in Keona's story to their own situation.

It must just be in us to be horrible to each other.

The next days were spent moving over the land, the thick Ponderosa forest finally giving way just west of Vale to the high desert landscape that Grayson remembered. A long carpet of sagebrush extended down to Vale from the hills, broken only in the basin by seas of wild alfalfa and wheat where they were once farmed.

They staked out a site next to a small lake. Though unimpressive, the water was clear and didn't smell stagnant. The map said they had camped at Pole Creek Reservoir, a man-made lake just a day's walk away from Vale. Grayson tucked the map away in his backpack and returned his attention to the wild hog roasting over the cookfire.

"I can't believe I'm gonna eat that," Juniper said, wrinkling her nose.

"Just you wait," Grayson said.

They had foraged wild potatoes, carrots, and onions from the surrounding area, which were now cooking on a flat rock at one corner of the cookfire. Everyone, shy of Juniper, was anticipating the feast borne by the land.

Grayson and Keona made quick work of the small but muscular boar, serving up a fragrant and flavorful meal that all, even Juniper, enjoyed. After eating, Grayson dug a deep pit for the carcass and covered it.

"I'm almost starting to feel bad for letting you do all the hard work, brah." Keona smiled. "Almost."

Grayson smiled back. "Help is always appreciated."

"Nah. Far be it for me to intrude."

The group all washed the clothes they weren't wearing and hung them to dry, happy for the abundant and clean water of the reservoir. Sated, they all nearly fell asleep simultaneously as their fire began to wane.

Grayson and Juniper were the exceptions; they took the opportunity to bathe in the reservoir, floating contentedly while listening to the breeze. Coyotes sang in the distance.

"I hope we'll have better allies in the Valerians," Juniper said. "I don't know who to trust after Kylie betrayed us all."

"I know. Me either. But the seven of us aren't gonna make it all on our own."

They remained silent. Juniper swam to Grayson, pressed her body to his, and put her arms around his neck. She kissed him, more deeply than she had ever kissed him before. Grayson returned it, holding her tightly as he walked her up on shore and set her gently on the grassy beach.

The thirty-foot walls had been visible from the outskirts of town. The refugees were relieved to finally approach their destination, the nearly week-long trek having worn them down. Hypervigilance and covering their tracks kept them engaged on the trail but fatigued their senses.

Logan's instructions for arrival on the back of the map were clear. Approach with hands held out to the side and long weapons held vertically by the muzzle. Announce loudly and clearly the challenge word *Malheur* three times. The answer should come back *Bully* three times. It sounded silly, but it would assure the safety of both the refugees and the Valerians.

The exhausted refugees approached the western gate, arms outstretched and their weapons held vertically by the muzzle, as instructed. Grayson monitored the movement in the parapet as they approached, which, predictably, heightened as they drew closer. When he saw that the sentries had clumped into a firing line, he knew it was time to call out the challenge. He halted the line of refugees.

"Malheur, Malheur, Malheur!"

There was a moment of silence. It felt too long.

"*Bully, Bully, Bully!*" came the reply. The line of sentries broke and hustled back to their posts. The huge locks in the solid gate *clunked* loudly as they were disengaged, and the gate doors swung outward.

Logan and Echo strode out to meet them, a short column of armed guards following a few steps behind. Grayson extended his hand and shook with both leaders.

"Good to see you, Grayson. I was beginning to wonder if you'd be making it."

"Thanks. It's good to see you too. How'd you know?"

Echo smirked a bit sheepishly. "From the beginning, the Rimrockians seemed too eager to use force by any means. So," she cast a glance at Logan, "we decided to eavesdrop a tad."

"How?" The refugees were led through the gate as Echo explained.

"We tapped into the compound's old public address system. As you know, it was a school once upon a time, and the speakers they installed in the early 2020s were two-way so school administrators could listen in on the classrooms. After all the school shootings, lots of schools started doing it as a security precaution.

"The planning committee for the project left notes behind. Everything back then was 'smart,' so the PA system was fully integrated into the school's LAN. They felt it would only be fair if *all* rooms had these speakers, even in the admin offices. Therefore, Kylie's office was included in the tap.

"We heard all sorts of fun facts. Her plans to eradicate both the Keepers and the Jiating, plans to plunder neighboring villages, and of course, the plans to kill her new greatest threats."

"Wait," Juniper said. "She was plundering villages? There was never any indication while we were there that she was doing that."

"We know. She kept it very quiet, even having her people use Keeper disguises before the Keepers were wiped out by the Jiating. Her strategy will probably change now."

Juniper let that sink in for a moment. That strategy likely meant that the Keepers that had sacked and burned Awbreytown were actually raiders from Rimrock. The anger bubbled up inside her. Grayson's gentle hand on her shoulder lowered her temper a bit. It didn't stem the single angry tear from escaping and tumbling down her cheek.

So much betrayal, so much anger. Juniper would no longer allow herself to believe that people were inherently good. Her faith had been shaken; her trust shattered. The Valerians would be no exception; she would watch them closely. Grayson was right, the seven of them couldn't survive alone. However, Juniper's era of blind trust in humanity was over.

TWENTY-TWO

"There's no sign of them anywhere. Wherever they went, there are no tracks, no broken stalks of grass, nothing. They were very disciplined about leaving no trace behind." Mason Twiss stood tall, though inwardly he feared Kylie's potential reaction. So far, she was taking it well. "We checked with Ochoco, and they swear up and down they haven't seen them."

"I don't believe that," Kylie said. "Ochoco is the first and *only* place they would have gone. With whom did you speak?"

"Several people, including the *de facto* leader, Alex. Just like the forest, there was no trace of them inside or outside the walls."

Kylie ground her teeth, something she hadn't done since she was very young. She hated losing control in this manner.

"There's every possibility they ran to Vale. It would have been the only other place they would have felt comfortable."

She slammed her hand into her desk. Twiss flinched.

"We have to assume we are no longer safe here. We'll be mobilizing to move the entire compound up to the Sisters facility."

"Kylie, we don't…"

"I know. It's highly inconvenient. We'll carry everything we can up there. Weapons, ammo, food, and water take priority over anything else. We leave in the morning."

Twiss's eyebrows knotted together even as he made a half-bow before leaving Kylie's office. When sure she was alone, Kylie buried her face in her hands and pressed her fingertips into her skull. The pressure began to relax the muscles in her face, in turn lessening the throbbing headache.

Nothing was going to plan. She felt she should have listened to her screaming inner monologue when she let the outsiders be walked out by Innes's team. Feeling stupid, she pulled a backpack from under her desk and walked out the front door.

Kylie waved at each sentry as she made her way down the stairs and out the east gate. She walked into the small ravine just beyond the east gate, where a copse of aspens stood at the bottom, their golden leaves dancing in the breeze. She deeply inhaled the clean and crisp scent of the aspens. She saw no hint of danger in the woods. Smiling, she knelt and set the backpack on the ground.

Kylie took off her coat and set it on the ground neatly. She then removed her shirt and set it neatly on the coat. The crisp autumn air lightly brushed her skin, raising goosebumps all over her torso. She removed the coiled cat o' nine tails from the backpack and stood up straight, letting the breeze course across her naked torso. Her arms, her shoulders, her nipples tightened; the scars across her back, however, were immune to the caress. She breathed in deeply yet again, then set the cat to its duty.

Keona spent some extra time at the range to keep himself occupied. He didn't relish the thought of engaging in battle against the same people he had just helped from certain annihilation. But that was exactly the course they were going to take.

Echo had called a meeting that evening that would more or less solidify Vale's position on Rimrock. Keona knew that position would be to neutralize the threat—a phrase that meant only one of two things, neither of which eased his troubled mind.

The little robot tapping at his feet annoyed him, but he moved out of the way so it could collect the brass he had expended. He sat quietly at the bench, cleaning the pistol he used that day. He still preferred the feel of his sword, though fighting from a distance sometimes had its benefits; such as not having to look into the eyes of someone you'd trained as you ran a blade through them.

Even before he found himself four hundred years in the future, he had been looking for ways to cut off violence. He had seen, and drawn, so much blood in his life that he was looking for something new. Something peaceful. It saddened him to know that it wouldn't be possible. Not until the last of the threats were cleaned up.

Keona returned to his quarters to clean up before dinner. The shower's hot water melted away the tension, but it couldn't wash away the memories. Keona gave up trying to forget. He shut off the water, dried himself, and dressed.

The other refugees were done with half their food by the time Keona went through the chow line and sat at their table. Ember set her head on his shoulder as he sat, and he answered with a short kiss on top of her head.

"Rough day?" Grayson asked.

"Mm." Keona shoved a spoonful of rice in his mouth. "Yeah."

"Echo tap you to speak at the meeting tonight?"

"Yep. You?"

Keona shook his head. "Nah. Guess she figured you were chatty enough for both of us."

Grayson let Keona finish his meal in silence. He could tell that Keona was unsettled. When Keona pushed his tray aside and focused on the coffee, Grayson knew he was free to speak. Unfortunately, the announcement over the speakers interrupted him as he was about to talk.

"Attention please; tonight's meeting has been moved up. All participants, report to the council chamber immediately."

Keona heaved a sigh and took another sip of coffee before standing, the mug still held tightly in his grip.

"Not gonna leave it, huh?" Grayson asked as he stood also.

"No cuppa left behind, brah."

They strode to the council chamber and were waved through by the guards posted at the heavy double doors. Echo was seated at the far end of the oval table in the middle of the room, the rest of the chairs empty as she awaited the arrival of the rest of the participants.

"Hello, Grayson. Keona." She stood and shook their hands. Logan came into the room and shook their hands also before taking his seat to the right of Echo. Grayson and Keona sat to her left.

"Sorry to pull you away early. We got some disturbing news that needed to be shared right away."

"Not a problem," Keona said, sipping again.

In a short time, the table was filled and the doors were closed. Echo stood and tapped the wall behind her. A high-resolution drone image filled the wall; a thick stand of trees pointed at the participants, and a tight column of people and equipment snaked their way through the middle of the trees. Echo tapped the wall again after moving to the edge of the image, and the paused video played. The people and equipment were moving steadily toward their destination.

"Kylie and her new lapdog, Mason Twiss, spoke last night

about evacuating Rimrock this morning and heading to 'the Sisters facility.' Given their number, we didn't believe that it would be a quick evacuation; however, at approximately five o'clock this morning, this column began moving to the west. Shortly after, another column left the compound. Shortly after that, another."

"They're spreading out their people to avoid having everyone offed at once in an attack," Keona said.

"Correct." Echo tapped the wall again, and the recorded audio of Kylie and Twiss talking in her office played. Grayson was impressed with Alex's ability to throw off the Rimrockians. He was less pleased knowing that the Rimrockians were relocating to a fortified position, albeit one with which he and his cohort were now intimately familiar.

"That doesn't make sense," Keona said, reading Grayson's thought. "Why would they move to a position we've already taken once?"

"Logan and I wondered the same," Echo said. "However, their trajectory appears to be taking them to a spot nearly due west rather than near the base of the Sisters peaks." Echo tapped the wall twice and a satellite image filled it. She waved her hands in front of the wall, which slid the image to the right, then parted her hands as if she were beginning a stretch, which zoomed in the image on a cluster of gray roofs in the forest.

"This is the old town of Sisters. These roofs belong to their old high school, the largest structure that existed at the time *Codagenesis* struck. We feel it's likely Rimrock is headed here. Kylie seems to have a preference for the old schools, likely because they were built to last with relatively light maintenance, as well as having been retrofitted for nuclear fallout and biological attacks."

Echo zoomed in tighter on the rooftop. "Unlike the roof in Rimrock, this roof is pitched, probably because of the history of snowfall there. Logan and I feel that the main defenses won't be elevated. They'll be concentrated at ground level with sniper hides and gunner's nests at strategic elevated points. The pitched roofs also make an aerial approach extremely difficult; if we go that route, it'll be a multi-pronged attack with fast-rope teams comprising a secondary element."

"It looks like the weakest side is the west. Does that track?" Keona asked.

"We think so, yes," Echo said. "The trees there will provide some concealment and cover, and there are few windows. That wing looks to be the old gym, so unless they've got scaffolding in there, there's less chance of an elevated shooting platform."

"I wouldn't put it past Kylie, though," Grayson interjected.

"Nor would I," Echo said. "So, we'll prepare for that. Lastly, since they've moved on, we'll lose the advantage of electronic surveillance; our team informs me they've attempted to tap into the old servers, but the system is completely offline, which means that the system is totally inoperable. Even at the site."

"No matter," Grayson said. "We know their capabilities, and if the site is anything like Rimrock, there won't be many surprises. Just to be safe, we should have a staging area here," he pointed to a clearing a few miles west of the site, "for aerial response in reserve."

"Agreed," Echo said. "We have several aerial assault vehicles with precision weapons and ordnance aboard ready to deploy."

"I thought you didn't?" Keona said.

"Not at Rimrock," Logan said. "That was by design. Since we knew of their plans, we elected not to show *everything* of which we're capable. Plus, as you said, we now know their capabilities in full, giving us the tactical advantage. These aerial assault vehicles can carry thousands of rounds of ammunition and up to eight guided missiles. Others we have in reserve can carry four guided ONC bombs." Logan pronounced it *ahnk*.

"ONC?" Keona asked.

"Octanitrocubane," Echo said. "It'll punch a hole in anything. Above ground, that is. If we need to penetrate underground facilities, we'll need to develop a ballistic casing for that."

"What do you have for ground assault?" Grayson said, getting more excited than he should.

"Well, what we had initially, but we also have repulsorlift vehicles ideal for rough terrain."

"What's that?" Grayson asked.

"Vehicles that float above the ground rather than needing wheels and tires," Echo said. "Very useful in the brushy environs of the high desert or the undergrowth over in Sisters."

Immediately, Grayson thought of the landspeeders and speeder bikes of the old *Star Wars* movies, vehicles that had been promised in his lifetime but never materialized before he was put in a stasis pod.

"That's excellent! Numbers?"

"Plenty of armored transports as well as several single-rider models for precision incursions," Logan said. "All are completely silent when run in stealth mode."

Logan brought up photos and spec sheets on the monitors. The transports looked like typical armored personnel carriers the warriors were used to in the 21st century, but these floated above the ground rather than using tracks or tires. The single-rider models didn't look at all like the speeder bikes of *Star Wars*, but more like personal watercraft with a flat underside and twin forward-facing machine guns at the front.

Grayson felt guilty about his giddiness, but the technology was too awesome not to be at least a *little* excited. Keona was torn; he wanted so badly to leave war behind him, but these machines were too beautiful not to appreciate.

"Looks like we have plenty of planning to do," Grayson said. "I'd also like to get some training on the repulsorlift vehicles.

Please."

"Of course." Echo had expected nothing less.

Kylie holed up in her new quarters as her people busied themselves outside, cleaning away the dust and debris of many years. Sisters had been abandoned for the better of three centuries, but Kylie's predecessors were big on contingencies. When they began turning people away, the fear became that a settlement would form that would resent them and gather to overrun Rimrock. Scouting parties pushed west and found that Sisters had a perfectly suitable building like the one they currently occupied. Work had continued secretly for many years to maintain the facility in the event they would ever need to evacuate their beloved home.

Kylie paced as she tried to gather her thoughts, but it had become increasingly difficult to focus. To torture her further, her clairvoyant abilities had begun clouding, especially since she had no "antenna" to work with any longer. Her vision had winnowed down to the mundane lives and personalities of her clan. There was very little information of interest to Kylie anymore, and that was unacceptable. Unacceptable or not, Kylie was going to have to use cunning rather than clairvoyance to help her clan survive.

A knock came at her door.

"Yes?"

Twiss stuck his head in. "Is this a good time?"

"No," Kylie snapped, "it isn't, but it doesn't really matter. What news do you have?"

"All of us have arrived. Everyone is settling into their quarters, except for the work crews, who are setting up the kitchen and the common area."

"Fine, thank you."

"Is there anything I can do for you? Get for you?"

Kylie wanted to scream but held her anger in check. Twiss was only looking out for her and wanted to make sure she was okay.

"No, Mason," Kylie said, smiling sweetly. "Thank you. Please join the others and make sure we're set up for dinner. Normalcy will help us adjust."

"Of course."

Twiss spun and left Kylie's quarters. She sat heavily on the edge of her bed, tears stinging her eyes. Never had it crossed her mind that *she* would be the one to lose Rimrock. She, the last of the Eastons, had lost her ancestral home because of a stupid mistake.

TWENTY-THREE

Grayson and Keona slowed the single-rider vehicles, which they had started calling speeder bikes. They dismounted at the maintenance area, where Logan waited for them.

"Those. Are. Awesome," Grayson said. "I can't believe how well they handle."

"Thank you," Logan said. "We take great pride in our craftsmanship."

Logan accompanied Grayson and Keona back to headquarters, where Echo was poised over the central screen.

"Ah, great timing," Echo said. "The Rimrockians have all arrived. It doesn't appear that they've begun fortifying their new position, which may work in our favor as we mobilize in the next few days. I'll keep the drones over the building night and day, see if we get any alerts."

"Excellent. We're ready to rock whenever you're ready."

"Almost," Echo said. "Come with me."

The refugees followed Echo to the weapons room. The walls were bristling with all manner of handheld weaponry. Most looked based on firearms with which they were already acquainted.

"Whoah," Grayson said. Echo walked them to a rack on the rear wall. Rifles stood standing in a tidy row.

"This is the primary weapon for ground forces," Echo said. "I'm sure you were probably expecting some sort of electromagnetic weapon or plasma gun, but—" Echo picked up a rifle, ejected the magazine, and showed them the top. Brass cartridges shined in the white light. The tips were a dull white. Echo rocked the magazine back home.

"Outstanding," Grayson said. "Although a rail gun *would* have been pretty cool."

"We found through much testing that the old way was still the best way. Plasma was too finicky and both it and the electromagnetic option required far too much energy storage for what we were trying to accomplish. Luckily, we were able to store enough power in the butt to do this." Echo pressed a button and the rifle disappeared. She still held her hands in a cradling position.

"Stealth?!"

"Yes. And it's not relegated to just the rifle." Echo set the rifle down and walked them to a bank of lockers. She opened the door and inside were sleek-looking uniforms in navy blue.

"Please tell me you're gonna make that disappear," Keona said.

Echo pressed a button on the collar and the uniform went invisible. "The suits are self-powering. They use the wearer's body heat and natural electrical conductivity to run consistent power indefinitely. When paired with the rifle, the suit transfers energy to allow it to remain cloaked as well, bypassing the rifle's battery to save its power. After all, what use is the tech if there's a floating rifle bobbing through the air?" She smiled.

"These are incredible," Grayson said. "This calls for a change in plans."

In the council chamber, Grayson laid out his new vision. With the stealth gear, he was confident they could mount a precision infiltration and eliminate the Rimrockian leaders without harming the noncombatants inside the compound. The aerial reserve would remain above the compound as overwatch. Logan and Keona would lead two fireteams straight to the rear door with Grayson acting as squad leader. Logan had gathered further intel from the drones that their primary defenses were focused at the rear of the compound, where an open attack was far more likely since the rear doors were too exposed and the hundred-yard leadup was a suicide run. No obstacles, no trees. Any trees that had tried to grow had been ripped up in its beginning stages to leave the fields open. This late in the season, the tall grasses had begun going dormant and were only about ankle high. This would cut down on the rustling noises as they passed through the fields toward their objective.

"Any questions?" Grayson asked.

"What time you wanna leave?" Innes asked.

As they exited the council chamber, Juniper approached and pulled Grayson and Echo aside.

"Are you still holding Zhang?"

Echo looked puzzled. "Yes, of course. He's being held as a prisoner. Why?"

"I'd like to speak with him. I think he may know more about the Rimrockians than he lets on. I don't believe he would've mounted an offensive of the caliber we witnessed without some assurance that he would be successful, even without the Sirens turning on him."

Echo was silent a moment. She looked to Grayson.

"Hey, don't look at me. Juniper is her own person."

"Very well," Echo said. "One condition—Zhang looks like he's out of line, we end the meeting. With or without your permission."

"Understood," Juniper said.

"May I tag along for observation?" Grayson asked Juniper.

"You don't need to ask permission," Juniper said.

"Formality," Grayson said, smiling. She knew he would have gone whether or not she approved.

The three descended into the lower levels of the command building, ramps zigzagging lower and lower. At the lowest level, Echo produced a proxy key and swiped it in front of the reader. The electronic pocket door *whooshed* open; it shut quickly behind them as they stepped through.

It bothered Juniper that she hadn't felt Zheng on their arrival, nor as they got closer to him.

"How is he being held?" she asked.

"I assume you mean the fact that you can't 'feel' him nearby," Echo said. "We have him in a kind of—ah—psychokinetic Faraday cage."

"A what?" Juniper said.

"We've put him in a box, basically, and we're flooding it with a broadcast of the frequency we used at Rimrock." Juniper nodded her head.

They walked a bit more in silence before arriving at another door. Echo paused before swiping the proxy key.

"Are you sure you want to go in there?"

"I do. I believe I can get more out of him."

"You're totally safe, and we'll be monitoring. Head to the door if you need anything or when you want out." Juniper nodded. Echo swiped the key and Juniper stepped in cautiously.

At the center of the room was a large steel cage; in the center of the cage sat Zhang in the lotus position.

"Hello, Zhang."

Zhang's eyelids opened slowly over his almond-shaped eyes.

"Hello, Juniper."

Hearing him say her name felt shameful but seeing him locked in a cage took the edge off her discomfort. She stopped a few feet away from the cage. Zhang unfurled and stood, placing his hands behind his back. He didn't take any steps forward, choosing to remain in the center of the cage. Juniper hated not being able to see what he was thinking or feeling. She would have to work on intuition alone.

"I didn't come here for pleasant conversation," Juniper said.

"I hadn't thought so. It *is* nice to hear a voice again…other than my own, that is."

"I imagine so."

"How may I be of assistance?" Zhang cocked his head slightly. "I believe that would be the only way you would come visit."

"It is." Juniper hesitated. "What do you know of the Rimrockians and their plans?" The vestige of a smile tugged at the corners of Zhang's thin-lipped mouth.

"Interesting." Zhang began pacing slowly, maintaining distance from the front of the cage. "Well, Juniper, I had hoped someone would arrive and maybe ask why we would want to eliminate Rimrock and all her occupants. It's simple. Kylie wished to destroy all other peoples and clans in the central territories. We, the Jiating, were of those, ah, 'other peoples.'"

"So were the occupants of Awbreytown," Juniper said, sadness and anger creeping into her voice.

"Yes, they were. Though, honestly, the only real threat we feared, at least for the last hundred years, were the Keepers. However, they had devolved to the point where they really presented no threat to us, except by the odd encounter in the woods.

"No, the real threat to the Jiating was the rest of you. The humans. You who had the capacity to plan. To love, to hate, to *feel*. We needed to better understand how you would try to eliminate *us*."

"Is that why you resorted to kidnapping and torturing us?"

"In part," Zhang stopped pacing and stood to face her. "Over the last generation, we realized humans were levels above the Keepers *because* of the innate things that make you all human." Zhang smiled again. "*Reason* was not one of those traits. I decided it would be best to remove the most dangerous of you from our vicinity to ensure our survival."

"Rimrock."

"No, dear girl. Just one. Kylie."

"Why her? Because she was clairvoyant?"

"Your predilection for seeing only a small part of the whole intrigues me, Juniper. Surely you know I would never fear a simple clairvoyant? You have *seen* how I perform among my minions, and the way in which I can travel between minds. No, Juniper. We did not fear Kylie because of simple clairvoyance. Her true nature is what we feared."

"What is she?" Juniper asked, her heart now beating rapidly.

Zhang was clearly enjoying building the tension. "Kylie is what the Navajo people called *yee naldlooshii*."

"A...what?"

"That's what the Navajo called them, anyway. We would call them 'shapeshifters.'" Zhang paused for effect. Juniper's brow simply knitted.

"Kylie possesses the ability to become virtually any mammal of equal size. She is likely the most dangerous creature ever to live. The particulars are quite unknown, but you can see why we were so interested in humans here. Ah, kidnapping and torture, as you say."

"You believe there are more than just Kylie."

"You're learning, Juniper. Yes. Of keen interest was her daughter."

"She never mentioned a daughter!" Juniper said.

"She never needed to, not when her daughter was already present," Zhang said, this time the smile crawling up the sides of his face. Juniper puzzled for a moment. Then realization hit.

"Mmm. There you go." Zhang reveled.

"Kylie is...*my* mother?!" Juniper felt panic. "But *how*? The

Keepers took my mother!"

"That she was, that she was. And it was by imitating the Keepers she and your father were able to escape. She pretended to be a guard taking your father to the slavemaster and they simply walked out of the camp. Alas, your father was a simple man and couldn't comprehend his lovely wife being such a vile creature. After their escape, he attempted to run off on his own and was killed by Keepers. They don't like it when their toys run off, you see."

Tears clouded Juniper's eyes. All these years. She thought she could remember her mother's face, but it had been so long, and she had been so young when her mother was taken, she just saw a blank spot.

"I don't believe you."

"My dear, why do you think we would have been so interested in *you*? Your potential was only proven on your escape. You did quite a lot of damage when you left our facilities."

Juniper began walking toward the cage. The door to the room opened suddenly and Grayson rushed in. He grabbed her around the waist and began pulling her backward.

"You're lying!" she cried, her hands grasping at Grayson's arms, trying to pull them away from her.

"I'd say I have nothing to lose," Zhang said, motioning to his cage with both hands. "What have I to gain by lying to you?"

Grayson kept pulling at Juniper, but there was a strength in her he hadn't felt before.

"How many are there? *HOW MANY?*"

"I have no idea," Zhang said. "It stands to reason, though, that you would be among their number."

Grayson finally succeeded in hauling Juniper out. The door slammed shut behind them. Juniper collapsed into Grayson, her breath coming in deep, racking sobs.

"I...I..."

Grayson sat against the wall and held her closely. Echo stood nearby in near shock. Juniper cried until she was gasping. Grayson cupped her chin in his hand and made her look into his eyes.

"It's gonna be okay."

Juniper's pupils were dilated, her breath shallow and raspy.

"It's going to be okay," Grayson said again, enunciating each syllable clearly. Juniper's face creased, her eyes watered. She nodded and set her head on his shoulder.

Grayson stood, hauling Juniper up in his arms. Echo hustled ahead of them as they headed back to the dormitories, opening doors for them. Grayson set Juniper on her bed and knelt beside her. He caressed her cheek with his hand; she responded by placing hers on top of his.

"I'm going to head back to the council chamber," Echo said, closing the door.

"My mother," Juniper rasped.

"Not anymore," Grayson said. "Not anymore." Juniper remained silent as she caught her breath and gathered her thoughts.

"That means the attacks, the ones where the Rimrockians were 'disguised' as Keepers, they must have been shapeshifters."

"I think so," Grayson said. "That would make sense. It looks like we're heading into an interesting fight."

"We have to capture her alive," Juniper said.

"She's not your mother anymore," Grayson said.

"I know, I know. It's not out of sentiment, Grayson. We need to know what *she* knows."

TWENTY-FOUR

The team was ready to roll. Juniper felt uneasy in her stealth suit, uncomfortable if only because she hated wearing something designed to make killing easier. She began to wonder if the Valerians, too, had some ulterior motive. There seemed to be no faction other than her own small clique that was honest in its objectives. She listened to the briefing as she squirmed in the suit, hopeful that this mission wouldn't last long.

Grayson saw Juniper fidgeting at the back of the council chamber, clearly uncomfortable. He tamped his desire to go comfort her, though he desperately wanted to. He hoped she felt the vibe he was putting out.

"Keona's team, Bravo, will be responsible for security at all times, and Logan's team, Alpha, will be the attack element. We'll clear the rear of the building and push toward our objective here."

Grayson pointed at the middle of the building. "This is the likely hiding place of most of the clan, simply because of its position within the building. It will be the best protected space on all sides, though it will limit their options for retreat. It may be elevated, which will give them a defilade that will assist in said retreat if they sound the alarm.

"We may be heading in with stealth suits, but bear in mind, our primary objective is clairvoyant. We'll be using suit-worn transmitters Logan created that will emit the frequency that has been proven to jam telepathic comms, but the transmission will be localized and will look like a void or shimmer in the objective's mind. Juniper has confirmed this with basic trials, so do *not* rely on it to fully hide your presence."

Taking away Kylie's name and labeling her with the sterile term *objective* appeared to give Juniper some measure of comfort during the briefing.

Keona sat quietly, his thumb toying with the fire selector on his rifle. He and Grayson had carefully toiled over the team selections the night before to build a squad that would be able to deliver the fastest precision strike they could conceive. He knew the plan forward and backward, and knew he would be successful with his part of the mission. Keona only hoped his team wouldn't let him down. He would also miss having his blade, but putting the stealth package on it would ruin the balance to which he had become accustomed and alter his proficiency; not to any measurable degree, but enough that he would notice. Regardless, it wasn't something on which he was willing to stake their success.

"We'll be assembled in a staggered column to maximize security on approach. From there, the environment inside will dictate formation and speed. Each team of four will have one psychokinetic team member as a backup in the event Logan's jammers fail. Trinity will run on Keona's team, Juniper with Logan. I'll be point on Logan's team."

"Reinforcements?" Hallie asked.

"Sixty second response," Grayson said. "Echo has several teams on standby that will be staged in swift aerials as well as a ground element to the west with repulsorlift vehicles for exfil if a hasty retreat is needed."

Hallie nodded.

Juniper took comfort in knowing that Ben, her oldest friend, would be safe in Vale. He knew his limitations, and combat was not his strongest suit. Ember would be hanging back as well. She was so very tired of the violence people did, and she wanted no part of it. Keona wished he could, for her sake, but he knew she would never remain safe unless that safety was secured by force.

"All right, everyone," Grayson called. "All aboard."

The teams loaded onto *Aviatrix* and settled into one of the landing craft, buckling into their seats.

"Gonna be a short ride," Echo said over the intercom. "Less than an hour. We'll roll stealth at ten minutes out."

"You haven't said much, Innes," Grayson said across the aisle. "That's unlike you."

"Yeah, well…" Innes paused. "It's not every day I'm tasked with huntin' someone I used to trust."

"I know it's tough."

"Do ya, now?"

Grayson looked Innes square in the eyes. "I do." Innes nodded.

As promised, the ride was fast. Much faster than the week it had taken Grayson's refugees to travel on foot.

"Ten out." Echo's voice broke the silence over the intercom. "Stealth engaged."

Aviatrix slowed to a mere 190 miles per hour as she was guided just above the treetops. The teams locked and loaded their rifles, getting ready to disembark immediately on touchdown. Each member reached up to their shoulder and tapped the frequency transmitters mounted there. The lights went out and a red glow filled the cabin.

"Craft deploying," Echo said. "Good luck."

There was a shudder and a quick dip in elevation as the landing craft, also cloaked using the stealth tech, descended from the belly of *Aviatrix* and sped into the treeline just beyond the north fields of the Sisters compound. The team members simultaneously tapped the collar button on their suits and engaged the stealth feature. Grayson saw each team member as a thermal figure in the facemask of his helmet.

Cool, he thought.

The team was pushed lightly into their seats as the craft slowed for landing, and a light jolt signaled they were on the ground. The rear bay door silently opened and each team member released their harness quickly before hustling out the door.

Grayson was the first on the ground, and he ran at a light jog, rifle cradled in his hands. The heads-up display on his facemask read no buried traps in the field, a tactical mistake on the part of the Rimrockians in his opinion. He chanced a quick look at the roofline of the old high school and the area just below, looking for any signs of movement. There were none. The HUD picked up a faint heat signature at the right side of the roof, but it ended up being a pair of doves.

Grayson signaled for the team to slow down as they approached the target door. They stacked along the wall behind Grayson and he tried the door handle.

Locked. He figured it would be. Keona moved up the column and grabbed the handle. He closed his eyes and envisioned the tumbler and pins moving inside the door handle and deadbolt; he began manipulating the pins until the faintest click sounded and the handle twisted in his hand. At the same time, the deadbolt disengaged. Keona opened the door as silently as he could, his concentration barely allowing even the smallest of squeaks. Keona stepped back and Grayson rushed into the building, rifle at the ready.

The HUD showed no personnel nearby, which, by the lack of response at the door opening, he expected. He wound through a mountain of supplies that had been stacked in the large space just beyond the door and halted just before the door to the atrium. He felt a hand squeeze his shoulder, and he opened the door.

There were no people to be seen.

Puzzled, Grayson looked over his shoulder and motioned for Logan to follow and for Keona to hold back for security. Both nodded, and Grayson pushed toward the double door on the right. Once again, Logan's team stacked against the wall. Grayson felt the squeeze on his shoulder and he opened the door.

The gymnasium on the other side, like the atrium, was empty.

What the hell? Grayson thought. He stood upright and glanced at the rafters. *Where is everyone?*

He immediately crouched into position again and exited the gymnasium. Keona saw him approach and readied to clear the other wing of the building, though it was unlikely anyone was there. But *where* could they *be*?

A thought suddenly and viciously hit Grayson. As quietly as

he could, he whispered, "Eagle Eye, are you monitoring, over?"

"Affirm, Wolf. Status, over?"

"All areas clear. No personnel present. Bring up your schematics, over."

"Up. Broadcasting to your HUD, over."

"Copy." Grayson used the controls embedded in the left gauntlet of his suit to manipulate the schematic in his HUD. The tangle of pipes and wires were almost too much to see through, but what he was in search of finally showed itself. He silently cursed himself.

"Eagle Eye, they're *under* the school, over."

Echo had seen what Grayson was looking at and shook her head just as he zoomed in on it in his HUD.

"Shit, Wolf. Copy. We didn't see that, over."

A vault door was hidden in the boiler room, denoted by a flat double-door and the ever-so-slight depiction of stairs beyond it. Several sets of trained eyes had gone over the schematic, but it was simply too subtle to see without knowing what should be there. Kylie's advantage had been years of scouting and planning.

"Scrum," Grayson said. The teams assembled near the wall in a circle, heads together, with three members facing outward for security. The thought was that blocking the center of the circle would limit unnecessary sound from traveling outside the circle when speaking, even silently.

"Okay, everyone. New plan. Single file, Bravo at front, Alpha to rear. I'll remain on point. We don't know the layout, but all fire will be funneled, so let's try not to fire unless absolutely necessary. Maintain element of surprise. Remember cover and concealment where available. We may be cloaked, but we're still flesh and blood."

The teams nodded. They stacked behind Grayson as he pushed farther into the building. They reached the door for the physical plant and halted. Keona swung around Grayson and ran the same lock-picking trick he had done on entry. Grayson pushed in first. The lone sentry looked confused when the door swung open by itself. Grayson pounded his left fist into the sentry's temple and caught the sentry as he fell, unconscious. Grayson set the sentry down gently and took up the lead again.

The first intersection arrived, and Grayson made the decision to bear left, believing the tunnel would lead back under the protected floors of the atrium and gymnasium. The tunnel soon darkened, and the HUDs switched to night vision. Unlike what Grayson had once used, this night vision was crisp and clear without any noise.

The next turn led to a door flanked by two sentries, and the card reader for the door was behind the sentry to the right. There was a single light bulb above the door to illuminate their position. Grayson motioned to Keona to burst the bulb.

The *pop* above the sentries didn't set off any alarm. Instead, the one on the right just said, "Not again," and huffed a sigh. He turned to swipe his proxy key and was stopped by a force he couldn't see. Grayson rent his neck quickly to the side and took the rifle from his hands. At the same time, Keona wrapped the other sentry's neck in a triangle grip, forcing downward until he heard a light *pop* and the sentry went limp.

Grayson retrieved the proxy key from the first sentry and readied. Keona squeezed his shoulder and Grayson swiped the proxy key at the reader. The door hissed open and they were in a large foyer that opened into a large room filled with bunk beds. Along the walls were doors leading to, presumably, the rooms of leadership personnel.

People milled about in various places around the room, none of them plainly armed. Keona saw a rather uptight-looking man walking out of a door at the right side of the giant dormitory and tapped Grayson. Grayson followed Keona's outstretched arm and saw the door to which Keona was pointing. Grayson nodded, and they began moving in a staggered column toward the door.

Something lurched in Grayson's gut.

There were about five men playing cards at a table a few yards to the left of the door they were going to. They were *watching* Grayson and the squad.

Impossible, Grayson thought. *Unless…*

The men snarled and suddenly bulged like balloons filling quickly with helium, becoming Keepers right before Grayson's eyes. The two youngest changed nearly immediately and began charging the squad.

"SHIT! COVER'S BLOWN! CONTACT FRONT!" Grayson unleashed a barrage of automatic fire at the shapeshifters, tagging the two charging. They fell, writhing, but not yet out of the fight. The other three were a touch older and were changing as they charged. The squads repositioned into a wedge formation and began laying fire at random shapeshifters that charged out of the crowd of noncombatants. The first five that had spotted them were on the deck, but they were slowly gathering themselves and getting up.

"Not good, not good," Grayson said to himself.

Juniper rushed at the door ahead of the wedge. Grayson peeled away and ran after her, shoulder-checking a shapeshifter that ran in from his left. The shapeshifter slid awkwardly across the floor on his back. Juniper closed the distance quickly and burst into the room. Grayson slid through the doorway on her heels and slammed the door shut behind them, swiftly covering Kylie with his rifle..

Kylie was crouched in the far corner between a bed and the wall. Something about her posture, her bearing, was wrong. Juniper approached slowly.

"We didn't come here to harm you, Kylie." Juniper's soothing voice seemed to be doing little. A growl rumbled deep in Kylie's throat. "We need you to come with us. We need to know what you know."

Kylie's crouch became deeper. Her skin seemed to ripple underneath her linen clothing.

"*I have no plan to comply,*" Kylie said.

"We know," Juniper purred. "But I think we can help each other. No matter how you feel about us, there's something else out there, isn't there?"

Kylie seemed to relax, if just for a moment.

"The Jiating in Sisters, they weren't the only ones, were they?" Grayson asked.

"*Your insight belies your stupid look yet again, Grayson,*" Kylie hissed. The rippling beneath her clothing eased, and she slowly stood to her normal height. Juniper stood her ground in the middle of the room.

"We have much to discuss. But not here."

"You intend to take me captive?" A sad smile flashed on Kylie's face. "I think not...daughter." Kylie appeared to change instantaneously into a giant wolf. Grayson raised his rifle and prepared to fire. Juniper placed her hand at the end of the barrel and forced Grayson to lower it. Kylie snarled.

"I will never call you mother. You tried to use me, then have me killed. I won't be like you."

Kylie lunged at Juniper. Grayson reached out to snag the flying wolf midair, but he didn't get the chance. Juniper's eyes crackled blue and she shot out her arm, fingers curled as if ready to catch Kylie by the throat. Kylie was suspended in the air, the look of shock registering even on her canid face. Kylie was unable to move at all. Grayson stood aside as Juniper turned and walked out of the room into the larger room. The shapeshifters outside that were still alive recoiled at the sight of their leader being hauled away with no physical tether, Juniper's glowing eyes striking fear deep within their chests. It looked to Grayson almost as though they were kneeling to Juniper.

Juniper cocked her head to the side and looked at Kylie, who couldn't maintain eye contact. Juniper switched direction and headed to the back of the room. Grayson and Keona followed, the rest of the squad providing security. Juniper stopped in front of another door—Keona stepped forward to begin unlocking it, but Juniper placed her hand on it and it crumpled like foil, falling to the ground with a loud *clang*. On the other side, Reed Newberry sat on his bed, haggard, hardly able to lift his eyes to see what was happening.

"Huh. Well, that's a neat trick," Newberry said. Grayson picked him up and threw him over his shoulder. The squad regrouped and began their exit, the rear security walking backward. None of the Rimrockians attempted to follow.

The squad exited the building to the rear. Echo had assembled a convex arc on the north field, anticipating a hot extract. Instead, she watched in fascination as Juniper—eyes ablaze in electric blue— calmly led a floating wolf across the field, the squad following closely behind.

"I didn't think you'd take your codename this seriously, Grayson," Echo said.

"It's…uh…it's a surprise here too," Grayson said, tripping on his words.

Juniper had said nothing since she went into her current state. They boarded the landing craft and ascended to *Aviatrix*, where Echo led them to the brig. They deposited Kylie and Newberry in separate cells.

Juniper, upon setting Kylie in the cell, quickly reverted to her normal self again. She blinked rapidly a few times before looking to Grayson. This time, Grayson was at a loss for words.

"What the hell was *that*?" was the best he could muster.

"I…I don't know. Suddenly, it just felt like…it felt like I could somehow make Kylie do what I wanted. Not mind control, but something else. I focused so totally on it that she just became…"

"A puppet."

"Yeah, kind of."

They walked together back to the bridge, where Echo stood waiting at the helm.

"We've got some chatting to do," Echo said.

"I guess we do," Juniper said sheepishly.

"Please join us for the debriefing tonight."

TWENTY-FIVE

The prisoners were safely rehomed in their new cells upon arrival at Vale after allowing them to bathe. Newberry was given a health screening and a flavorless nutrient paste to hold off the starvation that had begun to eat at what little muscle he had.

The team leaders gathered for their debrief in the council chamber. Juniper sat as close to Grayson as the chairs would allow. He put a comforting hand on top of her thigh.

Echo cleared her throat. "Well…where to begin."

"Start where we all know you want to," Grayson said. Echo met Juniper's eyes.

"I don't know how it happened," Juniper said, anticipating the unasked question. "I'm just as confused as you are."

"You channeled it," Keona said. "All the grief and rage inside you was focused like a laser beam." All heads swiveled toward him.

"When you saw Kylie, everything you've felt over the last weeks must have coalesced in your cells and targeted her when you saw her in that corner. Similar things happened to me during my testing; though not nearly as powerful as your manifestation."

"What are the guarantees that Juniper won't lose control of this ability?" Logan asked.

"None," Keona said, "but if she were going to lose control, she certainly would have before today." He gave her a knowing look and a nod. Juniper cast her eyes downward, grateful for Keona's vote of confidence.

"I concur," Echo said.

"Thank you," Juniper said quietly.

"All that aside, the mission was quite successful," Grayson said. "Recovering Newberry was a surprise, but he may also have information he's ready to let go. We're gonna have to interrogate all three prisoners to make sure we get as much intel as possible out of them.

"We have to be prepared for the likelihood that they won't talk," Logan said. "Our chem team has some lovely tongue-looseners should it come to that."

"As much as I'd love to stick the needle in myself," Juniper said bitterly, "I believe we'll have more success if I'm in the room during the interrogation."

"Agreed. Anyone have an objection?" Echo scanned the

leaders' faces. "Good. Equipment?"

"Equipment all functioned as expected. HUDs worked without a hitch. The emergency broadcasting system clearly worked as intended also, as you and the exfil team clearly mobilized at the first gunshot."

"Yes, we received the signal almost immediately."

"Good. We also had zero noise in the thermal and night vision components. The stealth suits were also flawless in deployment. However, we did learn of one weakness: the shapeshifters can see us even in stealth mode."

"See, or sense?" Echo asked.

"Unknown. But they definitely followed us with their eyes when we started walking toward Kylie's office."

"Wonderful," Echo said, sighing. She scribbled a note on her tablet with a silver stylus. "Weapons?"

"No complaints," Grayson said. "Fire rate was excellent, accuracy was at least eighty-five percent, very little recoil. Thoughts, 'Ona?"

"Same. Accuracy at ninety percent for me."

"Stop bragging guys, you're gonna make me blush," Logan interjected. Keona smiled.

Grayson continued. "No jamming or other typical malfunctions. They're the finest I've ever wielded."

Logan smirked. "Now I *am* gonna blush."

The leaders shared a chuckle around the table.

"Teams?" Echo continued.

"Cohesive, efficient," Grayson said. "We all flowed like we've worked together for years. I'm very pleased."

Echo scribbled on her tablet. She set it aside.

"All as I anticipated. Now it's on record. Now on to the more pressing business. Let's get Hallie and Trinity in here."

Logan stood and went to the door. Hallie and Trinity both looked at him as he poked his head through the crack and motioned them inside.

"Good evening, ladies." Echo invited them to sit. She paused a moment and sighed, allowing a small smile to form on her lips. "With the events culminating in today's capture of Kylie and Zhang's man Newberry, we have the distinction of being the most well-informed group of people concerning the geopolitics of the Oregon territories.

"We now know that the Jiating destroyed by Rimrock were *not* the sole faction of their race to be alive. We also now know that there are other, uh, mutations of humans that can change their appearance at will. We don't know how many, or their distribution, but we can be assured there will likely be others with other abilities.

"With further knowledge derived from future interrogations of the prisoners currently in custody, I am inclined to send out scouting parties to determine just how many more...people...are out there. Geographically, the land mass once known as North America was one of the largest continents on the planet. *Codagenesis* may have decimated humanity, but it seems the land is becoming populated once again, and we—humans—may no longer be the dominant life form."

The implications were staggering to Grayson. He hadn't even considered life beyond his old stomping grounds. He probably should have, but survival at the individual level had taken priority over the past few months. Keona stared ahead, having already considered the possibility.

"Hallie, I have to ask…did you have any knowledge about Kylie's ability to shapeshift?"

"None, Echo. She kept that secret *very* well-hidden."

"I had a feeling." Echo readdressed the group. "I would be eternally grateful if you would all join us. I know we're new to you, and I know you likely have some trust issues to work through, considering your last clan. Please, rest assured, we plan on being much more transparent with you. If you have any questions of us, you simply have to ask."

"When's dinner?" Grayson asked.

The tension drained out of the room as everyone let out a hearty laugh.

"I won't answer for everyone," Grayson said, "but I'd be happy to join the Valerians. You've given us every reason to trust your clan."

"I'm in also," Keona said. Juniper, Hallie, and Trinity all consented as well.

"Excellent." Echo stood. "I'm happy to hear it. I'm very excited about the next chapter. I hope the rest of you will be willing to join us."

"As am I," Grayson said.

TWENTY-SIX

Zhang was no longer resisting any questions. His time in captivity seemed to have weakened his resolve. Grayson watched every interview to be certain he wouldn't harm Juniper in any way. Juniper, for an untrained interviewer, did very well leading Zhang to answering her questions. Grayson observed this interview much the same as all prior; stoically, arms crossed, scowling.

"There may well be a group of defectors living on the peninsula separating the Columbia River from the Clackamas Sea," Zhang continued. "They were meant to find adequate facilities for their brethren, but instead fell in love with the freedom they had been given. I never made that mistake again."

"I'm certain you didn't," Juniper said. She unrolled the map Logan had printed for her and spread it out on the small table between them. She pointed to the peninsula he mentioned. "Here?"

"Roughly," he said. "Of course, I can't be certain they're still there. It *has* been some years."

Juniper rolled up the map. "Thank you, Zhang. That should be enough for today."

"I always look forward to our little conversations, Juniper," Zhang said, picking up his teacup and taking a sip. "Until next time."

Juniper stood and exited Zhang's cell. Grayson was waiting for her in the attached observation room.

"He's been providing some decent intel," Grayson said. "I wonder what's loosened his tongue?"

"He's been cut off from everyone and everything he knows. Most of them are dead. Plus, he's from a very social race, so he's probably genetically disposed to be chatty."

They exited the observation room and headed toward the council chamber. Echo was already seated inside when they arrived, anticipating that there would be news.

"Looks like we're headed north," Grayson said. "There's a group of Jiating living somewhere in Portland."

"Okay then. Let's get the team gathered for a briefing."

Within minutes, the team was assembled in the council chamber and seated for the meeting. Juniper recounted the interview with Zhang and the expected location of the Jiating defectors.

"We can't say with any certainty they'll still be there, but it will be worth the trip to investigate. If they've set up a permanent encampment, they may have established a new clan. Lacking any Morphs, they could possibly pose the greatest threat to humans in the area."

The Valerians had come to call the shapeshifters "Morphs" as calling them shapeshifters in routine conversation was cumbersome and slowed down discussions. Kylie, unlike Zhang, remained tight-lipped about her race and was reticent about her race's distribution and social habits. They had successfully infiltrated and manipulated the Rimrockians over the years, but there was no record of her people anywhere in the expansive Valerian library. They were, for all intents and purposes, a newly discovered race on Earth.

"Excellent," Echo said. "We'll need the approval of the Valerian Council before this excursion, considering the possible diplomatic overtones. I'll bring it to them at tonight's meeting."

The daïs in the council chamber was loaded with all of the Valerian Council members for the meeting. They chatted among themselves as they waited, their whispers the only sound that could be heard in the room. The meeting was closed to general audience, as the requests Echo would be making were classified as "secret."

Echo was a little warm under her collar. She hated asking these stuffy, self-important politicians for permission to do her job.

Madeline Lytle, the Council chair, rapped her gavel.

"Order, please, order." The soft murmur of conversation among the Council members ceased. They went through the regular procedure—roll call, establishing quorum, reading and approving the prior meeting's minutes—then on to the agenda.

"First tonight we have Commander Echo Larkwood of the Valerian Defense Corps with a proposal to scout the northwest region of the western territories," Lytle stated. "You have the floor, Ms. Larkwood."

Echo stood. "Thank you, Madam Chair." Echo walked confidently to the lectern. "We have recently gathered intelligence regarding a contingent of Jiating that had defected prior to the offensive on the bunkers in the Cascades. Our prisoner, Charles Zhang, has given us a general location, though the area is limited enough that few resources would be needed to conduct an effective search.

"At this time, I propose one scout craft with one pilot and one team of five, complemented with one surveillance drone equipped with one contingency ONC. The drone will be used for both visual and thermal sweeps prior to human incursion. The squad will then use the intel to search likely areas or hot spots. Estimated time of deployment is three to five days."

"Thank you, Commander Larkwood," Lytle said. "Your proposal is well-reasoned and thoughtfully planned. If the proposal is approved, you have the specifics at hand, yes?"

"I do."

"I expected as much," Lytle said, smiling. "I'd like to call for a vote. All those in favor?"

"Aye," called all but one.

"All opposed?"

"Nay." Morton Thrum's dour face barely cracked as he spoke his dissent. Lytle couldn't help but throw a disapproving look his way.

"Noted. Commander Larkwood, your proposal is approved. I expect a written copy of the full mission brief."

"Thank you, Madam Chair. I just so happen to have that for you." Lytle smiled and extended a hand. Echo walked forward with the printed brief in a sealed, marked envelope and placed it in Lytle's hand.

Echo turned and walked from the council chamber. As there were no other guests for the Council proceedings, Lytle immediately turned and addressed Thrum as the door closed behind Echo.

"Why is it you feel the need to cast a 'no' vote every time Commander Larkwood makes a proposal in this chamber?"

Thrum stared at her with his lifeless eyes. "Because I don't see the need for constantly supporting her warmongering. We have no reason to go beyond these walls to search for a fight."

"Really? And what is it that makes you believe that we're insulated from everything beyond these walls?"

"The walls themselves, Madeline. Nothing has gotten inside them since they were constructed."

"You're willing to bet your life on stone and mortar?"

"It's better than putting my life in the hands of people who only know how to use computers and how to murder with their hands. War is inelegant, inartful, and unintelligent. Our resources are better spent inside these walls, on our own people."

"Our resources cost nothing, Morton. You know this."

"And what if they anger someone we can't repel?!" Thrum slammed his hand on the council table and stood violently quickly, surprising them all. "All of these excursions to places unknown, and we get nothing but mission logs and reassurances! The last mission obliterated an entire *race* of people minus the two in captivity and *maybe* this unknown cabal of defectors in Portlandia. You wish to send…"

"Morton, sit down…" Lytle interjected.

"*I will NOT!*" Thrum shouted. "You wish to send a team looking for someone else to destroy without dissent? Then you are all mad fools. I will *continue* to vote against *any* military action—diplomatic or no—as logic and reason dictate I do so, sitting as I do amongst you goddamned idiots!"

The Council was stunned into silence, most of them, Lytle

excluded, with their mouths hanging open. Thrum composed himself and smoothed his Nehru jacket before sitting again.

"Please, Madam Chair, the next item on the agenda. I prefer not to extend these proceedings beyond the allotted time. I have other things to which I must attend."

Lytle regained her composure—mostly. "Um...next on the agenda..."

TWENTY-SEVEN

Grayson and Keona went over the gear one last time. They knew it would work just fine; it was just the ritual of it. They had prepared for the operation for a week with valuable input from Echo.

Keona stood and stretched. There had been little time between planning and drills to rest. The prospect of running yet another op weighed heavily on Keona, whose battle fatigue was beginning to show during drills. He knew the costs of failure. It didn't ease his weariness in the least.

Grayson could feel the tension in his friend and could see the fatigue in the lines of Keona's face. It worried him that his friend was in distress, and it worried him even more that he was unsure of how to ease Keona's burden.

"You know, you don't have to go on this one, 'Ona."

Keona looked at his friend and managed a tired smile. "You and I both know my honor won't allow that."

"It had to be offered to be rejected," Grayson said.

"It did. But I volunteered, remember?"

"I do."

"I just need a good night's sleep, I think. It's tough to get used to the quiet and the lack of immediate threats. I used to dream of an uninterrupted night's rest; now that I've got it, I can't sleep because it's too damn calm." They chuckled.

"I hear ya, bud."

"Ember's fitting in just fine, of course. I think she's finally over the shock of nice things being around all the time."

"I bet. A lifetime of being a slave would dampen a person's expectations."

"I kind of want the same things, brah."

Grayson had no reply prepared.

"All this blood, man...I just...I don't know if there's any redemption for me at this point."

"Of course there is, 'Ona."

"Do you really believe that, Gray?"

"...Fuck, dude, I don't know. I mean, we're four hundred years in the future and still doing the shit we thought would end long before now."

"Exactly."

They stood silently, looking around at the equipment. They looked at each other and then started out the door. As soon as they left the gangplank, it lifted into the belly of the scout craft and the door closed. The thudding of their boot soles echoed in the hangar as they walked. Keona stopped.

"I'm sorry, brah. I don't know what's going on with me."

"You're having a crisis of conscience. Totally normal." Grayson sighed. "I've dealt with it more than I've ever told you. I've been a fighter for as long as I can remember. Being a Marine only made it easier. But when I was deployed to Korea, man...the shit I was in was worse than anything I'd ever imagined. I saw and did things to other human beings that would curdle the Devil's blood. Through it all, I had to tell myself I was doing the right thing."

Grayson looked Keona straight in the eyes. "If I wasn't, dude? Then what the hell was I doing it for? We believed the North Koreans were minutes away from annihilating the U.S. with long-range nuclear weapons. That was enough for me. When I saw Jones lying next to me...that was the worst feeling I'd ever known, Keona. I was responsible for his death, and the deaths of all the others in my squad. And it made me question everything. *Everything*.

"You're fine, Keona. We're fighting for our future. We're fighting for Juniper and Ember, their future. If we stop fighting, Echo will find others to fight. The human race is on the brink of full dark, man. We just happen to be the two assholes with enough power to ensure they live on."

Keona smiled a touch. "Well, when you put it like that…"

They walked to the cafeteria, where the rest of the new Valerians had already commandeered a table. Grayson and Keona joined them. Grayson received a quick kiss from Juniper, and Keona a quick kiss from Ember. They spent the next hour eating and talking like a family. They told silly jokes, talked about the future, gave each other a hard time. The Valerian ale helped relax Grayson and Keona, finally a bit at ease after their emotional one-on-one earlier. Innes's guffaw could be heard even outside the cafeteria's doors.

"To tomorrow," Grayson said, lifting his mug. "Whatever it might bring."

"Tomorrow!" the group chorused, clanking their mugs together.

TWENTY-EIGHT

The scout craft glided silently over the landscape, desert giving way to the ponderosa forest, then the Cascade mountains. The west side of the Cascades suddenly gave way to a lush rainforest, the canopy bright green.

"Holy crap," Grayson said.

Though it wasn't raining, moisture began building up on the scout craft's windshield as they began their descent. Grayson had seen the landscape on his map, but he was having trouble believing his own eyes. They were above what was once Oregon City, now ruins at the east shore of the Clackamas Sea. Islands dotted the watery expanse, but one loomed large ahead. It was created by the tallest points in the area, Cooper Mountain and Bald Mountain.

They completed a flyby over the tops of the peaks of the island. Over the top of the Cooper peak, they spotted a settlement under the lightly thinned canopy.

"Well, we know it was populated recently," Logan said, banking right. There wasn't any visible movement. Juniper, in the co-pilot seat, tapped the console and brought up the thermal readout.

"Confirmed," she said. "Heat signatures are consistent with humans."

"Hope they don't mind a visit," Keona said.

Logan chose a clear spot just downhill of the settlement to land the scout craft. As he touched it down, he sent the coordinates to the surveillance drone that had followed them from Vale. Once the drone received the coordinates, it would immediately depart for the peninsula on the other side of the island's north channel.

Grayson led the disembarkment and gathered the team at the rear of the scout craft.

"I'll take point on the way up the hill. Keona, bring up rear security, please. Logan, since none of us knows how to fly this thing, stay in the middle and don't get shot, okay?" Logan chuckled and nodded. "Everyone else, find a position and fall in where you're comfortable. Mind avenues of fire and maintain muzzle discipline."

"Aw man, I was gonna just keep wavin' my barrel in Keona's face," Innes said.

"Last thing you'd do, old man." Keona said.

"Who you callin' old? I ain't *near* four hunnerd years old."

"Touché."

Grayson stifled a loud laugh and started up the hill. Juniper fell in right behind him, then Logan, Innes, Hallie, and finally Keona. Hallie had insisted on coming, as she felt the presence of so many men might make other feel threatened. She would be an unpleasant surprise if it came down to a fight.

The underbrush was dense, but it was fragile and easy to step through. Ferns and fireweed dominated their path, and the old cedars were wet and mossy. The air was oxygen-rich but heavy with moisture. They soon lit on a trail that appeared to head downward toward the natural harbor they had seen on approach to the island. The uphill side was going in the direction of the settlement, so it made sense to Grayson to use it.

"Heads on a swivel," Grayson said. The team tightened a little and immediately began scanning the landscape. Juniper began feeling a presence.

"*Halt!*" called a disembodied voice, just as Juniper was about to sound warning. Grayson immediately complied. He quickly covered the entirety of the area in front of him, but he couldn't find the owner of the voice anywhere in the dense forest.

"*Lower your weapons,*" the voice said. The team complied, ready to switch on their stealth suits and scatter at a moment's notice.

"We mean you no harm. We've come to gather information on nearby Jiating."

"Jah-whats?"

It hadn't occurred to Grayson or anyone else that the humans here might not know what the race was called elsewhere. "The skinny human-looking things with big black eyes." The pause that followed felt a little too long. *Did Zhang give us bad intel?* Grayson wondered. *Did we trip over the Jiating settlement?* It seemed unlikely, given that the Jiating preferred fully enclosed or subterranean accommodations.

The ferns next to him began moving closer. Grayson then saw the small, dark circle of a muzzle in the foliage.

"Don't move," the voice, now recognizable as a deep baritone, said. "What do you want with them?"

Grayson weighed his choices. The creature in the tangle of camouflage could be human, Jiating, or Morph. Confident in his team, he made his decision. "We want to exterminate them."

The muzzle remained motionless for a few moments, then dropped quickly. A hand pulled back the ferny hood to reveal a human man's face. The team all collectively sighed.

"Pleasure to have you here, then. Come on up."

The team followed the man up the trail to the settlement. On arrival, Grayson was surprised at the efficiency of the layout. Rather than the simple structures he envisioned, the houses were facsimiles of the houses he would have known; the exceptions were the rough cuts of the siding boards and the windows, which were just openings with thatched shutters instead of glass. The roofs were camouflaged to look like the rainforest from above, using leaves and branches from the cedars and oaks that comprised the forest. It was simple yet ingenious.

The man led them to the largest structure, a long, flat building at the rear of the settlement. He opened the door for the Valerians and allowed them in. He entered behind them and closed the door. In the middle of the room was a long rectangular table with chairs lining all edges.

"Please, take a seat. I'll go find our leader."

The Valerians sat at the table as requested, placing their rifles butt-down next to them and leaning against their legs, well within easy reach if things went sideways.

"Don't think I'll ever get used to being an envoy," Grayson said.

"Well, you're getting pretty good at it," Juniper said.

The man returned with a striking woman with fair skin, freckles, and bouncing red curls. She was dressed plainly in tidy clothing that resembled what had been worn at Rimrock, though hugging her very curvy frame a little tighter. The Valerians bristled a touch at the sight of it.

"Good afternoon," she said pleasantly, her voice a soft lilt. "My name is Tak Halsey. My associate is Lear Ainsworth. He tells me you're in our area for the purpose of hunting the Slims. Is this correct?"

"If that's your name for them, then yes, in a nutshell." Grayson said.

Halsey smiled as she sat. "That is excellent news. They've been a bit of a thorn in the side of the humans around here. We at The Bastion have been lucky to escape their intrusions, but the mainlanders have not."

"The Bastion?" Innes asked.

"Yes, it's what we call the island. It stands alone in the Clackamas Sea, surrounded by water on all sides. It is defensible in all directions. It seemed fitting to the previous generations."

"Quite," Grayson said. "What do you know about the Slims?"

"They've taken up residence at the top of the Sunset Cliffs near the north side of the peninsula. They've not been particularly hostile, but they have a habit of stealing things, usually cloth and tools."

That seemed unlike the Jiating Juniper knew, but she held her tongue. Grayson leaned forward and unzipped a pocket on his chest rig. Ainsworth started forward. Halsey put a hand out to stop Ainsworth. Grayson pulled out a folded satellite map of the area and smoothed it out on the table.

"Can you show us on this map?"

Ainsworth approached and looked at the map. He lifted his eyes to Halsey, who signaled her approval. Ainsworth pointed to an area free of any distinguishing characteristics.

"Here. There's an unusually high concentration of wild animals in this area, so it would be wise to be on alert if you go in."

Keona suddenly realized why the area looked so familiar. "It's the Oregon Zoo, brah," he said. "That would explain why there are a concentration of animals there. Most of the ones they kept were migratory, but would return to home territories sometime during the year."

"What kind of animals?" Hallie asked.

Ainsworth straightened. "Many, but the ones that seem to have the most in number are tall orange ones, fat gray ones, and big orange cats that hunt every living thing. The animals in the trees that screech and have faces like ours are unnerving, but mostly harmless."

Grayson and Keona shared a knowing look. It was going to be like an African safari in there.

"Do you know these animals?" Ainsworth asked, noting their nonverbal exchange.

"We do," Keona said. "The tall orange ones are called *giraffes*. The fat gray ones are called *elephants*. The big orange cats are called *lions*, and the tree animals with human-like faces are *chimpanzees*. Those animals were kept at a place called a zoo many, many years ago. These animals must be descendants of the ones kept there."

"How do you know these things?" Halsey asked.

"It's a long story," Grayson said.

"Then please, share a meal with me. I should like to hear your story. Lear, please have the cooks prepare a meal for us. And please change into something a little less botanical."

The feast that the setllement's cooks had prepared was excellent. The wild pig had been especially tender and well-seasoned. Halsey listened with rapt attention to the story of the two men who had slept through time. They were light on details when describing Juniper's journey, Kylie's true nature, and Vale's importance, but otherwise forthcoming.

"I must say, you've had an incredible journey," Halsey said. "I hope we are able to build an alliance that will carry forward for many years."

"As do we," Grayson said. "Humans seem to be few and far between in this age."

"Yes, well, the disease you call *Codagenesis* was highly efficient at what it did. We had no knowledge of Vale or Rimrock until today. We are rather insular, as you can imagine, and we simply wish to exist in peace. We were all startled by your flying machine, as we've never seen one. Lear was kind enough to quickly respond to determine what kind of threat you posed."

"Flight was abandoned by humans long ago," Logan said. "Vale was just equipped to continue the legacy of human flight. We thought it was a natural progression."

"You would likely do well to insert yourself on the peninsula with a little less attention," Halsey said. "There is a protected harbor below us where we launch our boats for supply runs. I'm sure Lear would have no objection leading you across the channel to the peninsula."

"It would be my pleasure," Ainsworth said, looking much more comfortable in his loose clothing and combed hair.

"Good. You can leave whenever you like, though you may wish to leave tomorrow at sunrise. Darkness here can be disorienting and very dangerous."

"We agree," Keona said. "Thank you."

"You're welcome. We can accommodate you here, or Lear can lead you back to your flying machine."

"We wouldn't want to put out Mr. Ainsworth," Grayson said. "We'd be happy to accept your offer of accommodation."

Halsey looked very pleased. She stood, and the Valerians stood with her. "Please, follow me."

Halsey led them through the dining hall and to a long hallway on the other side of the main wall. There were several doors along the opposite side of the hallway.

"Please, take your choice. Each room has two beds and a small water closet." Ainsworth stepped back to let the Valerians choose their rooms. The Bastion's guests closed the doors to their rooms once inside. Halsey motioned to Ainsworth and they retired to the dining area for tea. She enjoyed being a hostess, though The Bastion had not housed guests for some time.

Grayson and Juniper settled into their space quickly. Juniper cracked the thatched shutters a bit to let in fresh air. They hung their stealth suits in the small wardrobe and freshened up. Grayson joined the two beds and they crawled in, exhausted.

"Do you think this is going to be worth the trip?" Juniper asked.

"I have no idea. We're just gonna have to see how it works out. Honestly, I'm more worried about the friggin' lions than the Jiating."

"What's a lion like?"

"Have you ever seen a bobcat?"

"Maybe?"

"Big gray cat, no tail?"

"Oh, yes. They're great rodent control."

"Now imagine it nine times bigger and with a *tail* about as long as the average bobcat."

Juniper's eyes widened and she propped herself up on her elbow, brushing a strand of hair behind her ear. "You're joking!"

"Nope. Not at all. Average weight of a lion is close to four hundred pounds." Juniper shuddered a little.

"I hope we don't run into one."

"Or an elephant. They're known to charge humans over territory."

"Maybe we should just let the Jiating stay there…"

Grayson chuckled and ran a hand through her hair. "Maybe." They kissed and settled into the bed. Juniper reached over Grayson and snuffed the oil lamp on the side table. The light tapping of the rain on the roof of the building and the breeze rustling through the trees outside soon lulled the pair to sleep.

TWENTY-NINE

The Valerians gathered at the table and completed an equipment check before grabbing a quick bite to eat. Ainsworth had geared up in his organic ghillie suit, leaving the hood down while they ate and prepared. Logan brought out a tablet and opened the surveillance drone's app.

"There's a ton of thermal activity around the target area this morning," he said. "It's difficult to determine if any of it is Jiating."

"Well, we know they prefer being where there's little sunlight and temperature can be controlled, or at least mitigated," Grayson said.

"That could be problematic," Keona said. "There aren't any buildings visible under the canopy. Assuming any even survived the last four centuries."

Grayson turned to Ainsworth. "Have there been any Slim

sightings on the peninsula?"

"Not recently, and only near the seashore, here." Ainsworth pointed to the shores just north of the channel that covered the ruins of Beaverton. "The coves there are good for lazy but hungry fish. Beyond that, they rarely move about during the daytime. At least that *we've* observed, anyway."

"There might be another option for insertion," Logan said. "Instead of going through the channel and overland through the rainforest, let's go by air and set down here." He indicated a clearing on a dropoff just south of the search area. "We won't fly over them, and if we stick to the curve of the ridge we might be able to avoid being seen altogether. I don't see any raised structures, so unless they're sitting in the emergence zone, we should be good to go."

"How do you feel about flying?" Grayson asked Ainsworth.

Ainsworth beamed. "Please!"

A chuckle went around the table.

"Alright then. Let's get going."

"I wish you a safe journey and a safe return," Halsey said, appearing from the back rooms, a cup of tea cradled in her hands.

"Thank you, Tak," Grayson said. Halsey approached and gave him a quick peck on the cheek, smiling warmly as she pulled away.

Ainsworth led the Valerians back to their scout craft and embarked. Hallie showed Ainsworth how to use the seatbelt. He was so fascinated he buckled it and unbuckled it several times before sitting back in the seat.

Logan set the scout craft aloft and nosed north-northwest. The Beaverton Channel, as they now called it, sparkled in the filtered sunlight and danced with wind-whipped whitecaps. Ainsworth grinned like a child on a carnival ride, his eyes wide.

"I get to do this almost every day, and I still grin like that," Logan said, watching Ainsworth in the crew mirror above the windshield.

"I might have to run away with you and learn to fly!"

On the other side of the channel, Logan pulled up and began following the curve of the ridge that came down from the hills at the top of the peninsula. Logan kept the throttle to the minimum and skimmed across the top of the rainforest's emergence, occasionally hearing the light brushing of the tallest trees against the hull. The top of the ridge felt to Grayson like it was approaching a little too fast.

"Careful, Logan. We don't wanna crest that ridgeline."

"I got it, Grayson. Don't you worry."

Regardless of Logan's confidence, Grayson gripped his armrest a little too tightly, the metal and plastic creaking under his fingers.

"Easy, big guy," Logan said. "I know we don't use money any more, but I can find plenty of work for you when we get back to compensate for damages."

"Ha ha," Grayson said sardonically. "You don't get me killed today, I'll do anything you need back in Vale."

"I'm holding you to that."

The clearing suddenly appeared in the windshield and Grayson let out a sigh of relief, easing his grip on the armrest and taking up his rifle. The rest of the team did the same and set their free hands on their seatbelt buckles. Logan touched down gently and immediately cut the propulsion. The gangplank shot out from the tail of the scout craft and was mounted almost immediately by Grayson and Keona, rifles up, scanning for threats. They knelt at the bottom of the gangplank with their rifle muzzles still pointing outward. Grayson stuck a finger in the air and moved it in a circle, signaling that it was okay to move.

They trotted to the end of the clearing, the rest of the team tight behind them. The gangplank retracted and the door closed as the last of the team stepped off. They regrouped once concealed by the dense rainforest.

"Okay Ainsworth, you're point from here on out," Grayson said. "We'll provide security while you lead the way. Keona will be right behind you, and I'll be at the rear. You sure you're good with this?"

"Oh, yes. I've been around here several times, I'm confident I can get you to where you need to be."

"Copy that. Let's roll out."

Ainsworth pulled his hood up and began stalking through the trees. Cedars and oaks grew tall through the ruined foundations and rubble of once-proud mansions of the Southwest Hills. There were wide trails that had once clearly been the roadways that served the wealthy owners of those mansions. At the top of the ridge the team encountered a steep drop that required several switchbacks to traverse. The ground was suddenly very flat, and there were car-shaped mounds every few feet.

"Highway 26," Grayson said into his throat mic. Keona's thermal signature nodded up ahead. The arterial was once an east-west route that spanned the upper third of the state of Oregon, from Seaside to Nyssa and then on to Ogallala, Nebraska. Abandoned vehicles must have littered the highway in the days after the *Codagenesis* release, left behind as people scattered while attempting to outrun the inevitable.

The team pushed through the mounds until they reached a green wall and a gentle slope rising next to it. The slope would have been the on-ramp for eastbound Highway 26 from the zoo road in its former life. The team stacked against the wall.

"Last push," Grayson said. "We don't know what we're gonna find when we get up there." As if on cue, a chimpanzee screamed somewhere in the forest, and a lion roared at nearly the same time.

"The animals already know we're here," Juniper said. She felt the anxiety radiating in the air.

"Eyes peeled, then. We're hunted as much as we are hunters right now."

Ainsworth fell back one position and let Grayson take point. They moved slowly up the slope, pausing when unfamiliar sounds were heard. Hallie kept a vigilant eye on the top of the wall. Innes had strangely felt little need to speak on their sojourn, at peace with the rainforest, listening to every chirp, squeak, and squawk. The lion's roar had been the only thing to put him on edge; the most dangerous animal he knew was the wolf, but at least he *knew* that animal.

At the top of the slope was a wide trail running northeast. The team scanned the trees for any indication of being watched.

"Ainsworth, fall to the middle of the column," Grayson said. "We're gonna activate our suits, and I want you to be protected." Ainsworth did as he was told. The team then activated the stealth suits, and Ainsworth was a little taken aback at suddenly appearing to be alone.

"Need to get me one of those."

"Probably a little weird not seeing us. We got you. Innes will tap you twice to stop, once to go."

"Understood."

"Good deal. Let's go."

Ainsworth felt a firm tap between his shoulder blades and started forward. Innes watched Ainsworth through his facemask, making sure he didn't bump into Juniper. A chorus of chimpanzee screams rang out and echoed through the rainforest. Another lion's roar followed. The team paused to scan and listen. There were numerous thermal signatures all about them, but none were the size or shape of the animals for which they were on alert. Another burst of activity came from the canopy; the squawks and flapping wings of a flock of mountain toucans signaled that something had spooked them. The team focused its attention on the area directly behind their flight path. They crossed the wide trail and disappeared into the thickness of the forest again.

Grayson chose his steps carefully, trying to avoid rattling the ferns and grasses. Luckily, the dampness of the rainforest lent a bit of a sound buffer.

"Stop!" Juniper whispered suddenly into her throat mic. The column ceased immediately. "One o'clock high."

Grayson tilted his head to look in the direction Juniper had indicated. In the canopy were two chimpanzees, looking vaguely in their direction. They had likely seen the swaying of the ferns as the team walked through, Grayson reasoned. They wouldn't have been the cause for the flock to take flight.

"All clear," Grayson said. "Good eyes, Juniper. Keep it up."

The team continued until they all heard the rustling of leaves, followed by the sharp *crack* of several sticks. Grayson shot up his fist instead of issuing a verbal command. Innes tapped Ainsworth twice. The column stopped and knelt. Grayson's HUD thermal sensor picked up a large signature dead ahead, but it was obscured by a stand of tightly packed cedars. He tapped the top of his head, indicating he needed cover, and Innes moved out from the column and right behind Grayson. They inched forward, each step slow and deliberate.

The orange and yellow blob stopped moving, and the rainforest fell silent. The head of a bontebok, a type of antelope the zoo had housed, shot up and looked nervously around. It took a few tentative steps before another larger—and much faster—thermal signature darted out of the thick rainforest carpet and downed the poor beast. Grayson switched off the thermal reader and watched the lion wrestle the antelope to the ground and latch its jaws onto the bontebok's throat. He swept his rifle up and started looking in every which way for the same yellow-orange color in the vegetation. He didn't know much about biology, but he knew that lions hunted in packs. Thankfully, this one appeared to be male, so it would be hunting alone. Still, he didn't know how much of their habits could have changed with *Codagenesis* and centuries of evolution. At least now they knew what had set the birds off, anyway.

"On me, quietly." The team reconvened and pushed north again. After just a few meters, Grayson saw what appeared to be a cinder block wall. He signaled a stop and dropped to a knee.

"Logan, you have any historical map overlays on your fancy tablet?"

"Yeah, hang on." Logan brought out the tablet and tapped around, then watched the screen for a few moments.

"Looks like it's a building that's been there since your time. Those blocks must be self-healing concrete with elasticized mortar." Logan stowed the tablet and readied his rifle. "I'm thinking that's where they'd be."

"Same," Grayson said. "Juniper, you getting anything?"

Juniper closed her eyes and focused. "Nothing."

"All right. Stay tight. Ready?" Everyone nodded. Grayson readied his rifle and started through the vegetation.

On approach, Grayson noted the area immediately around the walls was cleared of any vegetation, and the blocks themselves looked pristine.

This thing was rebuilt, he thought. He pressed his throat mic and whispered. "This is what we're looking for. Rifles up."

The team stacked into a room-clearing column. They hugged the wall and moved to the first corner. Grayson cleared the corner and led the column to a door on the east side of the building. There was a proxy card reader mounted next to the door. Grayson motioned for Keona to move up. Keona surveyed the setup.

"Dunno, brah," he said. "If there's an alarm attached to that thing, I could trip it."

"Maybe, but we've gotta get in there."

"Let me see what I can do," Juniper said. "I think I might be able to keep the power going while Keona unlocks the mechanical stuff."

"Worth a shot," Grayson said.

"And the only one," Innes added.

Juniper placed her hand on the proxy card reader. A light crackle could be heard around her. Keona held out his hand and began willing the lock to undo itself. The light on the proxy card reader turned green and a light *click* told Grayson they'd done it. He grabbed the door handle and pulled.

The interior was dark. As the team filed in, each activated the night-vision module on their HUD. Keona closed the door quietly behind them. The hallway ahead seemed to stretch to infinity. Grayson moved quickly, trying to stay one step ahead of any counterattack. They had too quickly assumed there would be nothing here. Instead, they found a modern building with electronic security. That was *not* great news.

The first corner appeared and Grayson swept around it, finding no one waiting. The next corner bore left, and again he swept it. Ahead lay a door. Too late, he saw the infrared lights in the camera above the door as they activated with the team's movement.

"Shit…" The world went blindingly white.

THIRTY

"Put down your weapons," said a calm voice. The team did as they were told. "Now you may turn off your night-vision." Each member of the team did so, then blinked rapidly at the door ahead of them. The hallway lights were bright and the walls were a stark white; the combination of the two overloaded the night-vision modules and had blinded them all, even the tech-less Ainsworth, though to a lesser extent.

"Walk forward and through the door." The team moved, each holding on to the person in front. "Stop."

Once the temporary blindness began to fade, they were met with a line of Jiating pointing strange weapons at them, one standing apart with their hands behind their back. They were all dressed in simple human clothing, much like what was worn at The Bastion and Rimrock. Each wore a visor of some sort over their eyes.

"Who are you?" the Jiating leader asked.

"No one special," Grayson said.

To his surprise, the Jiating leader actually smiled. "Your levity suggests you are more than you wish to appear. Please, show yourselves."

The team did as they were told, deactivating their stealth suits.

"Impressive."

The leader removed the visor over their eyes and walked easily forward, keeping their hands behind them. "I am Jalen Coe. I suppose you could say I'm the leader of this little band. And you are?"

"Grayson Brooks."

Juniper felt nothing but calm in the room. Whatever their intent, the Jiating here posed no threat to the team.

"Grayson, they're all very calm. I don't think they intend to hurt us."

"Indeed," Jalen said. "And you are?"

"Juniper Scanlon."

Jalen's eyes widened, if that was possible. Jalen's hands dropped and they strode to Juniper purposefully. Grayson was about to intercept, but Juniper waved him off.

"Juniper Scanlon! I haven't seen you since your escape!"

"You...*know* me?" It was Juniper's eyes that widened this time.

"Of course! I was a student at the time you were captive. You were the reason we left Hope. We were all appalled by Zhang's desire to eradicate the Keepers and the humans. We left in protest. Of a sort." Jalen's demeanor changed slightly. "I organized the ruse of a scouting expedition to see if there were any humans in the north. We've lived here these past twenty years in relative peace, surrounded by the fauna that once lived in cages. Seems a fitting metaphor."

Jalen turned and motioned for the Jiating line to lower their weapons.

"It pleases me to say you are all welcome here. Anyone who cares for Juniper Scanlon is an ally to us."

Jalen gathered the team in a bright room with dark, comfortable furniture arranged in a circle. They were all offered seats on the plush chairs and sofas as Jalen settled into their normal seat. Several Jiating bustled in and out with mugs full of water for their guests and platter full of some sort of prepared fruits and vegetables. The Valerians recounted their journey, lightly abridged, as they ate from polished and sealed cedar bowls. The story was easier to tell than it had been at the beginning.

"I have to say, it's a bit of a relief we didn't end up in a fight," Jalen said. "I feel it may have been an uneven match."

"Probably," Innes muttered.

Juniper felt oddly at ease around Jalen and the other Jiating. They radiated no hostility, though, so there wasn't any reason to believe the Valerians were in any danger.

"How long did you intend to stay here?" Juniper asked.

"Until our natural deaths, likely," Jalen said. "It's not as if we would be welcome anywhere else in the territories."

"Didn't you worry that Zhang would send others after you?"

"Constantly. That's why we have so many security measures in place. We should have let the rainforest grow on the building, but even self-healing concrete can be made weak by too many intrusions.

"It's also why we developed our weaponry, which you saw displayed earlier. Zhang felt such things were unnecessary due to our advanced minds, but he was clearly mistaken."

"Yup." Innes set his bowl on the side table next to his seat and slurped from his mug of water. "But not by much. If we hadn't had Juniper around, we might not've figured out how to beat him."

"Us, I imagine is what you meant," Jalen said. Innes reddened. "I am still Jiating, though I am glad to not be possessed of a poisoned mind."

"Yeah...uh, sorry."

Jalen smiled patiently. "It's fine. I'm sure you meant no insult by it."

"Would you be willing to travel with us?" Keona asked. "I have a feeling the Valerians would be highly interested in either offering you shelter or at least providing incentive for an alliance."

"Actually, I would. I would appreciate the ability to bridge this divide between our races. Zhang and his family did irreparable harm to our coexistence. My I bring my husband?"

"I can't think of any reason not to let him come," Grayson said.

"I can," came a surprisingly baritone voice. A thicker Jiating entered the room and placed a hand on Jalen's shoulder.

"In her absence, there would be none to lead. Our clan is mostly self-sufficient, but, as with all groups, there must be one who takes responsibility for all."

"This is my husband, Zane Coe. Slightly overprotective, but likely correct in this instance. Our son is being groomed to be the leader of the clan, but…he's not quite there."

"Fully understood," Grayson said. "Is there someone you'd like to take in Zane's place?

"I think this would be the perfect time for our son to learn to be an emissary," Zane said. "We would like to send one more as well. For security."

"Of course."

The group began planning for the voyage. Ainsworth had been extremely distrustful at first but warmed to the Jiating during their planning. He reasoned that the Jiating, though strange, had never given his clan any trouble. The mainlanders had plenty of things stolen or sabotaged, but it was also true that the mainlanders were hostile to everyone; though they were especially wrathful toward the Slims. Granted, The Bastion was separated from all overland routes and an inconvenience to get to, but the Jiating had never tried to infiltrate it. That fact alone gave him hope that these creatures were legitimately attempting alliance with humans.

"Well, then, it looks like we're settled. We'll leave here in an hour. We'll have to make a stop at The Bastion to drop off Lear, but then we can be on our way and get to Vale before nightfall."

"Lovely," Jalen said.

"This is our son Killian," Zane said proudly, presenting the young Jiating. "Please take good care of him."

"We will," Juniper promised.

The Valerians and the Jiating group set out through the rainforest. Logan kept his tablet active to mark their progress back to the scout craft via GPS.

The hike took less than thirty minutes. Logan eased off toward The Bastion in a straight line, no longer fearful of being spotted by hostiles.

"You can land in the village square, I believe," Ainsworth said. "There should be plenty of room for your machine."

"Thanks," Logan said. "I think you're right. We'll touch down in a couple of minutes."

The village square was indeed large enough to receive the scout craft, and Logan made a light landing.

"I should probably go first, let Tak know we have visitors."

"Good idea," Grayson said, unbuckling his seatbelt.

Ainsworth trotted down the gangplank and entered the main building, emerging only moments later behind Halsey. Grayson and Keona met them at the bottom of the gangplank.

"I hear you've brought the Slims here?" Halsey's tone was colder than Grayson would have liked. Juniper, still inside the scout craft with the Jiating, felt the distrust radiating from her.

"We have," Keona said. "They wish to create an alliance with the humans. We're taking them to Vale to discuss what that might mean."

"Vale does not speak for the western territories," Halsey said.

"That may be so, but they are the most populous settlement in all the territories, at least to common knowledge." Keona didn't like the direction this was heading.

"*That* may be so—however, one population many miles away is unequipped to make decisions for those of us *here*. I shall meet these…people before you depart."

Halsey spun and walked to the main building without creating an opportunity for anyone else to speak. Ainsworth stayed behind.

"We'd better hurry. She means now."

They regrouped and hustled into the main building, slinging their weapons on their shoulders. Halsey was already seated at the head of the hall table on arrival. The Valerians and their three Jiating charges took seats at the table; the Valerians sat their rifles to their sides. Ainsworth stood behind Halsey and clasped his hands in front of him.

"Which of you is the leader?" Halsey said, her voice icy.

"I am." Jalen stood. "My name is Jalen Coe."

Halsey tipped her head back, appraising the Jiating. "What is it you wish to accomplish by aligning with the humans?"

"Simply peace." Jalen said no more. The silence felt awkward to Grayson, but no one else seemed bothered in the least. Jalen and Halsey stared at each other, neither breaking eye contact. After what felt like a very long period of quiet, Halsey stood.

"My name is Tak Halsey. I am leader of the clan here at The Bastion. I believe you are telling the truth. You have our support, and you are welcome when you wish."

"We thank you, Tak Halsey. We extend the same offer." The two smiled—Halsey tersely—and nodded to each other.

Grayson stood and slung his rifle on his shoulder. "We should get going."

"Of course," Halsey said. "I'll be joining you."

The Valerians were all taken by surprise at Halsey's self-invitation.

"Uh, sure," Logan said. "We have a seat for one more."

"Lear, I'm leaving you in charge until I return." Ainsworth nodded. "Let's be on our way." Halsey tossed her curls and began walking out the door. Grayson and Juniper exchanged amused glances before heading out close behind Halsey.

Once aboard and secured, Logan lifted off and shot eastward as quickly as the scout craft could go. As the scout craft cruised over the landscape, Halsey, Jalen, and Killian couldn't take their eyes away from the window. They watched as the Clackamas Sea gave way to the mainland rainforest, which gave way to the Cascade Mountains, which gave way to the Ponderosa forest, which gave way to the high desert. Logan continually checked on their guests in the cabin mirror. He smiled at their wonder.

Ever since Rimrock, the Valerians' world had been changing quickly and in ways no one could have predicted, least of all the Valerians. Now Logan was flying Jiating emissaries and a clan leader into his home to discuss the future of the Oregon territories. The Valerians had grown complacent in their bubble—Logan was both excited and fearful of what could come next.

THIRTY-ONE

Mason Twiss paced in his quarters. *Those filthy bastards.* He had been stewing ever since the Valerians took off with Kylie. This was unacceptable. He was at a loss, unable to think clearly. Several of his clanspeople had tried to help, but he snapped at them, figuratively *and* literally, depending on the form he had taken prior to their pleas.

A light rap at his door halted his pacing.

"*What?!*" Snapping again.

"Sir, I think I might have an idea." The mousy teen girl had been hovering around him for days.

"Out with it, then!"

"Do you remember when Kylie had those visitors back in Rimrock? The ones before the strangers came?"

"Vaguely. What about them?"

"They were…they were Alters, sir. Like you."

Twiss was immediately more interested in this girl. He spun to face her squarely. "How do you know this?"

"I was serving Kylie her afternoon tea that day. Gemma was sick."

Twiss closed the space between them. "Do you know where they came from?"

"East, sir. They kept talking about a place with yellow rocks."

Twiss smiled for the first time in days. "Thank you. You've been the most helpful of all the clan."

The teen's eyes lit up. "Can I get you anything, sir?"

"No, thank you. You've given me everything."

Twiss strolled out into the common area. The teen followed just steps behind.

"Everyone, may I have your attention, please?" He turned to the teen. "What's your name again?"

"Peri." Twiss smiled and stroked her cheek before turning back to the crowd that was gathering.

"Peri has given me very useful information that I intend to act upon immediately. I need four Alters to volunteer for a mission of the utmost importance."

Several of his shapeshifting comrades stepped forward, ready to volunteer. He pointed to the four he wished to accompany him and brought them forward.

"Thank you all who volunteered," Twiss said to the remaining

Alters on the floor. "Your courage will be rewarded." He turned to Peri. "Get them all double rations tonight. Let DuBois know he's in charge until I return."

"Of course, sir!" Peri ran off to let the kitchen helpers know of Twiss's request.

Twiss turned to his volunteers. "We leave now. If we push it, we can arrive at our destination in three days. We stick to the flats as much as possible, we change into whatever gets us there fastest. I'll lead, just match my pace."

"Where we goin', boss?"

Twiss grinned. "Yellowstone."

"One Trick to Lodge, over."

"Go ahead, One Trick, over."

"Inbound from the west with ten aboard, ETA five minutes, over."

"Copy. Pad 1A will be open. No other air traffic, clear skies, over."

"Copy, Lodge. One Trick out." Logan turned to the crew cabin behind him. "Alrighty, folks. When we land, be prepared for a lot of staring. Echo's been briefed, but I'm not sure what she's shared with everyone else."

"Copy that," Grayson said.

"You all say 'copy' quite often," Halsey said. "Is there really a need to duplicate so many things?"

"It's something we say to make sure the person on the other end of a radio transmission knows that we received the message," Keona said. "In our time, it just kind of carried over into normal speech patterns among our warriors."

"Ah," Halsey said. "Copy." She smiled. The rest of the cabin had a good chuckle as well.

Logan eased the scout craft over Pad 1A and touched down. The passengers unbuckled their seatbelts and stood to stretch.

"Goodness, that was fun," Halsey said. "I didn't realize there was quite such variety of lands in the territories."

"We live in quite a spectacular place," Logan said. He walked to the back as his passengers gathered their belongings. "Okay, everyone. Remember, the Valerians haven't seen a group like this before. Expect some stares, maybe even some hostility. Nothing will happen to you; I just want you to be prepared."

"Thank you, Logan," Jalen said. "It is appreciated."

Logan opened the door and stepped onto the gangplank. The new Valerians, Halsey, and the three Jiating followed closely. Echo waited at the bottom of the gangplank, smiling broadly. Juniper felt the unease in the crowd that had gathered to watch. Several of the armed guards shifted their weight from side to side, on alert for anything that might happen.

"Hello, all," Echo said. "Welcome to Vale. I'm Commander

Echo Larkwood of the Valerian Defense Corps." The group stopped in front of Echo.

The three Jiating stepped forward first. "I am Jalen Coe. This is my son, Killian, and our bodyguard, Atharv Robal."

"It's a pleasure to meet you," Echo said.

"I am Tak Halsey." She stuck out her hand. Echo stepped over and shook it amiably.

"A pleasure to meet you as well." Echo turned her attention to the full group. "Please, follow me. I've arranged your accommodations and they're ready for you. First, we invite you to join us for our evening meal."

Grayson and Keona took up seats outside the main group in the cafeteria. Juniper and Hallie followed.

"What do we think?" Grayson asked.

"I think it's going very well," Juniper said. "All is going according to custom. The overall feeling is one of relief and contentment."

"Feels legit, brah," Keona added.

"Guess that's gonna have to be good enough for me." The little cadre of new Valerians ate quietly, watching as the Jiating, the redhead, and the Valerian commander all chatted together over their plates. It was heartening to see diplomacy finally taking place.

A few minutes later, a group of folks the new Valerians hadn't met strutted into the room. In the lead, a woman with a humorless face, followed by some of the most sour-faced people Grayson had ever seen. The woman smiled and made some utterances. She swept her arm behind her, motioning to the people behind her, likely introducing them.

"Politician?" Grayson asked.

Keona nodded. "Politician."

"What's that?" Juniper asked.

"Person that talks a lot without saying anything, then makes promises they don't intend to keep." Grayson shook his head and finished his food. "Four hundred years couldn't reform those jackals."

The group disappeared as quickly as they had arrived. Grayson gathered up the plates from his compatriots and returned them to the kitchen. On his way back, he stopped to chat with Echo.

"What'd those creeps want?" has asked. Echo struggled not to spit out her mouthful of food. She swallowed and let out the laugh that had been trapped behind the potatoes.

"Valerian Council. They wanted to personally meet the new allies from the west."

"I see."

"Yeah. I have no idea what's gonna go down in the next few days. The Council is pretty secretive outside the public eye."

"Hmm." Grayson said.

"What?" Echo didn't like the big man's *hmm*.

"It's just...when politicians get secretive, bad things tend to happen. I mean, that's how it was in my time."

"Ours as well. I don't trust them beyond allotting resources."

"Hmm."

"That's the second time you've said that."

"I'll see what Juniper can find out."

Echo cast a wary look around the cafeteria. "That's an excellent idea. Just try not to stick out too much, yeah?"

"You got it."

They shared conspiratorial smiles. Echo's face contorted suddenly.

"What is it?" Grayson asked. Echo held up a finger and pressed into her ear with another.

"Drones are tracking a pack of wolves in the lowlands near the ruins of Burns," Echo said. "Big ones."

"Morphs?"

Echo nodded and stood. Grayson whistled across the cafeteria. Keona perked immediately and Grayson waved his crew over. They followed Echo to the command center. A high-resolution video was broadcast on the screen at the front of the room. The tech at the console was calmly controlling the surveillance drone that tracked the wolves.

"Moving at approximately twenty miles per hour, ma'am," the

tech said.

"For how long?"

"At least thirty minutes."

"That's not great. They're on a mission."

"Agreed," Grayson said. "And they're coming in this direction."

"ETA?" Echo asked.

The tech ran a quick calculation. "Just a little under five hours."

Grayson caught strange movement on the screen. "What the...? Guys—" The wolves had changed into hulking Keepers.

"Speed has increased to thirty-two miles per hour." The tech ran another quick calculation. "If they remain at that speed, they'll be here in just a little over three hours."

Echo stood up straight. "Let's prepare a welcome party, then."

THIRTY-TWO

"Hostiles sighted." Hallie kept her eye on the approaching Morphs in the rifle scope. She lay flat on the highest point on the Vale wall facing west.

In the council chamber, the Valerian Council monitored the events on the large screen across from the daïs.

"This is what happens when you prod the wrong viper," Morton Thrum said. No one acknowledged him. Madeline Lytle sipped at the water in front of her; her hand trembled lightly. Light perspiration glistened at her hairline.

"Nervous, Madeline?" Thrum smirked.

"A little, Morton, yes. These Morphs are an unknown in this world already so full of questions. So until they're gone, I'll be a little nervous."

"Good."

Grayson and Keona were staged just inside the western gate with Innes, Hallie, and Juniper.

Grayson met Juniper's eyes. "Anything?"

"No, nothing." Juniper's forehead scrunched up a little. "It's maddening. This is how they must have sneaked by me while we were in Rimrock. It makes no sense!

"Unless they're some sort of empath as well," Keona opined. "That might give them the ability to block, or just redirect your attempts to feel them."

"Could be."

Grayson racked the bolt on his rifle. "Either way, let's just wait on the word.

"Inbound, contact in five minutes," Hallie called over the radio. "Waiting for instructions, over."

"Copy." Echo watched the drone footage intensely. The Keepers were relentless, their arms and legs pumping in a furious rhythm that propelled them over the high desert floor as if they were flying.

Keona focused on his breathing. Juniper closed her eyes and did the same.

"Contact in four. Permission to engage?" Hallie flipped the safety switch on the rifle to *off*.

"Negative, Bounce. Over." Echo stood and stretched her neck.

"Copy."

The Morphs just kept running, churning the soft dirt into a pale cloud behind them.

"In three, over." Hallie was becoming frustrated.

"Do me a favor, Bradley," Echo said to the tech, leaning over his console. "Run telemetry, see what their probable route is." Bradley ran the app as asked.

"That doesn't look right. Does it?" Bradley ran it again. "Echo, they're going to go right by us."

"Bounce, stand down. Monitor only. They're gonna run right by us." Echo kept her eyes glued to the screen. "I sure hope you're right."

The Keepers closed the distance at their remarkable speed. Hallie set the rifle aside and rose to a knee, watching them run at the walls. When she estimated they were thirty seconds out, she saw that their line was definitely skewed north. They were going *past* Vale.

"I don't like this, Eagle Eye," she said. "Something's up."

The Keepers bypassed the Valerian walls and left nothing but footprints and a cloud of dust.

"I agree, Bounce. Pack it in. Debrief in five." Echo exhaled.

Twiss let the group relax every three hours, but they needed to push beyond Vale to put a safe distance between them and the humans. He determined that distance was the western bank of the

Snake River.

They slowed and rested by the edge of the water. They drank deeply, then lay back in the mud to cool their overheating bodies. Twiss sat and breathed calmly, deeply, replenishing the oxygen to his muscles. He was driven only by the need to get to his brethren.

"Twenty minutes, then we light out."

One of his compatriots groaned. "Come on, boss, can we stay a little longer? We're exhausted."

"No. The faster the better."

"Fine."

Twiss made note of the attitude.

After twenty minutes, they got in the river and swam across, then took off at a sprint across the high desert again.

Lytle met with Echo, Grayson, and Keona in the council chamber after the threat had passed. They sat informally in the gallery chairs, arranged so that they could all speak face-to-face.

"Why didn't they attack?" Lytle asked.

"We're unsure, ma'am," Grayson said, leaning back in the chair that was too small for him. "For a hot minute, it looked like they were beelining it for Vale, but they ran on by like we weren't even here."

"Like they were challenging us." Keona sat slightly forward, elbows resting on his knees. "I'm almost certain that's what they were doing. An intimidation tactic."

"Well, it worked on me." Lytle smiled sheepishly. "Do you think they'll be back?"

"Unknown," Echo said. "But I've got a surveillance drone above them, we'll keep an eye on them in real-time and report anything you should be aware of as soon as it happens."

"I appreciate it, Echo. Thank you for always looking out for our community."

"Always."

"In the meantime," Grayson broke in, "it would be wise to get set up for their possible return. Something in the urgency of their sprint makes me think that they have some sort of plan in mind, and it may include others."

"There's little to the east but mountains and deserts," Echo said, bringing up a map on the back screen. "There's really been nothing of interest that way in some time."

Keona watched intently as Echo navigated points east on the map. "Stop."

"What is it?"

"Right there," Keona said, standing and walking to the screen. He pointed at a spot on the map. "Zoom in there." Echo did.

"No..."

"You think?" Grayson asked, sitting forward.

"I think, brah. You believe that?"

"Care to enlighten us, Mr. Sage?" Lytle crossed her arms.

"That used to be the lodge at Old Faithful, a geyser in Yellowstone National Park."

"That place throws off all of our thermal readings." Echo changed the screen. The map was one giant hot spot, reading almost blank white.

"That's because it's one of the most geothermically active places in the west," Grayson said. "There could potentially be an army hiding in that reading. That building was right across the street from Old Faithful. If they've maintained it, it could hold, what? A thousand?"

"Depends on how they've configured it, but yeah." Keona rubbed his temple.

"You good, 'Ona?"

"Yeah, just a headache. I'll be fine."

Grayson kept an eye on Keona. "Echo, let's meet in the control room and hash this out. Keona, you wanna sit this one out?"

"Nah, I'm good. Maybe just need a cup of coffee."

"Please keep me updated," Lytle said, standing and shaking Grayson's hand. "And let us know if you need anything."

"We will."

Grayson accompanied Keona to the cafeteria and grabbed a cup of coffee also. "You sure you're okay, bud?"

Keona sighed. "I dunno, brah. You know I'm tired of all this shit. I just…I dunno."

Grayson gripped Keona's shoulder. "Whenever you figure it out, let me know."

"I will."

They meandered their way over to the control room and met up with Echo.

"All right," she said, "let's get started."

THIRTY-THREE

"They're gone!" Bradley yelled across the control room. Echo spun, startled.

"What do you mean, *gone*?!" She strode to the console.

"I mean *gone*. Their signatures aren't being picked up by visual or thermal."

"How long?"

"Five minutes, maybe?"

"Five minutes maybe, or five minutes for certain?"

"At least five minutes."

Echo stared at Bradley. The silence made him squirm. "Go take a break."

"I—"

"*Did I fucking stutter?!*"

Bradley leapt out of the seat and nearly ran from the room. Echo reached for the PA microphone. "Wolf, assemble team at control room. ASAP. One Trick, man the door now."

Grayson collected Keona and Juniper in the cafeteria and hustled toward the control room. Hallie and trinity met them in the hallway at the same pace. Logan met them at the door and swiped his proxy card to let them in.

"What's up?" Grayson asked.

"They disappeared just east of Boise. I have no idea why."

"We weren't' supposed to lose them until Yellowstone," Juniper said.

"No, we weren't. Are there any caves that long?" Echo asked.

"I have no clue," Grayson said. "'Ona?"

"I don't know either, bud."

"Awesome."

Echo's hands kept flying over the interface, different views scrolling on the main screen faster than Grayson could observe. "I've circled the area with the regular camera, thermal, even Doppler trying to get something, anything useful. There are no records of underground caves that stretch that far. I'm at a loss. Unless they're dead."

"Which we highly doubt," Grayson said.

"We don't know anything about their physiology," Keona said. "Could they turn into, I don't know, some kind of metal golem?"

"Highly unlikely, but excellent outside-the-box thinking," Echo said. The room went silent. "Nothing?"

"I'm afraid not, Echo," Grayson said.

"Well, let's get ready for the inevitable return, I guess." Echo slammed her hands on the console in frustration.

"It's okay, Echo," Keona said. "We'll do what we do best." He did his best not to wince as he said it.

Juniper hung back as the others left. She waited until she was sure she was alone with Echo.

"Can I speak to Kylie?"

Echo looked up at her. "You think you could get her to talk about capabilities?"

"It's worth a shot."

"It is." Echo pressed the push-to-talk button on the PA microphone. "Technician Millsap to the console. Now." Echo led Juniper out of the control room and to the elevator. Millsap ran past as quickly as his legs could carry him and flew into the control room.

Echo and Juniper rode the elevator to the lower levels silently. Kylie's cell was at the end of a long hallway deep underground, just to ensure that she would remain as far away from the Valerians as possible.

The elevator came to a stop and Echo and Juniper disembarked into the hallway. The sound of their footsteps were loud on the tiled floor as they walked to the last door.

"Ready?" Echo asked.

"Ready." Juniper took a deep breath. Echo scanned her proxy card and the electronic pocket door opened into an observation room. Beyond the five-foot-thick window was Kylie, pacing her cell. The embedded screen in the opposite wall showed a pleasant forest scene, much like what they had left behind in Rimrock. It was an unintentional yet perfectly fitting punishment for Kylie's transgressions.

Juniper pressed the intercom button. "Hello, Kylie."

Kylie stopped pacing and turned slowly to the window, a grim smile spreading on her face.

"Hello, daughter."

Juniper held in her rage. "Don't call me that."

"Not saying it out loud doesn't make it any less true," Kylie said, her speech slow and deliberate.

"No. I suppose it doesn't." Juniper paused. "Can your kind change into anything you want? Or just mammals?"

"Right to the point, I see." The smile left Kylie's mouth. "No, we can't change into *anything* we want. Only mammals."

"Are there any…enhancements you can make to the animal's skin, or temperature?"

Kylie grinned again. Juniper had given away the reason for the interrogation. Kylie laughed. "You lost them, didn't you? Oh, glorious, *ha ha haaa!*"

The laugh sounded to Echo a little unhinged. She pressed the mute button on the intercom microphone. "She knows what you're looking for."

"Of *course* I know what she's looking for," Kylie said. "I'm not an imbecile. And no, I won't tell you what I know. Just like the last time. And the time before that."

Juniper was afraid that might be the case. She backed away from the window. Her eyes began to glow a fierce blue. Kylie's own eyes went wide.

"Juniper, you can't..." Echo started to put a hand on her arm, but a crackle of electricity shocked her hand, causing her to recoil; the site where the electricity landed stung deeply.

"*where are they?*" A dark, hollow voice issued from Juniper's mouth; it had no sign of being Juniper's.

"I—I don't know. You know more than I do at this point."

"*yellowstone?*"

Kylie's eyes narrowed. A too-long pause gave Echo the confirmation she needed; the Valerians had been correct. "Possibly."

"*thank you.*"

Juniper's eyes returned to their normal dazzling blue and she walked out of the observation room. Echo followed tentatively and they walked in silence to the elevator bank.

"What happens inside your head when you do that?" Echo

asked, pressing the button to return to the surface. "Are you still here?"

"Yes. But I'm calmer, and I feel...everything. Down to the beating of the wings of a nearby fly. It's difficult to explain, but..."

"I think I get it. I'd only ask that you not do that indoors anymore."

Juniper smiled sadly. "Only if necessary, I promise."

Echo smiled back. "Let's just not tell anyone, especially the Council, of that particular...ah...manifestation of energy, yeah?

"Understood."

Twiss only lost one over the Rockies. Some medical condition had taken him out; they left him in the crags of some peak the name of which was lost to time. He counted the single casualty as a success. He only hoped his ruse outside of Boise had worked, having abandoned the original plan to stick to the flatlands beyond the high desert.

Twiss knew the Valerians had aerial technology that could track their heat signatures, so he'd made the quick decision at the wide river outside of the ruins of Boise that they would travel in the water as river otters. Large river otters, to be sure, but they could hold their breath underwater for a long period of time and still move somewhat quickly. They returned to other forms of quadrupeds and bipeds just beyond the remnants of a dam somewhere in the mountains.

Twiss and his two compatriots loped into the chalky, bare flatlands. Twiss had insisted they enter in wolf form to ensure they wouldn't be fired upon or torn apart. The only real benefit Twiss found in his wolf form beyond escaping suspicion was the enhanced sense of smell that necessarily followed the change. He used it now to sniff at the air.

There.

The unmistakable smell of his own kind. He looked at his compatriots behind him and gave a slight nod. They understood. All three regained their human form and looked for any sign of their brethren. A hillock ahead of them started to steam, and water began roiling near the top. Suddenly, the roiling water gathered itself up and started shooting skyward.

"Who are you?"

Twiss spun toward the male voice behind him. While he and his two companions had been watching the geyser eruption, five Alters had approached them from behind. They all leveled ancient rifles at the outsiders.

"Mason Twiss, Alter brother from the central territories of Oregon. We've come a long way to find you." Twiss stepped forward to offer his hand, but he was stopped by all five rifles training on him simultaneously. "Nice to meet you too."

"I don't know who you are, or what an 'Alter' is, but you're not welcome here."

Twiss took a decidedly calculated risk and changed into wolf form. He sat, curling his tail around his paws and staring unflinchingly at the man in the middle of the formation, clearly the leader. The man in the middle looked to his left and right and motioned to his crew to lower their rifles.

Twiss retook his human form and offered his hand without stepping forward. The leader hesitated momentarily, then stepped forward to shake Twiss's hand.

"I'm Dasan."

"No other names?"

"No."

"Are there any other 'Dasans' I might confuse you with?"

"Possibly."

This is going well, Twiss thought. "Well, Dasan, it's a pleasure to meet you. I've come a long way to ask for your help."

"Why? And how do you know of us?" Dasan took a step back to regain some distance from Twiss.

"Our leader, Kylie, was visited by members of your...uh...clan, some time ago in the settlement called Rimrock."

"I remember them. They told us of a group of our people living among humans in a secure compound far away."

"That was us. But we were forced from our home not too long ago by another group of humans who sought to hunt us down."

Twiss wasn't about to tell a long story; the half-truth would suffice. "We hoped you would be willing to assist us in an attack on the heart of their civilization."

"They drove you from your home? That is not right." Dasan appeared to quickly think over his options. "We will help you. Our ancestors were driven from their homes, too. We've lived in this place for as long as my people can remember. It may be time to take back what should be ours."

"We thank you for your help, Dasan."

"Thank me when it is done."

The group assembled quickly, more quickly than Twiss had anticipated.

Only a few had originally dissented, but they were quickly outnumbered and pressured toward assisting the outsiders. They mobilized rapidly, gathering only what they needed to survive. The rest they would find in the forests and mountains as they traveled westward.

A little more than four hours after arriving, Twiss was among the ranks of many of his own. He deferred to Dasan to lead, as his people were more likely to move at the pace he set.

"We go."

Dasan shifted into a wolf and took off at a trot. Twiss was next to him on the right. It was a perfect pace for a wolf pack with a long way to go, especially a pack that numbered near a thousand. For the first time since he lit out on his journey, Twiss felt at ease—maybe even a little hopeful.

THIRTY-FOUR

Grayson and Keona monitored the movement of the Valerian faction as they made their battle preparations, ensuring they understood the operational tempo of the response as well as the places where their skills would come in handiest.

"Well, brah, it looks like they're a pretty well-oiled machine," Keona said. "Guess we could sit this one out if we wanted."

"Yeah, I s'pose. So, I'll stick right here with the secondary. Game?"

"As much as I can be."

Grayson put a hand on his old friend's shoulder. "Look, I know you want out. To…retire, as it were. Let's just get through this."

"Yeah."

Grayson clapped his hand on Keona's should and walked off toward the control room. Keona hung back, watching the Valerian ants bustle about their anthill. He closed his eyes and breathed in deeply.

In the control room, the Valerians were tracking the movement of the Morphs.

"How long?" Echo asked. Millsap tapped away at the console and ran a few calculations.

"At current pace, approximately seventeen hours."

"At least we can see them again."

Grayson approached the console. "Jesus."

The mass that moved across the main screen was big, a blob moving quickly across the landscape of the former state of Idaho.

"Yeah. Estimated number is high hundreds to low thousand." Echo watched the mass intently as it crawled across the screen. "This isn't gonna be like the rest, is it?"

"Nope. They're an unknown. That they can turn into pretty much anything with tooth and claw is concerning."

"I'm not fighting any bears, Grayson."

"No worries. I will." They chuckled at Grayson's levity.

Twiss's companions were tired, their tongues lolling in their mouths. Sources of water were becoming scarcer as they pushed farther west. Even Dasan was showing signs of fatigue. That being so, they were all determined to follow through.

They pushed northward a little to hug the foothills in hopes of finding more water, which they finally did after a couple of hours. The entire group crowded the banks and drank deeply. Nearly all reverted to human form and filled water skins before they lit out again.

By sunset, the pack had enough. They settled down on the river near an old town, their muscles screaming, their stomachs growling. The decrepit remains of four giant silos and a red brick building were visible from the bank.

"I can smell them from here," Twiss said.

"Their town is just over the rise," Dasan said, pointing west-northwest. "We'll be fresh and ready in the morning."

"Excellent."

The Alters foraged for fresh onions and wild potatoes along the banks of the river. Some dove into the water and chased fish as river otters, bringing them up to the banks to share with the others.

After their feast, they stretched out on the soft, loamy earth and rested. All were exhausted from their long journey.

"They'll know we're here, Dasan," Twiss said. "They have technology that can see us from the sky."

"We know. But now they know what they can expect. We will not back down from this challenge. We rest tonight, we fight tomorrow."

"They've bedded down," Millsap said.

"As expected." Echo stood straight and stretched. "Go get some rest. I'll take over until your relief gets here."

"Thank you." Millsap stood and limped out of the control room. Echo sat heavily at his station and looked over the readings. The drone showed no scouting parties, only two sentries keeping watch near the river.

The door *whooshed* behind her. "How's it goin' in here?" Grayson asked, striding into the room courtesy of a shiny new proxy card.

"Fine. They just settled in for the night."

"Good. Need anything from us tonight?"

"No, we've got everything ready. Go on and get some rest."

"Absolutely. You too." Grayson was worried about Echo's dark eyes and disheveled hair.

"I will. Just another hour here."

Grayson left Echo to it and headed into the recreation room. Ben and Ember had joined Keona and Juniper there. It was the first time they'd all had leisure time together since their arrival.

Grayson sat next to Juniper, sinking into the puffy sofa. "Lord, you're gonna make me soft."

Juniper giggled and cuddled close. "Never."

"Ew," Ben said flatly, eliciting a laugh from the crew.

"Do you think we'll ever get to just *be*?" Juniper asked. "This is nice."

"Knowing the history of our races? Probably not."

"I was afraid you might say that."

Keona sat forward. "Whatever happens tomorrow, I'm done after. Ember and I are gonna take off." Grayson looked over at him. "I can't do this anymore, brah. My whole life has been killing or avoiding being killed. It's time for a break."

"I hear ya, bud. Where will you go?" Keona just smiled. Grayson understood. "Gotcha. Just keep in touch, yeah?"

"Of course."

They sat in silence for some time, just enjoying the ability to relax. *This* is *nice*, Grayson conceded in his thoughts. *Prolly just get lazy and fat if I let Juniper have her way.*

THIRTY-FIVE

A cold breeze washed over the camp. Twiss's nose twitched, having found a hint of his enemy's scent in the air. His eyes blinked heavily as he sat up, the rising sun hitting him full in the face. The golden rays pushed long shadows across the landscape, highlighting the wispy ground fog rising from the dewy grasses as it warmed the misted ground.

Dasan was already awake, watching the sun come up. His leathery face looked worn and weary as he stared eastward. Twiss stood and stretched, then turned human and stretched again.

"Rest well?" Dasan asked.

"As well as I could. Nice having a built-in blanket, though."

Dasan smiled. "It is. Our ancestors would have appreciated our gifts."

Twiss looked toward the low mountain, or the "rise" as Dasan had called it. Their enemy was so close. Twiss was buzzing with anticipation.

"When do you want to move out?"

Dasan hardly moved. "Now will be fine." He stood and gave a cry that sounded otherworldly. The Alters all around stirred quickly and were on their feet in moments.

"We'll need you to train us to do that," Twiss said, marveling.

"Wolf and Specter, they're on the move."

The radio pulled Grayson and Juniper out of a perfectly good sleep. Grayson reached over and mashed on the push-to-talk button.

"How long?'

"Four hours max."

"Copy." He sat up. Juniper groaned into the pillow. "Yeah. Me too."

They got up and prepared in silence, checking each other's equipment, and loading up their personal gear. Grayson clipped his helmet to his belt and slung his rifle on his shoulder.

"Ready?" he asked.

"Ready." Juniper stood on her tiptoes and wrapped her arms around his neck, giving him a long, wistful kiss. "Let's make it back here tonight, okay?"

"Planned on it."

They exited their room and made their way to the control room. Grayson opened the door and they met Keona and Echo at the console.

"Today's the day." Grayson watched the giant wolf pack loping across the arid landscape. "Weapons?"

"None that we can see," Echo said. "Doesn't make them any less dangerous."

"No. Alright. Keona and I will fall back to our positions."

"Thanks, Grayson."

Grayson and Juniper walked hand-in-hand to his station just inside the eastern doors.

"Be careful up there," he said, stroking Juniper's face.

"Better than cooped up here," she said. "Fight hard if they get this far."

"You know me."

"I do."

Juniper kissed him one more time, then put on her helmet and trotted away. Grayson put on his helmet and looked over toward the east doors. It was going to be a long day.

Dasan stopped at the top of the rise and looked down into Vale. The outer walls glistened in the morning sun, surrounded by lush green vegetation and brightly colored oak and quaking aspens getting ready to drop their orange and gold leaves. Dasan knelt and closed his eyes. The rest of his large clan did the same. Twiss mimicked the behavior, though he had no idea what they were doing, much less why he felt compelled to follow. Wordlessly, Dasan stood. The clan rose also.

Dasan unleashed that eerie cry again, which seemed louder and even more intense. His clan returned the cry. A shiver ran down Twiss's spine. *This is it. This is when we take back what is ours! And more!*

Dasan ran at full sprint toward Vale, then swiftly turned into a giant red-tailed hawk, alighting on the high desert wind. Twiss smiled and changed into his favorite wolf form. The rest of the clan and his compatriots became whatever carried them fastest toward their target. Twiss howled in delight.

"Tangoes incoming!"

The sentry's voice was nearly shrill over the radio. Juniper watched as the dust cloud from the east-southeast grew. The cry of a hawk split the air, and she looked up to see the largest red-tailed hawk she had ever seen diving toward her position.

"Sky! Sky!" she yelled. Half a dozen rifle barrels swung upward and rang out. Dasan easily swung around the bullets and picked up one of the Valerian soldiers, swooped hard left, and casually dropped him over the side of the building.

"They're flying, Wolf," Juniper called over the radio.

Grayson shook his head in disbelief. *Of course they are.*

"How many?"

"Just the one right now." They had decided to drop tactical communications when they didn't need to coordinate ground and air forces.

"Keep me updated."

"Yep." It was all Juniper could get out, as the hawk was coming back for another pass. Gunfire erupted from the eastern wall as the Valerians unleashed a barrage at the approaching wave. None but a few fell.

"Specter! East wall will breach!" Juniper ducked as the hawk barely missed her and the Valerian behind her. Too close.

"Specter, on it." Keona coasted over the ground and went up and over the wall, landing softly on the other side and drawing his blade. An Alter in the form of a mountain lion bore down on him quickly, then skidded to a halt just as quickly, its head bouncing away along the wall. Keona gauged the front of the line and coasted away toward the east gate.

Juniper couldn't get a bead on the hawk that was harassing them. It was too skilled at diving and dodging the rounds she and the other Valerians kept lobbing at it.

Dasan was having fun. He swooped around another fusillade and finally picked up another soldier as he was reloading. This time, Dasan flew upward. The Valerian beat at Dasan's underside the entire way. When he was at a satisfactory height, Dasan opened his talons to let the soldier fall, watching with macabre pleasure as the soldier descended. The terrified screams cut off abruptly as the soldier slammed into the ground.

That's enough for now, he thought, angling back toward his clan. He swooped in and rejoined the fight on the ground, seamlessly changing into a large brown grizzly bear.

Grayson listened to the muffled fighting from his position. The funnel that was his hallway felt like it was getting tighter by the second.

"Eagle Eye, what's the situation?"

"They're concentrating on the east wall, probably going for the gate." Echo zoomed out on the drone's camera. "Confirmed."

The east gate was just beyond the east doors Grayson was watching.

"Copy. Moving to the gate. Send reinforcements to my current position."

"Specter here. I'll join you."

"Copy."

Grayson stood and sprinted down the hallway and through the doors. As he approached the gate, Keona floated down from the top of the wall to join Grayson in front of the large gate.

"Good to see you, 'Ona. Sorry about what we've gotta do."

"Me too. But it'll be over soon, brah. There aren't enough of 'em to take us out." They fist-bumped and settled into their position, waiting for the funnel to spew forth their enemies.

Twiss changed mid-stride into a Keeper just beyond the wide gate. His two compatriots did the same. Striding along with Dasan, the three Keepers and the bear flung themselves at full force into the thick gate. It groaned and cracked pitifully. They reared back, and all four pounded into the gate again.

Grayson and Keona watched the gate flex and splinter on the inside.

"That's not great," Grayson muttered.

The third hit brought down the gate, and a flood of animals pushed through. Two Keepers headed straight toward Grayson and Keona and were met with Grayson's brute force; he knocked one to the side where it met Keona's blade and the other was pounded face-first into the packed soil at Grayson's feet. One Keeper and the bear slipped by as Grayson and Keona focused on the other dangerous animals flinging themselves at them.

Dasan turned and attacked Grayson from behind, knocking the big man to the dirt. Growling, Dasan attempted a bite. Grayson caught Dasan by the muzzle and forced his jaws open. Dasan's eyes grew wide at the force of Grayson's grip. He knew instantly that Grayson was no ordinary man. Thinking quickly, Dasan changed quickly into a man, his muzzle shortening and popping out of the large man's iron grip.

"What are you?" Dasan asked calmly.

"Neither man nor beast," Grayson said. The fighting grew more intense around them as reinforcements arrived and began pumping ammo into the animals.

Twiss ran down the hallway and was fired on by the Valerians at the mouth. Twiss's Keeper form dodged the rounds almost too easily, and he crashed into them, pounding one of the soldiers with the body of the other one. He threw them aside and pushed deeper into the building.

Sensing the shift in the battle below, Juniper leapt over the edge of the wall. Radiating her blue light, she eased to the ground and ran toward the east gate. A stray wolf was headed straight at her, but skidded to a halt and began retreating when her eyes crackled blue. She sprinted forward. It was time to put these powers to their test.

"Specter! East gate!" she called over the radio.

"Already there. They're pulling back."

"No, they're going to shift position."

Keona knew better than to distrust Juniper's instincts. "Copy, standing by."

Juniper rounded the corner and headed straight at Keona. "New idea! Grab my hand!" Keona cocked his head in slight confusion but stuck out his hand. Juniper grabbed it and immediately tapped into her power. Keona felt a jolt rush through his body as they rose above the wall and hovered in midair. They suddenly shared a single consciousness, aware of everyone and everything around them. They could see where everyone in Vale was at that moment, they could see every enemy outside the gates, they could see the second wave hiding in the brush. They could feel the anger and the fear rising from the ground forces.

Juniper inhaled.

The scream she let loose stopped everything in its tracks. The Valerians on the roof clapped their hands to their ears and fell to their knees; the pain was intense, even though it wasn't directed toward them. The Alters outside the wall, on the other hand, shriveled into fetal positions, knocked out of animal form by the sheer amplitude and mind-altering timbre of Juniper's scream. The second wave pulled as far back as they could, confused and frightened by what was happening at the front.

Dasan looked up at the duo hovering above Vale.

"We have made a grave mistake," he muttered.

"You have," Grayson said. "What was your purpose here today?"

"We were told you stole our cousins' homes in the place called Sisters. We came to avenge them."

"We didn't steal their homes. We infiltrated their home and took their leader, a Morph named Kylie."

Dasan's eyes widened. "Cousin Kylie? Why did you steal her?"

"We needed information from her. Plus, she tried to kill us after we helped her eradicate a race of people called the Jiating."

"I have been misled." Dasan's eyes clouded with grief. "Please, tell your gods to be silent."

Without correcting Dasan, Grayson hit the push-to-talk button on his throat mic. "Volt, stand down."

Juniper ceased her scream. Dasan let loose a cry, one that was less intense and underlined with lower tones. The Alters outside the wall picked themselves up off the ground and retreated to rejoin their comrades in the brush.

Juniper and Keona watched as the Morphs scuttled away. Their fear was now overwhelming.

"Who led you to us?" Grayson asked.

"A man named Twiss."

Grayson's face contorted. "Is he with you now?"

"Yes, but I believe he is inside. He ran by us all once we broke through the gate."

Oh shit. Grayson understood immediately. This wasn't a takeover attempt. It was a rescue operation. Twiss had played his kindred so he could gain access under the cover of attack.

"Take your people and go," Grayson said. "We have no quarrel with you."

Dasan nodded and ran off to join his people.

"Specter, Volt, tango inside. It's Twiss." Grayson unslung his rifle and sprinted to the east doors. Juniper and Keona alighted on the ground just outside the doors and entered a moment after Grayson.

Twiss strolled down the hallway, opening doors with the proxy card he'd stolen from the soldiers he'd killed after entering the building. Most of the cells down here were empty. He was at the last three doors. *Kylie* must *be in one of them,* he thought.

The first contained an emaciated Reed Newberry, sitting on the edge of his bed. The Jiating looked sadly up at Twiss and smiled ever so briefly. Twiss morphed into his wolf and stalked up to Newberry, who made no move to defend himself. Twiss lunged at Newberry, sank his teeth into the supple skin of Newberry's neck, and twisted violently.

Dripping Newberry's blood, Twiss returned to human form. He casually wiped his mouth with his arm as he tried the next door. Behind thick glass was the former Jiating leader, Zhang. Twiss smiled and promptly closed the door. The last door held his prize.

Twiss pressed the intercom button in the observation room. "Hello, Kylie."

"Mason!" Kylie was overcome. *"Get me out of here!"*

"On it." There were several virtual buttons on the control panel below the window. He found the ones he was looking for and pressed them in succession. Kylie's cell opened, the man-trap doors unlocked, and Kylie embraced Twiss in a brief hug.

"Thank you," she whispered.

"I've got a present for you."

Twiss led her to Zhang's door and opened it. Zhang, still confused by what appeared to have been a door malfunction earlier, stood watching at the glass. The realization of what was occurring struck him a little too late. He retreated as far as he could into the cell. Twiss ran through the control sequence in reverse, allowing Kylie to enter the cell. Kylie changed into a Keeper just before entering Zhang's cell.

Twiss reveled in the cries of the last of the Jiating being beaten to death by the woman he was fairly certain he loved.

Grayson, Juniper, and Keona reached the elevator. Grayson mashed the button and all three boarded. Inside, he massaged his pounding temples.

"This should have been a possibility we thought of," Grayson said. "I feel a bit stupid."

"We've been a little preoccupied," Juniper said. She placed a calming hand on the big man's shoulder.

"Yeah, brah, this was a long shot. We didn't have much intel on Twiss. Knowing he was capable of this strategy was improbable at best."

They rode the rest of the way in silence. When the doors

opened, they lifted their rifles and scanned the hallway. Nothing. Not a sound, not anything unusual.

They trotted down the hallway to Kylie's cell. Grayson passed his proxy card in front of the card reader and Keona entered the observation room on point, followed by Grayson, then Juniper. The cell was empty.

"Dammit!" Grayson lowered his rifle. "Where is she?"

Juniper's eyes widened. She could suddenly feel Twiss and Kylie.

"The elevator!"

The elevator door dinged. All three rushed out to see Kylie and Twiss dive into the safety of the front corner. They unleashed a barrage of gunfire. The doors closed, not a single round having found either Morph.

Enraged, Grayson threw down his rifle and charged to the doors. He stuck a hand in as if it were a blade and ripped out the left panel, then the right. There were no cables on this elevator; it was electromagnetic. There was no stairwell this far down—it ended somewhere around the fifth level far above.

"Of course," he said to himself. "*Keona!*"

Keona coasted over and looked up.

"Yep."

Keona stepped into the elevator shaft and went straight up. Juniper ran to him and clasped his hand.

"Go," Grayson said. Juniper kissed him. She stepped into the shaft, flickered blue, then floated upward. Grayson reached into the right side of the shaft and felt around. His instinct had been correct.

"They get the floaty powers, and *I* gotta haul my ass out the old-fashioned way."

Grayson started hand-over-hand. It was effortless, and he picked up speed. Suddenly, he didn't feel quite as bad.

Keona caught up to the elevator car just a few moments after it stopped above. There were no access panels in the floor of the car. He went downward and held out his hand at the doors for the floor below. Juniper joined him just as the doors opened and they dashed into the stairwell.

Crashing through the stairwell door one floor up, they turned and saw two wolf tails bounding down the hallway.

"No, no, no..." Juniper's heart pounded. She and Keona coasted down the hallway after them. They paused at the exit doors and quickly swept their rifles around the corners to ensure they weren't being ambushed. Pushing out the doors, they saw the hind ends of two pronghorn antelope blazing southward.

Keona and Juniper gave chase as fast as they could. Their energy was waning after having fought and levitated for so long. It was becoming evident that they were not above their human biology after all. The pronghorns gained distance and Juniper began falling behind. Keona pressed forward, but the pronghorns suddenly turned into golden eagles and caught a tailwind from the north. They quickly outpaced Keona, and he had to land to catch his breath. Clutching his side, he watched the eagles until they disappeared into the distance.

"Damn."

THIRTY-SIX

"Well, that was unfortunate," Echo said, pouring a measure of ale into her cup.

"Yeah," Grayson agreed, gulping his own ale and reaching for the pitcher on the table.

"I know it's not the greatest time to ask," Keona said, swirling the last of his ale in his cup, "but when are Tak and the Coes going back to Portland?"

"Tomorrow, why?" Echo drank.

"Ember and I would like to go."

"Sure, that should be fine."

"And we'd like to keep the scout craft."

Echo eyed Keona over the brim of her cup. She swallowed her ale and sat up, setting her cup gently on the table. "I can't make any promises on that, Keona. I have to ask the Council for permission."

"I figured that was likely, but I needed to ask. At the very least, I'd like to keep something on hand to communicate with Vale without having to bother the Coes at their compound."

"That, I can do without permission."

"I'll be grateful to have you there," Halsey said with a smile, sweeping into the room. "Although, I would have preferred you to ask me first."

"I think you misunderstand me, Tak, I was just hoping to catch a ride. Ember and I were going to find somewhere…"

"Nonsense." Halsey waved her hand as if flicking away a gnat. "You're very welcome to stay at The Bastion. I'll even make arrangements for you to live at the farthest house, so you won't be bothered."

"That's very kind, but…"

"I won't require anything of you. You and Ember can just *be*."

Keona was at a loss for words.

"Then it's settled." Tak took a seat and grabbed the pitcher. She sniffed its contents and winced.

"Oh, this won't do." She stood again and whisked away with the pitcher in her hand.

"Well, *I* was enjoying it," Grayson chuckled. Halsey was back in just a few minutes with three pitchers and a cup for herself.

"Now, *this* will do." She poured ale into each of their cups and Grayson's mug. Echo took the first sip and nearly swooned.

"What *is* this?"

"It's your ale, of course. With a slight modification."

"My God, it's *delicious.*"

Grayson and Keona sipped as well. It was almost like the craft beers they remembered.

"Oh, *that's* the stuff," Keona murmured. "Brah, I'm *totally* living with them."

Grayson barked a laugh. "I'll come visit. A *lot.*" Halsey swept in behind Grayson to refill his cup.

"How serious is it?" she whispered in his ear.

"Is what?" Grayson felt slightly dumb as soon as the answer left his mouth. "Oh. Very," he said quickly.

"Pity," Halsey said, smiling broadly. She stopped the flow of ale into his cup and kissed his cheek. As she swished away, he cast a pleading look to Juniper, who only laughed at his obvious discomfort.

After the group had drowned their sorrows in Halsey's ale, they gathered themselves up and cleaned up for the debrief in the control room.

Grayson, Keona, and Juniper were the only three at the table set up for the debrief, since they were the only ones primarily involved in the actions outside the general battle. Echo and Lytle sat at a table opposite. Ben, Trinity, and Hallie were in the room solely for support. Lytle felt the council chambers were too formal for the debrief, and Lytle wanted the team to be at ease.

"Thank you for meeting with me," Lytle said, smiling pleasantly. "I know things didn't go as planned but thank you for assisting us in that very strange offensive leveled against Vale."

"You're welcome," Grayson said. "This is our home now, too." *I hope.* "We'll defend it as our own."

"I have no doubt." Lytle smiled again and looked at the tablet in front of her. "It says here that the captive Kylie Easton escaped with a compatriot, Mason Twiss?"

"Yes, ma'am, Twiss led a contingent of Morphs to Vale under false pretenses. Their leader—whose name I didn't catch—was deceived. He believed he was leading his clan to avenge a wrong done to his people."

"His people to the east?" Lytle asked.

"No ma'am, to the Morphs that lived in Sisters."

"Ah, yes."

"The Morphs all retreated once their leader issued a command, some kind of yell."

"That's correct," Echo said. "I watched them head eastward again by drone."

"Good." Lytle set the tablet down. "How was it that Easton and Twiss escaped?"

"I can answer that, Madeline." Echo produced a slightly

bloody proxy card in a clear bag. "They used this to gain access to the lower levels. Twiss retrieved it from one of the soldiers he killed in the east entrance and used it to gain access to the prison. Once inside, he simply disengaged all the locks and set Kylie free."

"Don't we have security protocols in place to prevent that kind of activity?"

"Yes, but they're not automated," Echo said sheepishly. "They will be after today. We required a person to monitor movements, but everyone was busy with defense and no one caught the card activity real-time."

"I see. Well, I'm glad to know that won't be a problem from now on. I suppose it would have been easy to overlook, considering we've never had to deal with a threat inside our walls before."

"Thank you, Madeline."

"You're quite welcome, Echo. Rest assured, there will be no repercussions from the Council. Now, about this request?"

"Yes, Mr. Sage has requested to keep the scout craft when the Portland group departs for The Bastion."

"I see. And how will this benefit Vale, Mr. Sage?"

"I don't believe there is a direct benefit, Ms. Lytle." Keona fidgeted a bit. "However, there is an indirect benefit in having a scout afield to deliver news beyond drone relays."

"I'm inclined to agree. Thank you for asking permission. I assume you can fly one?"

"Reasonably well, Ms. Lytle."

"Good. You may keep it."

"Can you make that decision unilaterally, Madeline?" Echo asked.

"But of course I can. I *am* the Council chair."

"What about Thrum?"

"Oh, I'm sure he'll have a tantrum, but I couldn't care less. His impotent rage will be channeled into some other meaningless project to which he assigns himself, I'm sure."

"Thank you, Ms. Lytle," Keona said quietly.

"You're welcome, Mr. Sage. I hope you find the peace you're looking for out there. And please visit anytime." Lytle picked up her tablet and stood. "Very well. I believe I have all I need to make a full report to the Council. Thank you all very much."

"That's all?" Grayson asked.

"Yes, Mr. Brooks. That's all. I believe you all acted with tremendous courage and with the best interests of Vale at heart. I very much believe that you have all earned a place here, and I feel no need to subject you to anything further. Have a pleasant evening." Lytle left the control room.

"That was the strangest after action report I've ever experienced." Grayson leaned back in his chair and rolled his neck, a few pops emanating from the discs.

"Ew, I hate that," Juniper said, smacking his arm.

"Eh. Too bad."

Grayson and Juniper woke early to meet the Portland group at the scout craft. Keona and Ember huddled together at the foot of the ramp to receive their friends.

"You know, I take this as an insult." Grayson smiled.

"Whatever, brah. Just stay safe out here." The two men gave each other a bear hug.

Ember gave Juniper a gentle hug, then turned to give Grayson a hug. He barely even felt her, her touch was so light. Halsey and the Coes joined them at the foot of the ramp.

"I wish I could say it's been a pleasure," Jalen said, "but I'm afraid huddling in my quarters while beasts ravage the wall isn't my idea of *pleasure*."

"I fully understand," Grayson said.

"We'll make sure they're in cages before your next visit." The rare joke from Juniper made Grayson guffaw. Jalen smiled and led Killian up the ramp.

"Oh, parting. It's such sweet sorrow." Halsey flitted toward them.

"You've read Shakespeare?" Grayson asked.

"No; should I have?"

Grayson smirked and shook his head. "Well, yes, but I suppose his stuff would be hard to come by these days."

"You're a strange man, Mr. Brooks, but I look forward to your next visit." Halsey stuck out her hand in the custom of her new friends. Grayson and Juniper both accepted her handshake.

Keona took the helm and closed the rear door. The ramp disappeared into the hull. Ember took his hand as he nosed the scout craft west-northwest and eased the throttle forward.

"To a new beginning," she said, smiling widely. "I know a little about those."

EPILOGUE

"I didn't ask if this was something you wanted to do. I asked if it's something you were *willing* to do."

Kylie was getting frustrated with these talks. They seemed to be going nowhere. It had been a full day of arguing, pleading, and baking in the humidity. Their flight had taken them as far south as their knowledge allowed, and this place was home to their last hope.

The Sacramento Sea glistened in the late afternoon sun. Sutter Island was darkening as the sun began dropping behind the coastal mountains to the west. Formed when the polar ice caps had been destroyed, the Sacramento Sea had swallowed most of the former state of California, leaving the largest inland sea on the continent.

Krug sat forward, his muscles rippling as if trying to escape from his skin. Kylie was unaccustomed to the level of intelligence this group of Keepers exhibited. It was both unnerving and infuriating.

"Kylie, we have no reason to travel that far for a fight. We have all we need and want right here. Yuba provides anything and everything we could need and want."

"And what if they've tracked me here?" Kylie spat. "Or worse, followed?"

"Our scouts have no report of any followers." Krug paused. "I appreciate your frustration, but there really is nothing I can do for you."

" So, what is it you want? Food? Weapons? Women?"

"We have all that, Kylie. My answer is no."

"Fine. When they come for me, I hope they don't destroy you."

"What do you mean, *when* they come for you?" Krug sat up a little straighter."

"I'm a threat. I know where they are, their technology, their strengths and weaknesses. They know I won't be sitting idly by. I may be on the move, but they have flying machines by the *dozens* they'll use to track me. So, I ask again, what will you do *when* they come for me?"

"That depends. Will they try to hurt Yubites to get to you?"

"Yes," she lied easily. "They will destroy everything to get to me."

Krug shrank into his seat a little. The Keeper looked eerie, sitting there...*thinking*. After a short eternity, he blinked a couple of times and spoke.

"Then we will assist you. Does the rest of your clan feel the way you do about them?"

"Yes. They will do as I ask."

Krug stood. "Fine. We will travel north with you. We will need time to prepare."

"Do it. The sooner we can leave, the better."

Krug bent down and spoke slowly. "Kylie, it would behoove you to remember that *I* am the leader here. You *will* not give me orders." Krug's tone, confidence, and closeness made Kylie shrink a little in fear. It was an unfamiliar feeling, and she didn't like it.

"Of course, Krug. I apologize. I'm very tired."

Krug stood to full height again and looked out over the sea. He would miss his home as they traveled. Seagulls cried nearby. Gentle waves lapped at the shore. The seashore had been nearby for as long as he could remember.

"Rest well," Krug said. "We leave at first light."

Kylie smiled.

ACKNOWLEDGEMENTS

This story began as a collaboration with a friend in my early adulthood. It has taken twenty-one years to complete and has undergone so many changes that it was impossible to say where it would land. Grayson and Keona have been known by many names but have been virtually the same in character since their inception in 2002.

Building the world was easier than building the people, who had to have many layers and secrets. Many thanks to Jeffrey Linn of Conspiracy of Cartographers for his fantastic flood projection renderings of Portland and the Sacramento Valley, as well as Climate Central for the Surging Seas Risk Zone Map for providing detailed projections of sea level rise and the possible effects inland.

Thanks to my many mentors over the years for basic military and police tactics that assisted in the movement and decisions made in the battle scenes. Of particular note is the training I received at the All Phase Security Academy and USCCA.

To Kevin Smith, who has inspired me since I was a teenager, and who in October 2022 pumped me up at a screening of *Clerks III* in Sacramento. Kevin retold the story of his heart attack in 2018, and the lessons he learned from that near-death experience. He told us to chase the dream, and not put it off until tomorrow, since we never know if tomorrow will come. "Just fuckin' do it." Thanks, Kev. I fuckin' did it.

And, as always, to my wife Andrea and to my boys, without whom I'd have lost the passion for writing altogether. Thanks, honey. I finished this one.

Other Books by Wayne Campbell

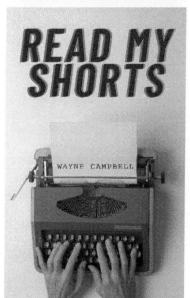